Hate To Want You

Hate To Want You
Copyright © 2025 Rae Quinn

All rights reserved. No part of this publication may be reproduced or transmitted in any form, including electronic or mechanical, without written permission from the publisher, except in the case of brief quotations embodied in critical articles or reviews. This work is a piece of fiction. Names, characters, places, and incidents are the product of the author's imagination or are used fictitiously. Any resemblance to actual events, locales, or persons, living or dead, is entirely coincidental.

Published by Rae Quinn
Cover Illustration by Elen Bushe
@elenbushe_art
ISBN: 979-8-9913334-2-9

Dedication

To anyone who doesn't believe in happily ever afters. It may take a while, but it usually happens when you least expect it.

Chapter 1

LAINEY

My heart pounds in my chest and the blood rushes in my ears as I'm pushed up against the wall. The stranger tangles his hands in my hair, our lips, tongues, and teeth clashing together as we devour each other.

The music from downstairs blasts through the house and I can feel the bass against my back. 'No Name' pushes my head to the side as he begins to suck on my neck and kiss down my shoulders. I'm panting and desperate as his rough hands begin to roam my body.

I didn't exactly come here tonight looking for a hookup, and I feel bad for leaving my best friend downstairs, but she'll understand after I tell her about how good this hot stranger got me off. At least, I hope it's good. I could really use the distraction right now.

In between kisses and sucks, the stranger tries to speak. His voice is deep, his breathing unsteady.

"Don't you want to know my name?" he asks. I shake my head, not needing to know his name to continue.

"It doesn't matter," I say against his lips, my eyes fluttering as his hand moves lower, stopping just above the waistline of my jeans. Knowing his name wouldn't change anything. I'm never going to see him again after tonight, and I just need the stress relief.

His lips find mine again, and this time, it's rougher, more urgent.

The guy tugs my hair as his other hands moves to squeeze my ass. My stomach flutters as the prospect of an amazing orgasm takes over my thoughts.

A light moan falls from my lips as No Name kisses down my neck again, and I momentarily forget we're still in the hallway and not behind closed doors. That is, until I hear a throat clearing and then the deep, familiar voice of the one person I cannot stand.

"Woah there, Barkley. Stand down. You look like you're trying to devour the poor guy," Holland Monroe, my best friend Ellie's twin brother, and the bane of my existence most days says with a mischievous grin on his smug face. Ever since we were little, he's been a pain my ass.

I pull away slowly, my cheeks burning with embarrassment and rage as my body comes down from its high. My eyes move slowly over to Holland, who is standing against the wall with his arms and legs crossed.

I can't help the way my eyes roam over his body. He's always been fit, especially with playing rugby.

His shaggy blonde hair is ruffled in a way that makes him look like he just had sex which does things to my lower half that it has no business doing.

The Dodger's rugby hoodie he's sporting looks almost a size too tight around his biceps, and the black jeans hug him just right. If the guy wasn't inherently annoying, I'd probably find him attractive. His personality ruins it all. That, and being my best friend's brother.

The smirk on his face makes me want to hit him, but I hold in the urge as I cling to 'No Name', barely even remembering he's there.

"You enjoying the show, Monroe? Does it turn you on?" I ask mockingly. 'No Name' looks between us both uncomfortably.

"Should I…" he begins.

"No," I say, much sterner than I meant it to be but it does the trick. He straightens and watches the scene in front of him play out.

Holland's eyes run up and down my body, stalling where 'No Name's' hands sit on my waist.

"You know it does. Wanna see how much?" he winks, and I roll my eyes, making a gagging face. Truth is, I don't think I'd mind seeing him, however I'd never say that out loud.

"You're disgusting. Don't you have anything better to do than watch me?" I ask in the snarkiest of tones. He shrugs, running his hand through his hair, then shoving them in his pockets.

"Ellie asked me to find you. She wants to leave, not feeling well or something. She seems to have had one too many drinks," he says, looking between my face and the hands that still rest on my waist.

Something unreadable crosses his face, but I don't think about it long before I look back to 'No Name' to tell him I have to go.

"I'm sorry. I have to go find my friend, but this was nice. Thanks for, well, you know," I wipe my thumb over my bottom lip seductively before giving him a small smile.

His hands fall to his side, and he looks a bit disappointed. I don't blame him, I was ready to go further and if the bulge in his pants is any indication, so was he.

My own disappointment floods my veins as I come to the realization that I'll be using my vibrator yet again tonight instead of having this hot guy give me what I need.

"Wait, you're really not going to tell me your name?" I smile, shaking my head. If he has my name, he'll likely try to find me, and I don't plan on ever seeing him again. He's nice enough, and he's attractive, but I'm not interested in having a redo.

"Nope," I tell him, slinking away.

I glare at Holland as I pass him, and he begins to trail behind me. I can feel his body heat against my back as I make my way down the stairs to find my best friend.

Ellie likes to party, but once she's done, she's done. Luckily, the party is at the Elite mansion, which is right across the street from our house off campus.

Holland follows behind as I make my way toward the stairs. Without turning around, I say, "you can go now. No need to follow me."

I hear the chuckle Holland releases.

"I have to go downstairs, Barkley. Don't get your panties in a twist."

Rolling my eyes, I continue down the absurdly elegant staircase. The Elite mansion is old and beautiful. Why they would give it to a bunch of men astounds me.

This is my senior year. Ellie and Hollands too. After our friends Ryker and Gwen graduated last spring, I thought our friend group would die down, but we've all remained pretty close.

Holland, his cousin Mason, and Ryker's younger brother Logan still live in the Elite Mansion. They continue to throw wild parties and act like total dumbasses.

Ellie, our other roommate Haley, and I still live in the same house we rented junior year.

Gwen and Ryker got together last Fall, and by the end of the spring, they were engaged. Their wedding is coming up pretty fast too. Gwen told Ryker they didn't need to get married so soon after their engagement, but Ryker insisted on having the wedding sooner rather than later.

So now it's January, and their wedding is in 3 weeks. Ellie and Haley are bridesmaids, and I have the greatest pleasure of being maid of honor.

When Gwen asked me to be her maid of honor, I sobbed like a baby. Gwen is one of my best friends and watching her get her happy ending almost made me wish it would happen for me. However, I'm not naive enough to believe in happily ever after. It's just not in the cards for me, and I've come to accept it… for the most part.

Growing up, my parents weren't around much. We had a nanny, a chef, cleaners, and I spent more time with them than I did mom and dad.

Dad's a lawyer, one of the most sought-after lawyers in Rhode Island, actually. Mom's a famous model. Together, they have more money than they know what to with and they used that money to take extravagant trips and buy me luxurious gifts to make up for the fact they never took me on said trips.

Being an only child, I was alone most of the time. My nanny, Erica, was nice enough. She essentially let me do whatever I wanted, whenever I wanted. That might sound like a dream to some people, but it was a lonely existence.

When I decided I wanted to attend Ellington University in Connecticut, my parents were happy for me, but I think they were happy they'd have the house to themselves, whenever they're actually there.

Sometimes, I think they took all those trips to escape me. The child they never wanted. At least, that's the way it seems.

All I wanted was love and attention from the two people that were supposed to love me the most in this world. But not even parents can be counted on. Their careers always came first, and I was an afterthought.

The only good thing that came out of that whole situation was my ability to be independent. I don't need anyone. I'm perfectly fine on my own, and that's the way I prefer it.

That might explain why I've never been in an actual relationship. I lost my virginity in high school to a boy that made me feel like I was his world. Only to turn around and sleep with Izzy Carter, my sworn enemy.

Since then, the only kinds of relationships I've had are the kind where we fuck and don't even know each other's names. Quick and easy, no strings. That's worked perfectly well for me so far.

Ellie's family moved in next-door when I was eight. We quickly hit it off, and she became my best friend. Her annoying twin brother started tagging along just to bother Ellie, and in turn, bother me.

As we got older, he got more annoying and more protective over Ellie, which of course we found aggravating as hell.

With them attending the same college, and us living on the same street, it's only gotten worse.

Holland and I aren't enemies, but I wouldn't call us besties either. I tolerate him because he's my best friend's brother, but I wouldn't be torn up about it if he wasn't here.

When I hit the ground floor where the party is full swing, the music blasting and the people drinking and smoking, my eyes wander.

I spot Ellie, her shoulder length blonde hair and pink dress standing in a corner by herself. She looks like she'd rather be anywhere but here.

I don't blame her, now that my night's been ambushed by Satan himself. Okay, maybe that's an exaggeration. Holland isn't Satan. He's actually a good guy, always has been. Which has always been aggravatingly annoying because it makes him more appealing.

I'd never admit this to anyone, but I've definitely had a fantasy or two starring Holland Monroe. It's hard not to when I've seen him almost every day since I was eight.

"Finally!" Ellie exclaims as I approach. She looks a bit spooked, and a lot mad.

"What happened? Are you okay?" she shakes her head, looking down to the ground. I can feel Holland stiffen as he walks up beside me.

"Ellie? What's going on? Did something happen?" Holland growls. The anger immediately taking over his body is palpable. Ellie looks back to me, her gaze only landing on her brother for a second.

"I…" she takes a shaky breath. "I went to get some fresh air on the deck, and Danny Larson was standing outside…" my blood begins to boil, and I can feel Holland stand a bit taller as he listens to his sister.

"He tried to…" Holland cuts her off before she can get out whatever she was about to say.

"Did he fucking touch you? If he laid a finger on you, I'm going to kill him," he spits. Ellie cowers a bit, but she continues to explain.

"He forced himself on me. I tried to push him away, but he was too big. He kept trying, and somehow, I was able to gather enough strength to knee him in the balls," she says. She straightens a bit. "I rushed inside before he could do anything else," Ellie explains. She seems more pissed off than anything.

My own anger begins to grow as I hear a low noise from beside me. Holland looks like he could burst at any moment. I'm honestly a little worried being so close to him.

When it comes to Ellie, he is wildly overprotective. Especially when it comes to guys.

Holland begins to move through the crowd as Ellie and I trail him. A few dancing bodies bump into us as we maneuver our way through.

"Holland, wait," Ellie calls, but Holland doesn't stop.

"I'm going to find that fucking prick, and when I do, he's fucking dead," Holland calls back.

Ellie and I exchange a worried look before continuing to follow Holland through the sea of people.

We come to a stop when Holland finds exactly who he was looking for.

Danny Larson, captain of Ellington U's hockey team stands with a drink in his hand and a smile on his face as he chats with a group of guys who I assume are his teammates.

Holland walks up to him, pushing him backward. Danny's drink spills over the lip of the cup as he stumbles backward.

"What the fuck, Monroe?" he yells, attracting the eyes of many other students in the vicinity. Great.

"Stay away from my fucking sister, man," Holland throws a punch at Danny's face and chaos ensues.

Fan-freaking-tastic. Here we go.

Chapter 2

LAINEY

A crowd has gathered around us to watch the violence unfolding. People cheer, while some others look horrified. Ellie cries harder as she watches Holland pound the shit out of Danny.

I hold her to me for comfort as her small body shakes.

"Holland! Holland, stop!" she yells, but he doesn't stop. It's like he doesn't even hear her. He's in a blind rage. If it were anyone else, I'd probably find this extremely attractive, but it's Holland.

"What's going on?" I hear a familiar voice call over the chatter. Logan Steele and Mason Howard rush into the small space, grabbing Holland and pulling him off of Danny, who is lying in a bloody heap on the floor.

Holland looks feral as the two guys pull him away. His knuckles are bloody and busted, his hair falls in his face, and a bead of sweat drips down his face as his chest heaves.

"What the fuck, man?" Logan asks, sounding completely lost. Logan is a good guy, nicer than his brother. Ryker was moody and unpredictable. Logan is the complete opposite.

Logan is calm, cool, and collected like ninety-nine percent of the time. He's rational, and he always tries to see the good in people.

We didn't really know him until he started actually hanging around us more when Ryker left. I don't think they fully get along, but I think they're working on it. A lot happened in the spring semester. Their family is kind of messed up, much like all of ours are.

"I know he's a dick, but why are you attacking Larson?" Mason questions Holland who is still seething with anger. His nostrils flare as a few of the hockey guys help Danny to his feet.

Danny swipes the back of his hand under his bloody nose while staring at Holland with disgust.

"He tried to touch Ellie," Holland grits out. Mason and Logan share a quick glance before looking over to Ellie and me. Their faces shift once they realize the tears on Ellie's face.

Logan rolls his eyes, his head falling forward as if he's contemplating his next move. Mason's face gets red as he glares at Danny. All three of these guys can kick some serious ass, but we don't need that right now.

Right now, I need to get Ellie out of here.

Danny scoffs. "She wanted it. That's why she came out there. She knew I was out-," Holland lunges for Danny but before he can get to him, Mason and Logan are tugging him back.

"You son of a bitch," Holland yells. Danny's lips turn into a smirk, and my body shivers. I don't really know the guy, but I've heard enough to know that he's a sleaze ball. If I wasn't trying to comfort Ellie right now, my knee would hit his balls so hard they'd pop out of his mouth.

"Holland, let it go. I'm taking her home," I tell him, hoping that my words will bring him down a bit. Holland doesn't get mad often. He's the kind of guy that lets most things roll off his shoulder.

Not when it comes to the people he loves though. He'll do anything to protect them. That I've learned first-hand throughout the years I've known him.

Holland's body visibly relaxes, and Mason and Logan let him go. He straightens out and looks Danny dead in the eye.

"Don't ever look at my sister again, you got that?"

Before Danny can answer, Holland pushes his way through the crowd of onlookers and heads for the front door. Ellie and I follow closely behind while Mason and Logan stay behind to help remedy the party.

The chill in the air feels good against my clammy skin as we walk across the street to our house. Holland doesn't say much as we approach.

"I'm going to go in and take a shower. Thank you for making sure I was alright, Laine. Holland, I appreciate that you didn't kill Danny so I didn't need to bail you out of jail," Ellie teases. Holland shrugs his shoulders casually, as if he didn't just beat the shit out of someone.

"I do what I can," Holland smirks, his hands in his pockets. I roll my eyes at his very 'Holland' response.

When the door clicks shut after Ellie disappears inside, I take a deep breath and look at the black sky. No stars tonight, only a crescent moon and a few streetlamps lighting the small street.

"This is not how I thought this night would end," I chuckle to myself.

"Yeah, seems like you expected to be getting railed by some guy tonight, aye Barkley?" I narrow my eyes at him.

"Yeah, I was… And?"

Holland holds both hands up in surrender.

"Nothing, nothing. Good for you," he says as he shoves his hands into his pockets. I give a curt nod and begin to turn toward my front door.

"It's just…" Holland continues. My head falls back in annoyance. Of course he has more to say. When doesn't he? "I thought you had standards, Laine."

God, he's the worst.

Placing my hands on my hips, I look him up and down. "I do. I've never slept with you."

Holland smirks, not at all offended by my comment.

"Not yet," he winks, and I gag.

"That is never going to happen, Monroe. Nice try," I sling back, whipping around to walk into the house.

"Whatever you say, Bug."

Slamming the door in Holland's face before I strangle his cocky ass, I shudder at the nickname. He only calls me that when he's trying to get a rise out of me.

He doesn't need to call me a nickname to do that though. His existence does it naturally. I wonder if Ellie would be heartbroken if her brother disappeared off the face of the planet?

Fights like the one that just happened never surprise me, really. The Elites are always finding new ways to get into some trouble. Holland was never really a hot head until last year when everything went down with his dad.

Ryker, Logan, Holland, Mason, and their friend Patrick took down their father's empire. I don't know all of the details, but apparently their dads were doing all kinds of illegal shit with their business.

When the guys found out, they confronted them and forced them all to step down. Since Ryker graduated in the Spring, he took over his father's position as CEO of the company.

Holland has a share of the company too, as well as Pat and Mason. But Mason and Holland decided to finish school before they took their official positions.

It amazes me that Ellie, Haley, and I had no idea any of this was happening right under our noses. But Gwen kept it pretty hush hush for Ryker's sake.

Their fathers were all part of the Ellington Elite when they attended Ellington University. The guys are what they call "legacies". Born into a life of wealth and popularity.

The Elite is the most powerful group on campus. Everyone knows they hold a lot of power here, and that means people fear them. Although not all the girls got the memo.

Women are constantly throwing themselves at them. I wonder if they know they're wasting their time.

Chapter 3

HOLLAND

The sounds of metal on metal, the grunts that fill the large space, and the blasting music in my ears aren't enough to drown out my racing thoughts. My arms are sore, and my legs are on fire as I finish my last set.

Mason moves out from spotting me, running his hand through his hair.

Grabbing my water bottle off the ground, I chug a good amount of water before setting it back down and wiping my face off with a towel.

I've been pushing myself a lot harder recently since I've come back from my injury. I've been out of commission for six weeks now. Since our rugby season already started, that means I've missed valuable time on the pitch.

I fucked my knee up pretty bad at practice, and I've been recovering ever since. It's been absolute hell not being able to play with the guys. Having to sit on the sidelines and watch my team play without me.

So, when my physical therapist and my doctor told me I could ease back into my gym routine and back into practice, I didn't even hesitate.

I've been sitting on my ass for too long now, and I was beginning to go stir crazy.

This season's already weird as hell without Ryker. Ryker was our fly half, and a damn good one at that. Now that job was given to Ryan Hirshnick. He's not bad, but he's nothing compared to Ryker. Our buddy Patrick was our captain. When he left, that position was handed down to me.

Since my best friend graduated, it's been kind of weird to be here without him. Of course, I still have my cousin Mason, and Ryker's brother Logan. But Logan's nothing like Ryker.

In fact, for a while, Ryker and Logan didn't really get along. They didn't totally dislike one another, but they weren't like normal brothers.

With their dad being a total dick and turning out to be a criminal, they've grown a lot closer.

Last semester ended pretty fucking weird. Ryker, Pat, Mason, and I all found out our fathers were doing some illegal shit, and we shut that shit down real quick.

My father and uncle, Mason's dad, were part of a big crime circle in New York. There was a lot of illegal activity involving money laundering, drugs, and prostitution going on behind the guise of their night club business.

They owned six night clubs in the city. Each one was searched thoroughly for anything that could be illegal, and when they were cleared, Mason and I took over.

Being seniors in college still makes it kind of difficult to run six different night clubs, especially since we're in Connecticut. We hired the best of the best people to run the clubs while we're away at school.

It's been working so far. We haven't had any problems, and we've made a lot of changes to the clubs, so they have no remnants of our fathers.

All I know is that I have to crack down this semester and at least try to pass my classes so I can graduate and start my life away from Ellington University.

The university itself is great. It's old and the architecture is crazy. The professors are some of the best of the best, and most of the students come from wealth, fame, and legacy.

The guys and I are all legacies. Our fathers went to Ellington back in their day, and they were part of the Ellington Elite, the big men on campus.

Being part of the Elite was a privilege, or so they say. Professors let you get away with shit other students would probably get shit for. Kids on campus either worship the ground you walk on or run the other direction in fear.

You can't be an Elite unless your father, grandfather, or great grandfather was a member, making this 'club' really exclusive.

To me, it didn't make much sense. We're basically just a glorified fraternity. I wouldn't even say that we do anything important. We just have a shit ton of money and respect. I guess I can't really complain about that, can I?

My head is still reeling after last night with Danny fucking Larson fucking with my sister. Ellie may be my twin sister, but I've always felt like I had to be the protective brother. Everyone tends to think I'm older than her because of that.

I honestly can't believe Larson would try something with MY sister on MY turf. The guy must be a special kind of stupid.

And Barkley. Finding Lainey shoved up against a wall by some fuckwat who didn't even look like he knew what he was doing. That shit made my blood boil.

I'm not a fucking idiot. I know Lainey gets around. That's her MO. Since high school, she's been pretty open about her sexuality. Honestly, good for her. I like that she doesn't take shit from anyone and doesn't care what anyone thinks about her.

It makes her that much more interesting. Lainey Barkley has been in my life since we were eight, and one thing I've always loved to do is get her riled up.

I don't know why, but knowing I can make her so angry, so annoyed, it makes me feel… powerful. Like I have some sort of hold over her like she has a hold over me.

Again, I'm not an idiot, and I'm certainly not blind. Lainey Barkley is hot as sin. Long tan legs, a waist that's to die for, an ass like no other, and dark curly hair that makes her greyish eyes stick out.

She's every guy's wet dream. It's no wonder she has guys all over her at all times. It's been like that since we were teenagers. It's always bothered me, watching guys throw themselves at her.

I was never sure if it was because I was jealous or because I saw her as a sister. But when my dick started to get hard at the thought of her, and I would jerk off to her face in my head, I knew it was the former.

Obviously, that piece of information I've kept to myself. Not even my boys know about it. Ellie especially doesn't know how often I fantasize about her friend sucking my dick.

Lainey acts like she wants nothing to do with me. She acts like I'm nothing but an inconvenience, a thorn in her side, but I know she feels something too. You can feel the tension like a fucking rubber band about to snap.

For some reason though, she doesn't want to act on her desire. I guess I could say it's because of Ellie being her best friend. Or maybe I've completely misread the signals. Maybe Lainey Barkley hates my guts and actually despises my existence.

If that's the case, she's shit out of luck because I'm not going anywhere.

"Yo, Holli. What's going on? Are we done or what?" Mason asks, breaking me out of my thoughts. Fuck. I shake my head, regaining my composure.

"Yeah, sorry. Let's get out of here."

Chapter 4

HOLLAND

"You know you need to get a suit, right? Like a presentable one that doesn't look like you got it when you were fifteen," my sister says in a smartass tone.

Rolling my eyes, I grab the old suit out of my closet and look it over.

"It's not that bad," I say, not sure if I'm trying to convince her or myself.

Ellie scoffs. "You're kidding right? That thing would not fit you. You need a new one."

She's not wrong. This thing looks like it would fit a child, not a twenty-two-year-old man, but I don't want to have to go out and buy a new one.

Money isn't an issue here, but my distaste for shopping and trying things on is. I do look damn good in a suit though, so maybe it's worth getting a new one.

"Can't I just wear sweatpants?" Ellie's eyes widen in horror, and I have to resist the urge to laugh.

"To a wedding? How are we even related?" she asks, hopping off my bed and heading for my door. I think I may have met her quota for annoyance today. She's just so east to rile up. "Gwen would kill you if you showed up to her wedding in sweatpants. Get a suit. You have like two weeks."

With that, Ellie lets herself out of my room, leaving me alone with my too small suit.

Well, this is just great. The last thing I want to do is go out and get a new suit. I wonder if Logan and Mason already got theirs. We're all groomsmen, and we were told to get black suits with some light blue flower thing for the pocket.

Ryker's been keeping us updated on the wedding planning, and as expected, Gwen hasn't really been high maintenance. She's got a pretty laid-back personality, so that's not surprising.

She was adamant about the light blue being their color scheme. Ryker didn't really care about the colors, so he let her have it.

Pulling out my phone, I send a text to Mason and Logan, really hoping they haven't gone and gotten their suits already.

The Elite Three ☹

Me

Have you guys gotten suits for this thing yet?

Mason Howard

Yup, and I look hot.

Logan Steele

"This thing". You mean the wedding?

Mason Howard

Have you not gotten yours?

Me

...

Mason Howard

Bro... you know you got like 2 weeks, right?

Logan Steele

Monroe, Gwen's gonna kill you if you don't have a suit.

Mason Howard

You should go to this place I went in the city. Rupert's on fifth. There's this hot chick who get's real handsy when she's taking things in, if you know what I mean. Seems like she'd be into some freaky shit.

Me

What is wrong with you?

Logan Steele

Something is seriously messed up in your head.

Mason Howard

Don't hate me cuz you ain't me.

Logan Steele

Me

You've both been no help. Thanks.

Tossing my phone onto the bed in annoyance, I grab a sweatshirt out of my closet and pull it on. Swiping my phone and my keys, I head downstairs and into the driveway where my Mustang sits.

I dread things like this, and I really don't feel like going alone. Usually Ryker and I would do these things together, but he's not here. Fuck him for graduating, honestly.

Starting the engine, I check my mirrors, and my eyes catch on a small figure across the street sitting on the screened in porch. The thing is heated so you can sit there all year round and look out at the snow falling outside, making it possible for Lainey to sit out there in the middle of January.

She's reading a book, her dark hair sitting on the top of her head in a mess. She's got one leg under her, and one pulled up against her.

Suddenly, I get an idea. A really, really shitty idea that in no way could ever be considered a good idea but for some reason I can't seem to talk myself out of it. She's totally going to hate this, but I can't help myself.

I pull out of the driveway, pulling in front of Lainey and Ellie's house. Rolling my window down, I call out to Lainey.

"Whatcha doin, Lainey Bug?" I ask, knowing the name will piss her off, but I'm a prick, so I don't care. She looks up from her book with a death glare, and those grey eyes make my cock stiffen. God damnit, Holland. Get yourself under control.

"What do you want, Monroe?" Lainey asks, a bit of snark in her tone. God, she's hot.

"Wanna go for a ride?" I wink and Lainey rolls her eyes.

"With you? No," she deadpans, looking back down to her book. I shake my head, a smirk growing on my face.

"Come on, Barkley. I gotta get a suit for this wedding. Don't make me go alone," I pout, my lip jutting out and everything. She doesn't even look up.

"You haven't gotten a suit for the wedding yet? You know you have like, two weeks, right?" My eyes roll as my head falls back on the headrest in exasperation. Like I haven't heard this already.

"No, I didn't. I've been… distracted," I tell her, thinking about the recent weeks and how hard I've been working to get my body back in shape for this season. I haven't really even thought about this wedding, which I guess is pretty shitty considering Ryker is my best friend.

"Distracted? By what?" Lainey asks, finally looking back up from the book in her lap. I shake my head, not wanting to get into it.

"Will you just get in the damn car? I need someone to tell me which suit looks best on my figure," I tease, which causes Lainey's nose to scrunch up in a way a rabbits would. Why does it make her look so damn cute though?

"Why don't you have one of the guys go with you? Are they tired of you too?"

"Ha. Ha. No, they're busy. Come on, do you want me to get on my knees and beg? I'll get out right now and-" Lainey stands abruptly, dropping her book on the chair and walking toward my car.

"Fine, I'll go with you. Not because I want to, because I don't, but so you don't cause a scene in my front yard."

She opens my passenger side door and slips in. The Ellington Dance Team sweatshirt she's wearing is a bit oversized, and the jeans she's got on are tight against her toned legs. She's got no makeup on, making all of her natural features stand out.

The small freckle under her eye, the scar on her cheek from when we were twelve and she fell from the tree in my front yard and a stick cut her. She didn't even cry. Just got up, dusted herself off, and got up to climb the damn tree again.

She's always been tough, and that hasn't changed a bit since we've gotten older. Lainey isn't the type of girl to complain or make waves. She goes with the flow, but she'll stand up for what she believes in and the people she cares about.

When we were in high school, Ellie was picked on by this one prick, Jameson Karrick. He'd harass her and make her feel uncomfortable. I'd knocked his head in a few times, but that didn't seem to deter him from being a grade A jackass.

One day, Lainey had had enough of Karrick's bullshit. She went right up to him without saying a word, punched him straight in the nose, shook off her hand, and walked away like it was the most normal thing in the world to punch someone in the face in the school hallway.

Of course, this led to a week suspension, but with her parents pretty much absent ninety nine percent of the time, there was no one there to yell at her or be disappointed in her.

My mom was always there for Lainey. Since her parents were always away, Lainey spent most of her time with a nanny, but my mom always made sure Lainey felt like she was part of the family.

It was normal for her to always be around hanging with Ellie. They'd always be off in Ellie's room, painting their nails and watching stupid TV shows, staying up late giggling and keeping me up.

We'd always bicker because Lainey was a know-it-all, and she was always around in my space. Not much has changed since then. She's still a know-it-all, and she's still always in my space since her and Ellie live together, and across the street from the Elite mansion.

Only now, instead of annoying me, she turns me on without even trying. Without even knowing she affects me, and fuck. As hot as she is, Lainey Barkley kind of fucking scares me.

Chapter 5

LAINEY

We pull up to a nice building on the outskirts of Connecticut. The sign on the front reads "Porter Brothers Suits Co."

The red brick building looks old but charming. I'm sure it looks absolutely beautiful in the summer, but right now the bricks look dull after being covered with snow, and the sidewalk is covered in brown slush. Still, the place has an expensive feel to it.

Holland gets out of the car first, and I watch as he moves in front of the vehicle, coming to my door and opening it for me. My eyes narrow before stepping out onto the pavement.

"Since when are you a gentleman?" I ask. Holland runs a hand through his shaggy hair, a strand falling in front of his eye.

With a teasing smirk, he says, "I'm always a gentleman. Give me a chance to show you," he leans in closer, whispering in my ear. "In bed."

His breath against my ear is warm, and it causes a small shiver to run through me, and not because it's like thirty degrees outside.

He pulls back and winks at me, the asshole. He's always making sexual jokes and giving me things to envision in my head. Like his face between my legs, or him behind me as he…okay, Lainey. That's enough.

Holland and I will never be a thing, even though I can admit that the guy is seriously attractive. Why'd he have to grow up to be hot? It would really make my life a whole lot easier if he were ugly.

The way his sexual comments now make me feel things in my vagina make this whole thing more complicated. Because I find him annoying, and arrogant, and occasionally sweet and protective, and God damnit. I need to stop.

I shake my head and roll my eyes, hoping I look more unaffected than I actually am.

"You're disgusting," I tell him, pushing his chest so he backs away from me and starting toward the building. It's cold as shit out here and if I don't get inside now, I'm going to freeze to death.

I can hear Holland's deep chuckle as we come into the foyer of the luxurious looking men's warehouse. Immediately when you walk in, you can feel the energy change. This isn't your typical suit and tux shop. This is where fancy, rich people come to get five-thousand-dollar suits and accessories. People who have more money than they know what to do with.

I can't say much because I grew up wealthy. Really wealthy, to be honest. At any major inconvenience in my life, my parents would send me extravagant gifts like a new car, or a trip to Cabo. But I never used any of that stuff to make myself look better.

No one at school knew how wealthy I was, even though the school consisted of many wealthy families from around the area. I never advertised that I had money. It wasn't really important to me. It wasn't what I wanted, or what I needed.

What I needed was for my parents to actually be there, to actually give a shit about their only daughter. I didn't care about fancy cars or clothes, big houses or crazy vacations. All I wanted was to be a family.

But that wasn't what I got. So, I took what I could get. Eventually I stopped fighting it. I started accepting their gifts and accepting the fact that I would never have the family I wanted. Life was less disappointing that way.

To the right of the large foyer, a large, beautiful mahogany desk sits with a young, well-dressed gentleman behind it. His black hair is slicked back with too much gel, and he looks kind of uncomfortable in the suit he wears. He's typing on a computer, and when he notices us, a friendly smile appears on his face.

"Well, hello there," he greets us in a voice that could only be described as 'customer servicy.' "Welcome to Porter Brothers Suits Company. I'm Marcos. What brings you in today?"

Holland gives him a polite smile. "I need a suit for a wedding. Black, please," he tells the man. Marcos continues to smile, and I'm surprised his cheeks don't hurt from smiling so much. I don't think he's stopped since he saw us.

"Right this way," Marcos says, leading the way to a large room. The large chandelier that hangs from the ceiling is incredibly beautiful. There are two brown leather couches in the room, with two accent chairs sitting the middle edge between them.

Suits, ties, and shoes line the surrounding walls, and it smells like cedar, leather, and man. The place looks wealthy and almost exclusive. I'd almost feel bad for sitting on the decadent furniture, but then I remember that's what it's there for. So I take a seat while Marcos shows Holland all of the options.

I catch myself watching as Holland walks around the spacious room, noticing his muscular legs from years of playing rugby, his huge arms in the long sleeve shirt he's wearing, his megawatt smile as he talks to Marcos.

I grab my phone from my hoodie pocket and see a missed text from Ellie.

Ellie Bear 🐻

Ellie Bear 🐻

Did you get abducted?

Do I need to call the cops?

Me

No, I'm fine. Did you know that your idiot brother hasn't gotten a suit for the wedding yet?

Ellie Bear 🐻

Yep. He told me this morning. I seriously can't believe him.

You know what, yeah, I can. He's a dunce. Did he kidnap you?

Me

Yup. Sitting at this really nice men's shop waiting for him to pick a damn suit so I can go the hell home.

Ellie Bear 🐻

Tell him to hurry up. I need you.

Me

What's wrong? Are you okay?

Three dots appear as Ellie begins to type back, but before I can see what she said, Holland walks out of the dressing room dressed in an elegant black suit that makes me feel some type of way.

"Well?" he asked, spreading his arms dramatically. "Do I look like someone who has their life together?"

I can't help the snort that comes out of me. "Sure, if your life is about attending business meetings and arguing over spreadsheets."

"Spreadsheets are important," Holland states, turning to inspect himself in the three-way mirror. "How else would I keep track of my growing empire?"

"Empire?" I ask, raising an eyebrow. "Is that what we're calling your fantasy football league now?"

Holland turns back to me, grinning. "Laugh it up. You're just jealous you weren't drafted into greatness."

"Oh, yeah, devastated," I reply, mock dramatic. "Anyway, the suit's fine, but it's not *you*. Too serious," I shrug.

He frowns, tugging at the lapels. "I can do serious."

"You couldn't do serious if you tried," I tell him, leaning back with a smirk. I don't think Holland's ever been serious a day in his life. That's just not his personality. The only time he can be serious is when he's playing rugby, or when he's threatening to beat people up for looking at Ellie the wrong way.

"Challenge accepted," he says, his tone dropping to an overly stern voice. He strikes a stiff pose. "I am here to negotiate world peace."

I burst out laughing, not able to contain it. I slap a hand over my mouth. "Stop! You look like you're about to fire someone."

"Maybe I am," he teases, gesturing to me. "Starting with you."

"You couldn't afford to fire me," I shot back, crossing my arms. "Who else would tell you when you look ridiculous?"

"Fair point," Holland admits, disappearing back into the fitting room. "What's next on your list of sartorial demands, Your Highness?"

I shrug, sinking back into the couch. The suit he had on was hot as hell, but it was missing something. It wasn't him. "Something less funereally, more weddingy."

Holland's voice comes through the curtain. "Weddingy?" he questions. I fold my arms over my chest, even though he can't see me.

"Yes. Weddingy."

"I don't think that's a word in the dictionary," Holland calls back, and I can hear the amusement in his voice.

"Don't question me, Monroe. I know what I'm saying."

"Woah there, killer," Holland says as he steps back out from the fitting room. "Remind me why I brought you?" he asks, his lips pulled up into a smirk.

My breath hitches, and my heart begins to race in a way that shouldn't be possible. It was perfect. The jacket hugs his shoulders in just the right way, and the fit is much less funereally. He looks… delicious. Oh, shut up, Lainey. He's a pain in the ass, and he's annoying.

"Well?" he inquires, his grin growing wider, probably because I look like I'm ready to pounce on him.

Shit. "Does this one fit your outrageous standards, Lainey Bug?"

I blink, regaining my composure. "It's… alright."

"Alright?" he repeats, his eyebrows shooting up. "That's all I get? Alright?"

I shrug, trying to look unimpressed. "I guess you clean up *alright*."

His head tilts to one side, like he's studying me. "Has anyone ever told you that you suck at compliments?"

"I'm just honest," I reply, standing and making my way over to him. I don't know why I'm moving toward him, but for some reason I can't stop myself. "But yeah, this one works."

When I'm right in front of him, I brush an imaginary piece of lint off one of the sleeves, and when I look up, Holland is looking at me.

The fun, lighthearted air between us shifts, and suddenly I'm very aware of how close we're standing. He must feel the weird energy too, because he stiffens a bit.

I clear my throat and step back, shoving my hands in my hoodie pocket so I can't make any stupid moves.

"So, are we good to go? I have to get home. Ellie needs me," I tell him, starting to walk out of the room.

"Uh, yeah. We're good to go," he states, walking back toward the fitting room and calls over his shoulder, "I'm holding you responsible if I look better than the groom."

"Not a chance," I shoot back, continuing my way back to the front of the shop to wait for him.

Chapter 6

HOLLAND

The drive home was pretty quiet. I didn't try to force conversation, and Lainey didn't seem to mind the silence. Honestly, I think she preferred it.

She's really hard to read most of the time. You can never tell what kind of mood she's in, which is why I find it so strange that she's the funny one in their little friend group.

Gwen was the book smart, quiet girl. Or at least, that's what she seemed to be until she got with Ryker. My sister is quiet, and she doesn't get into trouble. She's been that way since we were kids.

Their other roommate, Haley, she's a bitch. Like she's nice to them, but she reminds me of a feral cat.

Ready to pounce at any second if someone even looks at her wrong.

Lainey though, Lainey is the one that keeps everything lighthearted and cool. She's the one with all of the advice and the one that will kick some sense into you if you need it.

She's not afraid to speak up and tell you exactly what she's thinking, and to be honest, that's one of my favorite things about her. She's not afraid to tell me to fuck off or to let me know when I'm being a prick. Not afraid to tell other dudes to fuck way off if they offend her or bother her in any way.

I used to think that made her a bitch, but now I think it makes her strong. She never had anyone there to help her grow up, except the nanny that I'm pretty sure just let Lainey do whatever the fuck she wanted, and my mom when she could.

I used to feel bad for her as a kid, because even though my dad was a prick, and he was barely around, I at least had my mom who was always there for Ellie and me.

When we pull up in front of Lainey's house that she shares with Ellie and Haley, Lainey jumps out of the car and shut the door. I roll down my window before she can disappear inside.

"Thanks for coming today," I tell her. She shrugs, as if it's no big deal.

"It's not like you gave me much of choice," she snaps back. I smirk, loving the bit of snark in her tone.

"You know you loved every second of it, Barkley. Don't act like you didn't enjoy seeing me all dressed up," I tease, and Lainey looks completely unaffected.

"I would have rather stepped on Legos repeatedly than have been there with you all day," she smiles, but it's not a friendly smile. It's a 'fuck you' kind of smile, and my dick twitches in my pants. Why does her attitude turn me the fuck on?

Just then, the front door opens, and my sister pops out, looked at Lainey and then glaring at me. Her small stature makes her much less intimidating than she thinks she is.

"What the hell, Holland? You can't just kidnap innocent girls off of their front porches," Ellie says, a playful kind of anger in her tone. I shrug.

"Barkley's anything but innocent," I chaff, watching Lainey for her reaction. She glares at me, and I give her a little finger wave. She lifts her hand as if to wave back but instead raises her middle finger with a sweet as can be smile.

Bringing my hand to my chest and placing it over my heart, I say, "Come on, Lainey, baby. You know that turns me on."

Ellie makes a disgusted noise. "Ew, Holland. You're such a guy. Can you please just go?" she begs. I laugh at her expression and give Lainey one last look. She looks like she could kill me, and for some fucked up reason, that makes me want to stay and find out just how mad she actually is.

But I don't. I give Lainey one last wink before driving the rest of the way to the Elite mansion and pulling in the driveway.

Grabbing the new, absurdly expensive suit from the back seat, I haul it inside, heading straight for my room. Thankfully, I don't run into anyone in the hallway because I really just want to jump in the shower.

I wasn't completely teasing when I told Lainey her flipping me off turns me on. The fact that she's pint size and can hold that much rage inside of her is hot as fuck.

Most girls would be terrified to talk to me, let alone flip me the bird and tell me to fuck off.

Maybe it's because we've been playing this game since we were kids, maybe it's because she's got this off-limits factor to her, or maybe it's because she's able to pretend that I don't affect her when I know for a fact I do.

But no matter who or how many girls I fuck, no matter how much I try to tell myself that Barkley is forbidden fruit due to being my sister's best friend, I can't seem to help the fact that my dick gets hard every time she's around.

Maybe that makes me a fucking idiot with a death wish, but I never said I was smart.

After hanging the suit up in my closet, I strip down and turn on the shower. The hot water cascades over my head and down my back as I stare at the drain. I watch as the water gets sucked down and try to distract myself from thoughts of my sister's best friend.

Unfortunately, staring at the shower floor doesn't help much. Thoughts of Lainey Barkley take over my mind, and I can feel myself getting worked up.

The way she acts like she's unaffected, the way she takes no shit, the way she stands tall and strong no matter what she's going through.

The way her jeans hugged her ass and nearly brought me to my knees today.

My hand slowly drifts downwards, my fingers brushing against my hardening length. My teeth sink into my lower lip as I imagine Lainey's soft touch that makes me ache with need. The thought of her hands on my body sends shivers down my spine.

The thought of her making out with that guy at the party the other night. How she twisted her body with his, how her fingers tangled in his hair, how his hands moved over her perfect ass. It shouldn't turn me on so much. What the fuck is wrong with me? Why does she have to be so damn tempting?

I picture Lainey's lips, full and pink, and wonder how they would feel against mine. How they'd feel around my…

My fingers tighten around my dick, stroking slowly as I envision Lainey's hands replacing my own. I imagine her kneeling before me, her eyes locked on mine as she takes me into her warm mouth.

The fantasy is so vivid, I can almost feel her tongue swirling around the head of my cock, her soft moans filling the room.

"Fuck, yes," I groan, my eyes fluttering shut as I increase the pace of my strokes. I picture Lainey's hands roaming over my body, her fingernails gently scraping my skin. The thought of her exploring every inch of me, discovering my most sensitive spots, makes my breath catch.

My mind continues to race with scenarios, each more erotic than the last.

I imagine Lainey pushing me against the shower wall, her wet body pressed against mine, her hands gripping my ass as she urges me to take her. I can almost feel her hot breath on my neck, her soft moans turning into desperate pleas as she begs me to fuck her.

My strokes become more urgent, my breathing ragged as I envision Lainey riding me, her tight pussy bouncing on my cock.

My balls tighten and my hand moves faster, my body tensing as I groan loudly, cum shooting out in hot bursts, hitting the shower wall and mixing with the steam.

As I catch my breath, I lean against the cool tiles, my heart still racing. The thought of Barkley down on her knees for me, sucking me off… fuck. This is bad.

I've always had this attraction to her, ever since she stood up to me when we were kids when I stole her freaking cookie. She pushed me to the ground and broke the cookie in my face. That's when I knew this girl was different from the rest.

That and ever since her tits grew and she started wearing more revealing clothing. I just don't know why it's affecting me so much now.

Turning the water off that has now turned cold, I step out of the shower, the cool air hitting my skin. The feeling that Lainey is becoming an obsession, a temptation that I might not be able to resist for much longer is kind of pissing me the fuck off.

My sister would absolutely kill me if I went after Lainey, Lainey would probably kick me in the balls if I tried anything, and I should not be feeling these things for this girl.

I'm so fucking fucked.

Chapter 7

LAINEY

"I'm really sorry Holland kidnapped you. Do you want me to kick his ass?" Ellie asks, bringing two mugs of coffee into the living room. She takes a seat next to me and hands me my mug. I probably shouldn't be having coffee this late in the day, but it smells too good to pass up.

I chuckle at the thought of Ellie, who is shorter than me, trying to beat Holland's ass.

"I'm fully capable of kicking his ass myself, El. But no, it's fine. I was bored anyway," I tell her.

It's not entirely true. I was perfectly content sitting on the porch, reading my book.

She rolls her eyes. "He's so annoying. I mean, you don't even like him. Why would he think you'd want to go with him anywhere?" she inquires, her face scrunching up in disgust. Her and her brother do get along, believe it or not, but they butt heads… a lot.

I shrug. "Does anything he does ever make sense?"

"No, I guess not," Ellie says, taking a sip of her coffee. "Did you see the text from Gwen?"

My eyebrows furrow in confusion. I haven't really checked my phone since we left the shop. I shake my head.

"No, what happened?"

"She's freaking the hell out. I think the wedding jitters are finally hitting her. She might come visit this weekend," Ellie explains. Just then, a door opens from down the hallway and Haley appears, looking exhausted.

"I heard Gwen's coming home?" she asks, a smile growing on her face. She pads over to where we're sitting in the living room and plops down next to me on the couch.

Ellie nods. "We should plan something to get her mind off of the wedding for a bit. What do you think, Lane?"

"Yeah, I think that's a good idea. We never did a bachelorette party. Maybe that's what we'll do. I'll plan something," I tell my friends. I'm usually the one that has to plan things like this anyway since Ellie doesn't go out much without me, and Haley is always busy.

I don't mind making the plans, especially because I feel like I know my friends better than they know themselves most of the time.

While they're shy and soft spoken, I'm loud and I go for what I want when I want it. I don't even think twice about it or the consequences. This has gotten me into trouble in the past, but at least it helps me feel something other than emptiness.

I wouldn't say I'm depressed or anything like that. I think I do quite well on my own, and ever since I accepted that this was my life, and my parents would always be shitty parents, I stopped being so sad about it.

I know Ellie feels bad for me. Whenever she brings up going home or her mom, I can feel the way she deflates a little, like she thinks she's going to offend me or make me feel bad.

It's crazy because I know I have a shitty home life, and it's not been easy growing up alone, her family is going through shit too.

Ever since last year when Ryker, Holland, Mason, and Patrick confronted their fathers for the shady business they were doing, things have been rough in the Monroe household.

Ellie and Holland's mom wanted their father out of the house for all the lies he told her. For putting their family in danger. I can't say I blame her, but I know it's been hard for all of them.

Mr. Monroe has been out of the house for about seven months now, and I imagine that's been hard for Ellie and Holland to wrap their head around.

But Ellie is really good at putting aside her issues and feelings to make sure everyone around her is happy. She'll talk about how she's feeling, and she'll vent to me when she needs to. Unlike me, who bottles up all of her feelings and refuses to show anyone any weakness.

I have to be strong. I've had to learn to rely on only one person, and that's myself. Of course, I know Ellie would always be there for me, and when Gwen was here, she was always trying to get me to share my feelings.

Showing weaknesses only gives people a chance to exploit them. Call me a pessimist, but I'd like to think of myself as a realist.

No one in life has it perfect. No matter how much they try to put on a front of the ideal life, there's always something sinister beneath the surface. If more people would realize that there'd probably be a whole lot less disappointment in the world.

Even with my unfortunate circumstances, I had to find ways to keep myself entertained. In high school, I partied a lot, more than a young girl should have. Without actual supervision and someone telling me no, I did whatever the hell I wanted.

I was out practically every weekend either at someone's house party or up at the local community college hanging out with guys much too old for me at the time. But why would I care? No one else did.

Getting drunk, fucking random guys that would show me the slightest bit of attention, and forgetting about my problems was my specialty. I can't say much has changed since high school.

I still party, and I'm still finding less than healthy ways to deal with my feelings, ways that would make my mother cry with disappointment if she actually gave a shit about me.

All this to say that I'm pretty good at being the life of the party, and making sure everyone has a good time.

Ellie claps her hands together, breaking me out of my thoughts.

"Perfect! I'll tell Gwen to prepare the bail money," she teases with a wink. I roll my eyes.

"That was one time, and that cop had it out for us the second we walked into that bar," I huff.

"Maybe because he knew we were underage and should not have been there," Ellie laughs. She's not wrong.

"I promise I won't plan anything illegal, and now we're old enough to drink, so there shouldn't be any problems."

Ellie and Haley laugh, and I smile. I don't know where I'd be without my friends, and I don't even want to think about it. They're one of the only things that keep me going.

"Alright, well I'm going to bed. It's been a long day," I tell them, standing up from the couch and stretching. Haley looks at me, confusion in her delicate features.

"What did you do today? I thought you had no classes today," she asks curiously. Before I can give her an answer, Ellie steps in.

"My idiot brother forced her into going to get a suit for the wedding with him," she explains, rolling her eyes. Haley looks at me, her expression almost knowing. I don't know what she's thinking, but she clearly thinks she knows something.

"Oh, did he now? And you went?" Haley asks. I nod nonchalantly.

"He threatened to get out of the car and make a scene. I figured I'd save myself the embarrassment and just give in," I explain, shrugging. I would rather him not get down on his knees and beg in front of everyone on our street.

Haley nods slowly. "Right, yeah. That makes sense," she gives me a narrow-eyed look, like she thinks there's more to the story. Well, there's not.

"Yup," I say. I don't know what else to say. Why is she being so weird?

Beginning to back out of the living room and toward my bedroom, I say, "Alright, well I'm going to take a shower and go to bed. Night."

"Night," I hear Ellie and Haley call back as I shut the door to my bedroom and take a deep breath.

I don't know what was up with Haley, or why she was acting like she knew something I didn't, but I didn't like it.

All I know is that I have to start coming up with a plan for this weekend. It shouldn't be too hard. Maybe we could go into the city for the night. That could be a fun reprieve from the reality of life, and I could use that right now.

Chapter 8

HOLLAND

My ears ring as I lie on the ground, trying to recover from the hit I just took from Luke Hunter, the teams left center.

This is my first time back on the pitch in a while. Working out and shit in the gym hasn't really helped prepare me for getting back to the game. I knew it was going to be difficult. My knee is fucking killing me, and I'm trying really hard to ignore the searing pain it's causing me.

I haven't really told anyone that my knee still gives me trouble. Not Mason or Logan, and not my doctors. I don't want to sit on the sidelines anymore. It's been long enough.

It's not like I plan on going pro or anything. That's never been my plan. The other Elites and I wanted something physical we could do to get our anger out, so we chose rugby. Ever since we joined the team, I've taken it pretty seriously.

I do also really enjoy it. The physicality, the adrenaline, the competitiveness. It makes me feel alive. It doesn't hurt that the team also gets a lot of attention from the girls on campus.

Being an Elite *and* on the rugby team pretty much makes me a God on campus. Not many people know about what happened last year with my father and his company, or that I'll be taking over said company when I'm done with school.

We're playing Ridgewood Academy this weekend the guys are working extra hard tonight. Ridgewood is a rough team to beat. Their guys play dirty, and our guys don't back down from a challenge. It always makes for interesting games.

That just means Coach Shaw is working us to the ground, making sure we're ready for Friday's game. It's Wednesday now, and we have practice tomorrow too. Mason, Logan, and I got a group text last night from Ryker reminding us he's coming into town this weekend for his bachelor party, not that we needed a reminder.

So they'll be at the game on Friday. I'm just glad we don't have practice for the rest of the weekend so we can actually spend some time with them before they leave. They've been living in the city since they graduated. Ryker taking over his family's company and Gwen being a teacher.

They're doing well for themselves, and I'm glad they found each other. Ryker needed someone to pull the stick out of his ass.

"Alright, boys," Coach Shaw barks, his voice cutting through my thoughts and the ringing in my ears. Mason shows up next to me just then, extending his arm to help me up. When I'm on my feet, Mason eyes me warily.

"You good?" he asks, looking down at my knee. I give a sharp nod.

"Yeah, I'm fine."

"Set it up. Holland, let's see if you can get that ball out clean this time," Coach bellows.

Not even acknowledging Coach's works, I get myself into position. I crouch low at the front of the scrum, my hands poised and ready. The pain in my knee distant as I try to focus on what's happening in front of me. My teammates pack in around me, the forwards forming a solid wall of muscle.

"Crouch!" Coach shouts.

I bend further, my fingers brushing the damp grass.

"Bind!"

Our tight-head prop, Payson Rawley locks arms with me, our grip firm and unyielding.

"Set!"

Then we're off.

"Get it, Holland!" I hear Mason bark from somewhere behind me. My foot shoots out, expertly hooking the ball back toward my side. The motion was fluid, practiced—a result of hours spent perfecting my technique.

The ball skids into the hands of our scrumhalf, Warren Lund, who darts away, passing it down the line.

"Good hook!" Coach shouts as the forwards break apart and scramble into position.

The play moves quickly, the ball weaving through the backs as the team executes our set play.

I jog forward, staying ready to support, my body thrumming with adrenaline. Our inside center breaks through a tackle, then offloads the ball just before being brought down.

I take the chance to scoop it up, barreling straight into a defender without hesitation.

The hit was hard, but I stay upright, driving my legs to gain speed before being brought down.

I felt the weight of bodies pile on top of me, the chaos of the ruck forming around me. The wind feels like it's been knocked out of me, and that's how I know I'm out of shape. God damnit.

"Support!" I call, holding onto the ball as my teammates crash into the ruck, securing possession.

Warren darts in, plucking the ball out and passing it wide. The backs surge forward, finishing the play with a diving try in the corner.

The team erupts in cheers as I push myself to my feet, panting but grinning.

"Nice work, Holland," Coach calls from the sideline. "That's the kind of grit I want to see on game day! Alright, we're done for the day. See you guys tomorrow."

"Thanks, Coach," I mumble, wiping the sweat from my brow. My teammates clap me on the back as we all head for the locker room.

Mason jogs over to my side, a teasing grin on his face. "You enjoy getting flattened, or is it just a hooker thing?"

I smirk. "Better than standing around waiting for the ball like you backs."

"Keep telling yourself that," Mason says, jogging ahead of me.

I shake my head because my cousin's an idiot. Trying not to walk with a fucking limp, I make my way into the locker room where the rest of the guys are already showering and changing into street clothes.

I find an empty stall toward the back, stripping down and stepping into the hot water, and it feels good against my clammy, sweat covered skin.

I know I'm going to be in pain tomorrow for practice, and especially for Friday's game., but I have to push through it.

Honestly, I could just say fuck it and quit., but I'm no quitter. I don't really care if we win or lose, but I know my team does. So I have to stay strong for them. I've got no idea why I was given the captain position, but I won't let my guys down.

When I've successfully scrubbed all of the mud and grass off of my body, I step out, wrapping a towel around my waist before heading to my locker.

Of course, Mason is still here waiting for me. He's a loyal fucker, and I like that about him. We always have each other's backs.

He stands from his spot on the bench he was sitting on and grins at me.

"We're going out," he states, as if that's a final decision. Giving him a questioning look, I dig through my gym bag to find clean clothes. I pull them on, careful with bending my leg as I step into my sweats.

"Who's we? I'm going home. I'm starving, and I need sleep," I tell him, slinging my bag over my shoulder and heading for the door. I can hear Mason's footsteps as he follows behind me.

"You, me, Logan, and some of the guys from the team. We're going to Rascal's," he says matter-of-factly.

"*I'm* not going anywhere."

Walking through the parking lot to my car, Mason strolls up next to me, pouting.

"Come on, man. I can't go without my wingman," he tells me, sagging in a pathetic way. I shake my head and chuckle.

"Sorry, Mase. Not tonight," I say as I toss my bag into the back of my car and get in the driver's seat, starting it up immediately because it's cold as fuck out here. A moment later, I sigh, rolling my window down.

"Are you getting in the car, shithead? Or are you going to walk home?" I ask, annoyance laced in my voice.

Mason sighs obnoxiously. "Fine," he grumbles, throwing his bag in the back with mine and taking the passenger seat. Once he's in, he looks out the windshield with his arms crossed, not making eye contact with me.

Shaking my head, I say, "you're such a child."

He still doesn't acknowledge me. Now I'm getting annoyed. "Say something."

His head slowly turns toward me, his eyes narrowed.

"I'm not mad, I'm just disappointed," he looks back down to his lap. Oh, for fucks sake.

"Oh, fuck off," I tell him, rolling my eyes and finally pulling out of the parking lot to head home. Mason laughs and I just shake my head, not saying anything for the rest of the way home.

LAINEY

Ellie, Haley, and I are dressed up and ready to go two hours early. The game against Ridgewood Academy doesn't start until seven, but we were all so excited to see Gwen that we got ready early so we could meet up before the game.

I haven't seen my other best friend in months, and it's been terrible. We talk practically every day, but it's not the same not seeing her every day.

Luckily, back home in Rhode Island, we don't live far from one another, however, she's been living in the city, so that hasn't been much help either.

I'm just glad they didn't move somewhere further, because I don't think I'd survive her being that far away.

Ridgewood Academy is a rival school to Ellington, and their rugby team is rough. They often don't play by the rules, but somehow, they always get away with it. It's like they're paying the refs to look the other way or something.

I like the sport, and I know quite a lot about it. Ever since Holland joined the team, Ellie has dragged me to every single game. I've sat in the cold for hours on end watching her brother play, watching him probably closer than I should have.

At first, I loved the violence, and I loved watching Holland get thrown to the ground. It brought me a sick sense of peace. Now, I actually enjoy watching the game. Although, I still do enjoy watching Holland get his ass handed to him. The cocky little shit needs a good ass kicking now and again.

I remember last year when I dragged Gwen to her first rugby game, before she would admit to having feelings for Ryker who was the team's captain at the time. She didn't understand the game at all, and I had to explain what was happening.

Now, in a little less than two weeks, she'll be marrying him in one of the most romantic cities in the world. Why they chose to have their wedding in Italy is beyond me, but I am not complaining. I've never been out of the country before, and I'm dying to get the hell out of this town.

"Gwen's going to meet us at Café Grind," Ellie says as she puts her coat on. She's dressed in her green and white Ellington University sweatshirt and beanie, her blonde hair peeking out at the bottom the hat.

"Of course she is," I smile to myself. That girl and her coffee. She is coffee obsessed. She would spend hours in that little café on campus.

Haley chuckles. "She's probably only come to visit to go back there." We all laugh and nod.

"Yeah, you're probably right," I tell her.

Taking one last look in the mirror, I pull on my Ellington U winter hat and my coat, combing my fingers through the long, dark hair resting over my shoulders. My lipstick is red, making it stand out against my hair and my grey blue eyes.

Deciding I look good enough, I say, "I'll drive."

When we get to campus, we walk into the tiny coffee shop and sit at a table in the corner. We all order drinks as we wait for Gwen. I take a small sip, trying not to burn my tongue when I hear a familiar voice.

"I'm back, bitches!" Ellie, Haley, and I all look up at the same time to see Gwen enter the café, walking toward our table. I'm the first one out of my seat as I squeal and jump her, almost knocking her over.

"Shhh," I hear from around us, but I don't even care. My bestie is back, and I've never been so relieved to see another human being in my life.

"Hey, Lainey," Gwen chuckles. "It's nice to see you, too."

I pull back slightly to look at her face. My hands grab her cheeks and Gwen's eyes go wide. I look into her eyes and move my hands around her face like I'm trying to feel every inch of it. Gwen laughs, pulling my hands away.

"What the hell are you doing, Lane?" she asks, still chuckling.

"I had to make sure you were actually here and this wasn't a bad trip," I tell her, my face as straight as it can be. She smiles.

"Well, I'm really here. You're not tripping," she assures me. I hug her again and she wraps her tiny arms around me. I bury my face in her neck.

"I missed you so much," I say.

"I missed you, too."

"Alright, move. I wanna hug!" Ellie exclaims, pushing me aside to bring Gwen in for a hug of her own.

After the greetings, we sit down together, drinking our coffee and chatting. For a minute, it feels like old times, being all together and gossiping. I forget that this hasn't been our normal for a while now, and it feels good to have all of us in the same room again.

An hour later, we're on our way to Ellington U's athletic wing. Sports are pretty popular here, so Ellington allotted an entire space for every sport to play and practice.

The stadium is lit up with big, bright lights. The sound of the crowd is roaring, and it makes my adrenaline spike. I love this atmosphere. When the school comes together to cheer on our team, and we all have a common enemy.

My stomach is rolling, and I can't tell why I'm feeling anxious all of a sudden. A shiver runs down my spine and I'm not sure it's from the cold.

"Lainey, you okay?" Gwen asks, her elbow hitting my arm lightly. She gives me a small smile.

"What? Yeah, of course. I'm fine," I assure her, but I don't even know if that's the truth. "Where's Ryker by the way?"

Gwen shakes her head and chuckles lightly to herself. "He's with the guys in the locker room. Coach Shaw was ecstatic to have him back."

"That makes sense," I laugh.

We make our way to our seats, sitting down and bundling up because it's so God damn cold. I pull my gloves on and tug my hat down a bit.

"I want popcorn," Ellie announces. "Do you guys want anything?"

I look between Gwen and Haley who both shake their heads. Deciding I should probably eat something, I nod.

"Yeah, I'll take some."

Ellie scoffs. "Well come on then. Get your butt up and come with," she orders. I look at her with a pout which causes her to put a hand on her hip.

"I can't, my legs are broken."

"Get your lazy ass up or you get nothing," she tells me. I groan dramatically, standing and walking toward her.

"God, someone's touchy," I say sarcastically. She swats me on the arm, and I turn around to see Haley and Gwen watching our interaction with smiles on their faces. I stick my tongue out at them, and they crack up.

Ellie grabs my arm and leads the way through the stands and straight to the concession stand. Ellie orders two popcorns and waters as I stand to the side scrolling through my phone. It's always crazy down here, especially at a big game like this one.

People are everywhere and any normal person might think this was overwhelming, but I feel comfortable. Growing up with no one around you makes you appreciate when you do have others there. Even if you're not necessarily talking to them.

My phone is suddenly knocked out of my hands, falling to the floor. Shit.

"Shit, I'm sorry," a familiar male voice says. He leans down to retrieve my phone and our eyes connect as he hands it back to me.

"No Name?" I ask, my head tilting to one side. It's the guy from the party the other night. The guy I *almost* had sex with. The guy I totally would have fucked if Holland Monroe didn't cockblock me.

A piece of his wavy brown hair falls onto his face before he runs a hand through it to push it back. He really is attractive, and I kind of regret not finishing what we started. He smirks, looking a bit nervous.

"Yeah, I guess?" Right, I never actually called him that to his face.

"Sorry, I didn't get your name when we were, you know," I say, and he chuckles.

"Yeah, you wouldn't let me tell you." I nod slowly.

"Right, yeah. Sorry about that, and sorry we didn't get to…" I drift off, hoping he'll finish my sentence in his head. He does.

"Yeah, that kind of sucked. Is your friend okay?" he asks, sounding actually interested to know the answer.

"What?" My eyes narrow in confusion. "Oh, yes. Yeah, she's fine now," I hike a thumb over my shoulder to where Ellie stands, paying for our popcorn and drinks.

His eyes move from my face over to Ellie. He nods and smiles.

"Good to hear," he says, smirking, then extending his arm to shake my hand. Seems a bit trivial since his tongue has been in my mouth. I take is, his large hand encompassing mine.

"Hi. I'm Archer, and you are?"

My mind freezes and I debate telling him my name. He seems like the type of guy who gets attached and I'm not in any space for that.

"Come on," he coaxes. "Tell me your name."

Alright, what can it hurt. "Lainey."

Archer smiles, his perfect white teeth shining brightly. He looks like he'd be an accounting major. Like he grew up with a perfect family and has never actually felt pain. A small pang hits my chest as I think about how different my life is from that.

"See, that wasn't so bad, was it?" he teases, and I can't help but smile. "Well, it's nice to meet you, Lainey."

"I think we've already met. But it's nice to re-meet you, Archer."

His smile grows, and then I realize he hasn't let go of my hand yet. He follows my line of sight down to our still attached hands and then drops his.

Tucking his hands into his pockets, he clears his throat before asking, "Would you want to get dinner sometime?"

My heartbeat stutters, because what the hell? I was not expecting that. I mean, I shouldn't go, right? I'd probably wreck him, and he seems like a nice guy. No guy I've ever hooked up with, or almost hooked up with, has ever asked me out. This is new territory for me.

Of course I've gone on dates, and I've tried the whole monogamy thing, but I'm not so sure it's for me. I've never really had anything stable in my life other than Ellie, Holland, and Gwen. I can't imagine a man wanting to stay with me when my own parents couldn't even stay.

My brain races as I try to come up with a good reason to tell him no. I'm emotionally unavailable. I'm damaged goods. I'm not worth it. Archer deserves someone that's fully invested, and that just isn't me.

Archer looks from Ellie back to me, his eyes studying my face and I can feel my cheeks heat. I'm a pretty confident woman, and I don't get flustered easily, but I'm feeling pretty damn flustered right now.

This guy is sweet and kind, and I already know he can kiss and make me feel good. What harm could going to dinner with the guy do, Lainey?

"Well?" Archer asks, looking hopeful.

"I'm sorry, I don't think so," I tell him, and I watch the hopeful look fall right off of his pretty face. God, I'm an asshole, but I'm doing him a favor.

"Oh, really? Is there a reason?" he asks, a look of disappointment filling his face. Crossing my arms over my chest in a protective manner, I shrug.

"I don't do dates," I say simply. I won't go into my tragic past or childhood trauma. Keeping it simple and frank is easier. I know he'll think I'm a whore or a bitch, but that's better than him developing any kind of feelings for me.

Archer nods slowly, although I know he doesn't understand.

"Right, okay," he says, his hands moving to his pockets awkwardly. "Well, then, it was nice seeing you again, Lainey."

I'm such an asshole.

"You too, Archer."

"See you around."

Ellie looks between us as she shoves a piece of popcorn into her mouth as if this has been some form of entertainment for her.

"See you," I tell him, secretly hoping I'll never actually see him again.

God damnit, Lainey. Why can't you be normal? Archer seemed like a nice, decent man. He could have been a great thing for me. Why'd I have to go and ruin a chance I had to be possibly be happy?

"Oh my god, who was that? He's seriously hot," Ellie squeals as she grabs my arm. I shake my head and chuckle in half amusement at her reaction and the fact that I'm such a mess.

"I uh, almost hooked up with him the night… the night of the incident with Danny," I explain, seeing Ellie stiffen a bit when she hears Danny's name.

"What do you mean *almost*?" she questions, her brows furrowing. I'm not going to tell her it's because I went to check on her, she doesn't need to know that. She'll feel guilty as hell.

"I stopped it. I wasn't feeling well," I lie. Ellie looks like she wants to question me more, but thankfully she doesn't.

"Oh. Well, you should've said yes to that date. He seemed sweet."

Nodding, I grab the box of popcorn from her, popping a piece into my mouth.

"Yeah, that's the problem. I'd ruin him," I tell her matter-of-factly. "Come on, let's get back to our seats."

Ellie shrugs, following me through the crowd which has started to cheer louder as the teams start to head onto the pitch. I watch the Ellington guys set up and get in their positions.

And when we're back at our seats, and I'm sitting back down on the cold bench, I notice that my eyes aren't focused on the whole team. They're focused on one person. Holland Monroe.

Fuck.

Chapter 10

HOLLAND

Tensions run high as we take the pitch and Ridgewood's team follows suit. Some of the guys shoot death glares at each other, and I can already tell this is going to be a rough game.

My blood is already boiling since I saw Lainey talking to some guy at the concession stand. I don't know who the fucker was, but they sure looked pretty friendly.

Not that you fucking care, Holland. You do not care if she's talking to a hundred guys.

She can do whatever she wants. She is not your girlfriend, she's not *yours*.

So why do I have the urge to go find that prick and punch his lights out for even touching her?

"Holland, dude. What are you doing?" I hear my fly half, Ryan, ask as he pats me on the back. We're not close, and I don't know if I'd even consider us friends, but we're on the same team and he's a good enough guy.

Shaking my head, I try to get rid of every thought that doesn't involve this game. "Nothing, I'm good."

"Okay, man," Ryan says, running toward the rest of the team. "Let's fucking do this!" he shouts.

I shake my head and chuckle softly before heading over to join him.

The crowd is going crazy, a sea of green and red as students and faculty show support for both teams. My eyes scan the people, and then they catch on a familiar head of dark, wavy hair, the top of her head covered in an Ellington U hat. She's snuggled up next to my sister and Ryker's girl, Gwen. Ryker stands by Gwen's side, and their other roommate is jumping up and down with excitement.

"Go number 2!" Ellie screams as she waves to me. I chuckle lowly and wave back. My sister has always been one of my biggest supporters, even though we get on each other's nerves more than ninety percent of the time.

My eyes wander back to a pair of greyish blue eyes, and I swear my dick twitches just from the bit of eye contact. Lainey starts to jump up and down with Ellie, cupping her hands around her mouth and screaming, "Go Ellington!"

With that, she looked back to me and without any hesitation and huge grin on her face, she flips me off. It's so unexpected and so her that I can't help the laugh that bubbles out of me. I'd flip her off right back, but there are a lot of eyes on me right now, and I don't want them thinking I'm the asshole.

Instead, I hold up my hands in the shape of a heart in her direction and wink, laughing when she acts like she's gagging.

"Yo, Monroe. Come on," Mason calls for me. Tearing my gaze away from Lainey, I turn around and get into position.

The floodlights burn down on the pitch, casting long shadows across the muddied grass. The air is thick with tension, a mix of sweat, earth, and the unmistakable scent of competition. My eyes lock with Ridgewood's hooker, Tommy Crawford. He gives me a devilish grin and I reciprocate.

"You sure you're ready for this, Monroe?" he asks, his voice cocky as ever.

"I asked your mom the same thing when I fucked her brains out last night, Crawford," I say, giving him a wink. The grin falls from his face and he growls.

"You're fucking dead, Monroe."

I laugh loudly, and that seems to piss him off even more. God, it's just too easy.

I run my tongue over my teeth and grin mischievously. I'm sure I look crazy, and that's what I'm banking on.

"Bring it on, Tommy Boy."

I adjust my grip on my green Ellington U shorts, rolling my shoulders. As hooker and captain, I'm basically at the heart of every scrum, every battle, every hard-fought inch of territory.

It's a lot of pressure, but I love it.

Ridgewood has a reputation for playing dirty, and so far, tonight was no exception. Late tackles, high hits, shoving in the ruck. Things are escalating, and fast. I can feel the tension bleeding off of my guys and theirs.

But I'm not rattled. If anything, I'm thriving.

"Stay tight," I mutter lowly as me and the guy's crouch into the scrum. "They want us angry. Don't give them the satisfaction. We can't let them win because we can't keep our heads."

Across from us, Ridgewood's front row sneered, their prop, a hulking figure with a permanent scowl, spitting onto the grass.

"Nice speech, Captain. Hope it sounds as good when you're eating dirt," the big guy says. I think his names Allen or something stupid like that.

I can't help but grin at his juvenile trash talk. "Guess we'll find out soon, won't we?"

The referee raises his whistle. "Crouch! Bind! Set!"

Our packs slam together in a violent collision, bodies straining for dominance. I can feel Ridgewood's prop twisting illegally, driving up under my chin in an attempt to disorient me.

I bite down my frustration, keeping my form, hooking the ball cleanly back to my scrum-half.

But Ridgewood won't fucking let up.

The moment the ball is out, their flanker slams into me, late, high, deliberate. I go down hard, skidding across the mud, elbows scraping against the rough turf.

The whistle doesn't blow.

The crowd erupts, jeers and shouts filling the air. I barely have time to shake off the hit before the Ridgewood player is standing over me, pressing a heavy forearm to my chest.

"How's that dirt taste, Monroe?" the Ridgewood flanker sneers.

Rage boils inside me and I know I'm about to lose my cool. Instead of trying to stop the anger from boiling over, I give in, because fuck it.

My hand shoots out, shoving the Ridgewood player off as I spring to my feet. The shove wasn't hard, but it was enough. Enough to ignite the powder keg.

Players from both teams rush in, shoving, grabbing, and shouting. I look up just in time to see some guy from Ridgewood heading straight for Mason. Fists are flying, and I duck away from a stray elbow as I jog over to where Mason is throwing punches at Tommy Crawford.

With a growl, I yell, "back off!"

Yanking Crawford by the back of the shirt, I tug him backward, causing him to stumble to the ground. Crawford gets one good punch in, right on my jaw, before the whistle blows.

"Enough!" The referee storms between us, shoving us apart from one another, his face red with fury. "One more move like that and cards are coming out!"

Slowly, we all make our way back to position, but the tension remains, and I honestly just want this fucking game to end at this point.

My jaw clenches as Crawford passes me to get into his position, and I can't help the glare I'm shooting at him. I can feel the ref watching my every move, and against my better judgement, I stay rooted to my spot.

"Keep it clean," the referee warns, locking eyes with both Tommy and me.

I exhale sharply, trying to hold my eyes back from rolling. Instead, I nod.

For the rest of the damn game, my mind is elsewhere. All of the thoughts running through my head, and almost all of them involve a five foot three, dark haired woman that for some reason has stolen all of my focus.

She never used to get to me like this. I used to be able to push the thoughts of her away. Sure, I've thought about what she looks like naked since she grew tits, but it didn't used to take over every single brain cell I have.

Lainey Barkley is dangerous, because she doesn't even have to try to get my attention. She's always had it, and I have a feeling it's going to get a whole lot worse before it gets better.

Chapter 11

LAINEY

I usually get really into the games, but tonight I wasn't as into it as usual. I can't figure out why.

Maybe it's because I have planned this weekend out to a T for Gwen's bachelorette party. I've kept everything a secret, which is actually really hard for me because I suck at keeping secrets.

I didn't even say anything when Ellie and Haley tried to coax it out of me with my favorite wine and ice cream. That usually works pretty well.

I've held strong, and really I want it to be a surprise for everyone. I think Holland or Logan planned something for Ryker tomorrow night too, so the bride and groom will have one night of stress-free fun before getting back to wedding prep.

That's exactly what they need. It's exactly what *I* need. I haven't heard from mom or dad in weeks, and yeah, I'm okay on my own. Yes, I'm used to it, but how have they not checked in at all in *weeks?* It's like they've completely fallen off the face of the earth or have completely forgot they even have a daughter.

I don't usually wallow in self-pity, but I haven't had any of my usual distractions in a few days, which is why this weekend will be good. I'll be able to put my parents, or lack thereof, to the back of my mind.

As we wait outside the locker rooms for Holland and Mason, Ryker's brother Logan catches up with us, a grin on his face as he approaches his brother. Ryker brings him into a hug, patting his back like guys do whenever they hug another dude.

When they pull away, Ryker chuckles softly.

"There he is," Logan says, a teasing lilt to his voice. "How's life in the big city without me?"

Ryker shakes his head. "It's great. Better than this shithole town."

"Shithole? It's not that bad, man. I got a new girl," Logan begins.

"Did you? Better than that cheating bitch Adrianna, hopefully," Ryker comments in disgust. Logan laughed and nodded, shoving his hands in his coat pocket.

"Yeah, a lot better. Her names Charlotte, and she's really fucking great, man. She's in the bathroom," Logan explains, turning around to look toward the bathroom where a small blonde girl is walking this way, a shy smile on her face as she approaches.

She's cute, her hair in two long, blonde braids over her shoulders. She's wearing a hat identical to mine, and her blue eyes are bright enough to see the color even in the dark.

Logan's smile says it all. He's clearly into this girl, and I'm honestly surprised I hadn't seen him with her at the Elite mansion. I wonder if she's not a partier. She honestly doesn't look like she would be. She looks really uncomfortable in this setting, being surrounded by virtual strangers.

Logan scoops her into his side, leaving a kiss on her forehead which causes her to smile brightly.

"Here she is. Guys, this is my girlfriend, Charlotte. Char, this is my brother Ryker, and his fiancée Gwen," Logan gestures toward them. Gwen reaches out her hand to shake Charlotte's hand. Charlotte takes a minute before taking Gwen's hand with a small smile.

"Hi! I'm Gwen, it's great to meet you, Charlotte," Gwen introduces herself with her warm and welcoming smile. She gestures toward Ellie, Haley, and I. "This is Lainey, Ellie, and Haley."

I give Charlotte a big smile. Taking her hand in mine, I pull her into a hug.

I'm not a shy girl. I've always been outgoing and confident. I'll always say what's on my mind, especially if I don't like you. But I'm also really friendly. That's something that my teachers in elementary school always said on my report cards that my parents never got a chance to look at.

Honestly, it's a miracle that this is my personality with growing up essentially alone, but maybe that's what caused it. I was tired of being alone, and I wanted people to like me.

Now, I don't care who likes me or not. If you want to be my friend, great. If you don't, well you can fuck right off. It's not going to bother me. I have Ellie, Haley, and Gwen. I guess you could say I have Holland too, since he and Ellie are my oldest friends.

I pull back from Charlotte, and she looks even more uncomfortable than before.

"Hi, I'm Lainey," I tell her, even though she already knows this.

Her small smile returns as she says, "nice to meet you all."

"Careful, Barkley. You're going to scare the poor girl off," a familiarly irritating voice calls from behind me. Charlie looks past me to the owner of said irritating voice.

Releasing Charlie, I turn to face Holland and Mason who look showered and victorious. Ellington won the game, so that makes sense. I'd feel pretty victorious too.

I narrow my eyes at him as he approaches with his big, stupid grin.

Turning back to face Charlie, I give her a sympathetic look. I crook my finger for her to lean closer and cup my hand around her ear.

"Ignore him. He's not completely right in the head. Doctor's say his brain is like, ten sizes too small for a twenty-two-year-old."

Ryker and Mason snicker behind me as Haley, Ellie, and Gwen giggle. I look back to Holland whose eyes are narrowed on me, but he looks more amused than angry.

Charlie looks confused as hell, and I almost feel bad. She looks from me to Logan, who looks like he's trying not to laugh.

"We've been over this, Lane. Nothing about me is small. Come over here and I'll prove it," he licks his lips before shooting me a devilish smirk. I roll my eyes out of habit.

Reaching out for Gwen, I grab her shoulder, trying to steady myself. Gwen grabs my arm, helping me stay upright.

"What's wrong? Are you okay?" she asks, clear concern in her voice. I continue to hold onto her, holding my stomach. I can feel my friends' eyes on me, but I keep going.

"Y-yeah. I just… I thought I was going to die there for a second," I tell her before straightening and looking Holland directly in the eyes. "I felt a bit claustrophobic with Holland's ego taking up so much space."

"You're funny, Barkley. Real funny," Holland nods, crossing his arms. He looks like he wants to say more, but he refrains.

We continue to glare at each other, stuck in this battle of who will have the last word.

"I'm confused, are they friends or not?" I hear Charlie whisper a bit too loudly into Logan's ear. He chuckles before replying.

"Yeah, this is normal."

"Okay, you two. Stand down. Don't scare away our new friend," Ellie says as she throws her arm around my shoulder.

"I'm fucking starving. Are we going to get food or what?" Mason asks, clearly getting a bit irritable. "I'm literally going to fade away and die from hunger."

Mason grabs onto Ryker, acting as if he's withering away to the ground. "This is the end. Tell my mom I love her, and don't let her in my nightstand," he whines pathetically.

Ryker shakes him off, shaking his head.

"Get off me, asshole. I see you're still dramatic as fuck."

"Do you see what you've left us with, man?" Holland asks.

"Listen, you try not eating for eight straight hours and then playing a game of rugby," Mason groans.

"You ate right before the game, Mason," Holland deadpans.

"Well, it feels like it's been days."

Rolling my eyes, I grab Gwen by the arm and start walking toward the parking lot.

"Come on, shitheads. I wanna get drunk," I call over my shoulder.

Let the weekend begin.

Chapter 12

HOLLAND

Coming to Party Glowers wasn't exactly what I had in mind when we decided to get food. The club, previously owned by my father, and currently owned by, well, me, has not been one of my party spots lately.

I guess it pisses me off that it was used as a coverup for a lot of illegal shit that Ellie and I had no clue about. We brought our friends here, and half of Ellington's campus comes here to get shitfaced.

Knowing that we might have all been in danger and my father never said anything sends a rage through my body.

My father was a decent man, as far as we knew growing up. We never had any reason to believe he was doing anything nefarious behind our backs. Mom never seemed to ask questions either, so there was nothing that set off alarms.

Sure, we grew up wealthy, just as wealthy as Lainey's family, if not wealthier. Ellie and I knew our father owned several night clubs and other various businesses, so we assumed all of his money came from those.

I don't think either of us expected to find out that a lot of that money was coming from selling drugs and other things.

Since he lost all of his control over the club, I've turned it around a lot, into something legit. I've asked Ellie for a lot of help in remodelling ideas and such, and she's really enjoyed having something to do.

We have people here all the time to do the hands-on work, and we kept most of the employees that previously worked here since they knew the club better than we did.

I don't feel as guilty bringing my friends here anymore since we've cleaned it up, and I don't have any concerns about dad trying to get it back since he's spending a long while in prison.

I think it's been hard for my mom, not having him at the house and us being away at school. She's been putting on a brave face, and she hasn't really complained, but I know she's lonely.

Mom doesn't usually show her feelings, which is probably where I get it. Ellie wears her feelings on her sleeve, and you'll always know when she isn't happy. Me? You wouldn't know if I was dying inside. I've never been one for sharing feelings, which might explain why I've never had an actual girlfriend.

The thought of telling a girl my deep, dark secrets makes me physically cringe. I can't imagine someone knowing so much about me.

"What can I get you?" Sherry, one of the original bartenders at the club asks me with a sexy smirk. Sherry is attractive, with big tits and blazing red hair that falls down her back. The small black top she's wearing shows off the ample amount of cleavage she has, and my eyes automatically move in that direction before moving back up to her face.

"Whiskey, please Sherry," I say, giving her a wink.

"You got it," she replies. I watch as she turns around and walks away to make my drink.

"Hey," Ryker's familiar voice rings through the loud music blasting through the club. He leans next to me against the bar, watching the table that consists of his fiancée and the rest of friends.

Logan brought his new girl, Charlie, who looks completely out of her element. I feel kind of bad for the girl, honestly. She looks like she's going to cry.

I'm happy for Logan though. Charlie seems like a nice enough girl, and his ex was a bitch. They'd been together forever, and she cheated on him with Ashton fucking Davis. Ashton was a prick who messed with Gwen last year, and clearly didn't know when to quit.

Ryker clears his throat as Sherry sets my drink down on the counter.

"Anything for you, hun?" she asks Ryker.

"Yeah, I'll take a whiskey, too. Thanks," he tells Sherry who smiles and walks away once again.

His gaze moves back to the table where the girls are laughing at something that Mason probably said. He watches Gwen like he doesn't want to miss any of her movements, and I catch myself doing the same as I watch Lainey take a sip of her drink.

"I can't believe my wedding is two weeks away," Ryker shakes his head in disbelief.

"I can't believe you're getting married," I tell him, taking a sip of my whiskey and enjoying the feel of it going down. "I never thought I'd see the day."

Ryker scoffs, crossing his arms over his chest and leaning his back on the bar. Keeping his eyes trained on his girl, he smirks.

"Neither did I. But Gwen kind of changed everything I ever thought I wanted. A good girl will do that to you," he explains, and I can feel his eyes on me as mine lock on the one girl I shouldn't fucking want.

If she wasn't my sister's best friend, I don't think I'd feel so dirty for wanting her, but Ellie would kill me if I went after her best friend. Wouldn't she?

I mean, I've never really asked her about it, and to be honest, I've never been interested in asking her since I never planned on doing anything. But lately, watching Lainey with other guys has made my stomach churn and has caused an irrational amount of rage to build inside me.

I've always been protective of Ellie, even though I know she's tough and she doesn't really need my protection. But I'm her brother, and that's what brothers do. That protectiveness trickled over to Lainey since she was always around.

Back in high school, when Lainey started dating and guys started fawning all over her, that's when my protectiveness really started.

What if it wasn't protectiveness at all though? What if it was always just jealousy? I mean, sure, I would get pissed when a guy would make her cry, or if I saw the guy treating her like shit. But I always thought that was because I was trying to shield her from getting hurt.

I knew the way she grew up, I know how lonely she was, even if she tried to tell everyone she was perfectly fine. I could always see straight through her façade.

She thinks she's perfected it to a T, always trying to act like nothing bothers her, like she isn't hurting. But I know her, and I see her. She may not think I do, but I do.

I've always thought that her parents were shitbags for letting their daughter feel like she wasn't important. Like they couldn't care less about their own flesh and blood being home alone all the time.

I used to have dreams where her parents would come home, and I'd confront them about being such shitty parents and how Lainey deserved better.

I had imagined it so much that it started to feel real. It started to burn itself into my memory, and I could recite exactly what I'd say to them to this day.

Of course, Lainey doesn't know about that. She doesn't know how much I wanted to protect her from the pain it was causing her. How I wished I could take it all away because she didn't deserve to feel so alone, so insignificant.

"I see you still haven't done shit about that," Ryker says, making my gaze turn from Lainey back to him.

My brows narrow in confusion. "What?"

He nods his head toward the table again, and I know he's talking about Lainey. He'd asked me about her last year, and I'd told him it was nothing. We just enjoyed getting on each other's nerves.

I don't think he believed it, and to be honest, I don't even know if I believe it.

"Her," Ryker states.

"Who?" I ask, acting as if I haven't got a clue who the hell he's talking about.

Ryker rolls his eyes. "You know who. The drunk girl hanging all over my fiancée. The one that you've been pretending you don't have feelings for since the day I met you."

I scoff. "I don't know what you're talking about, man. I don't have feelings for anyone."

Ryker laughs, grabbing his drink off the counter and taking a large gulp. My nerve endings feel like they're on fire, partly because of the whiskey and partly because of the confusing as fuck feelings swimming around in my head.

I've known this girl since she was eight. I've seen every part of her, the good, the bad, and the ugly. I never once imagined I'd feel... *something* for her. I'm so fucking confused, and of course Ryker would call me out on my bullshit.

"Yeah, right. So, you don't have a problem with Colton Kent having his hands all over her, do you?" Ryker questions.

My head snaps in the direction of the table where sure enough, Colton Kent, another Elite member takes Lainey's hand and drags her to the dancefloor.

My heart pounds loudly in my chest as a surge of anger and jealousy take over my body. What the hell is he doing? My fists clench at my sides as I watch Lainey wrap her arms around Colton's neck.

They begin to dance to the upbeat music, him turning her around so her ass is practically grinding on his dick.

Lainey's smile makes my already racing heart thrum faster and I have to fight the urge to go over there and physically remove her from his grasp.

Ryker's soft chuckle brings me back to the conversation at hand.

"That's what I thought. You have feelings for that girl."

Grabbing my glass, I down the rest of my whiskey before slamming it back down on the bar.

"You don't know what the fuck you're talking about," I bite out, stalking toward the table where my sister and the rest of our friends are.

Ellie's brows furrow as I slump into the seat next to her. "What's wrong with you?"

I shake my head and avoid looking at her. "Nothing," I grumble.

"You seem pissed off. Are you alright?" my sister asks, concern lacing her tone.

"I'm fine," I say firmly. I don't mean to be a prick, but my emotions are running haywire, and I feel like I might explode as I watch Lainey and Colton dance like no one's fucking watching. I'm fucking watching.

For some reason, I can't tear my gaze away. It's like watching a car wreck. I want to look away, but my body is forcing me to stay rooted in place, watching as Colton's hands roam over Lainey's body.

When his hands begin to slowly lift the hem of her dress up her thigh, I think I see red. I am not going to make it out of here without a murder charge if I keep watching this.

"Dude, you look like you're about to burst. Do you need another drink?" Mason asks, a smirk on his lips.

"No. I don't need another fucking drink," I seethe.

Mason holds his hands up in surrender, and for a minute, I almost feel bad for snapping at him, but when my eyes find Lainey again, the anger overtakes me.

Don't cause a scene, Holland. Don't cause a scene.

"No need to bite my head off, Holli. I was only trying to help.

I shake my head, looking down at the table.

"I said I'm fine. I don't need help."

Feeling Ryker's knowing gaze on me, I look up with an expression that I hope conveys how pissed off at him I am. He didn't really do anything, but he made me think about the feelings I've been having toward Lainey. Feelings I've been trying to avoid. Feelings I don't even understand.

My fingers tap anxiously on the table as I wait for my anger to settle, but the more I watch that pricks hands move up Lainey's thigh, the more I want to tear him apart.

She moves closer to him, like she's enjoying his touch, and that pisses me off even more.

Keep your head, Holland. You don't need a murder charge on your hands. You are too pretty for prison.

When Colton's hand slips fully under Lainey's dress, and she makes no move to remove it, my patience runs out.

Jumping up from the table, I barrel through the crowd to where the asshole and Lainey are dancing. They don't see me approach, too busy feeling each other up.

I've seen Lainey with a lot of guys over the years. I've seen her making out in corners, in dark rooms where she thinks no one's watching. I've seen it and it's never pushed me to act this way.

The already confusing as fuck feelings just got a hell of a lot worse.

Chapter 13

LAINEY

The feeling of alcohol running through my veins has me feeling more relaxed than I have in days. The music in the club is loud, and I can feel the bass in my stomach.

I wasn't sure how tonight would end, and I didn't really have any plans. I was going to chill out with my friends, get a few drinks, and dance the night away. But somehow, I found myself in the arms of a stranger once again.

I don't know his name, but I think he's an Elite because I've seen him at the mansion.

He's attractive enough, and my drunk brain really doesn't care. I'm having a good time, and that's all that matters right now.

The lights above me flash around the large space in different directions, and I'll admit, I may have had a bit too much to drink because I'm starting to feel dizzy.

I don't know what's going on with me lately. I don't know why I'm feeling so off, so unlike myself. It's like things that didn't bother me before are all coming to a head and making me feel emotions I'm not used to feeling.

For as long as I can remember, my parents have travelled and been gone for long periods of time. When I was little, it really bothered me. I would have nightmares, and Erica the nanny would have to come soothe me in the middle of the night.

I would cry when it was Parents' Day at school, or at recitals where everyone else's parents were there, and it would always be Erica sitting the audience for me.

When I met the Monroe's, Mrs. Monroe would cheer for me, but it was never the same as having a parent there.

My parents should have been my biggest supporters, my loudest cheerleaders, my allies, but I wasn't so lucky. I got the parents that were barely around, that made me feel like a burden, that tried to shut me up by throwing money at me.

As if that would make up for them never being around.

I was an angry kid because of it. I got mad easily and threw tantrums when things didn't go my way.

I would defy teachers' orders and refuse to do my work. I may have been friendly, but I was also a pain in the ass more often than not.

As I got older, my attitude was still there, but I wouldn't say it was as bad. I got more used to not having them around, and then I grew to prefer it.

The sex, drugs, and drinking were easier to do in parentless household.

I wonder what my parents would say if they ever found out about any of that. Would they be disappointed? Would they even care?

Probably not.

Either way, it hasn't really taken a toll on my emotions in a while. Lately, I've been thinking about it a lot. Last I heard, they were somewhere in Spain. Mom had texted me a picture of a beach they were at. That was the first contact we'd had in weeks.

I received that text five days ago in my psychology class. I haven't mentioned it to anyone, especially Ellie because she'll get pissed and want to take matters into her own hands.

I've looked back at it every day since, wondering what they're doing and where they are now. Honestly, I probably should have gone to a therapist when I was young, but no one ever even suggested it. Now I kind of think it might have helped.

Having Ellie and Holland was a great distraction, and moving away to college was even better because I no longer had to be in that house, alone. Now, I have Ellie and Haley, and I'll even throw Holland, Logan, and Mason in there.

We spend enough time at the Elite mansion that I'd say we're all friends.

The guys' hands landing on my ass catches my attention and breaks me out of my thoughts. My eyes open and my body instinctively moves against him. I'm not planning on going home with this guy, but I can have a little fun while I'm here.

Letting him move me, I relax into his grasp, letting my mind shut off.

It only lasts a minute before we're interrupted by a hulking, six-foot two brick of a man who is standing so close to us, I can practically feel the heat radiating off of his body.

Holland stands with his fists clenched at his sides; his face pulled into a scowl. He looks angry, but I don't know what for. He was fine earlier. Did something happen while I was dancing?

It takes a minute for the guy I'm with the realize I've stopped moving and we are now being watched. His movements slow and he clears his throat awkwardly.

"Oh, hey Monroe. I didn't know you were here tonight," he says sheepishly. Is he afraid of Holland? Holland isn't scary, at least he's not scary in my eyes.

He is a very tall, very muscular, very intimidating rugby player, but to me he's still the eight-year-old boy I used to climb trees with.

"Colton," Holland says bitterly. "I'm gonna cut in."

My eyes narrow in suspicion as Connor looks at Holland like he has six heads.

"W-what?" he asks.

Holland takes a step closer, making the guy step back.

"Get lost, Kent."

Colton looks from Holland to me, and I'm pretty sure I look just as confused as he is.

"Oh, shit. Sorry, bro. I didn't know you guys were a thing," Colton rubs the back of his head, taking another step back.

My eyes widen when what he just said finally registers. I look at Holland, waiting for him to tell the guy we're not a thing, but he doesn't say anything.

"We're not," I tell him, feeling Holland stiffen slightly at my side. Colton looks confused as hell, and honestly, that's how I feel right now. Confused as all hell. What is Holland doing?

"Get out of here, Kent. I have to talk to Lainey, alone," he spits. My eyes narrow so much I'm practically squinting as my body starts to buzz from the mix of alcohol and anger.

This wouldn't be the first time Holland has tried to involve himself in my love life, or lack thereof, and I swear to God, he does it on purpose just to piss me off. Like he doesn't want me to be happy, or at least content.

I don't get myself wrapped up with his shit. Why does he feel like he has the right to mess with mine?

"Go away, heathen. I'm dancing," I bite out. Holland gives me a challenging look, begging me to fight with him.

"Not anymore, you're not. Come on, we're all leaving," he tells me, grabbing my elbow and pulling me toward him and away from Colton who looks a bit too stunned to speak.

Yanking my arm out of his grasp, I dig my heals in, not allowing him to pull me any further.

No one around us sees what's happening. They're all too drunk and preoccupied to pay any attention, which is good because I might commit murder right now. Ellie might be a little upset at first, but she'll get over it.

"I'm not going anywhere, Holland. You're not my keeper," I yell at him. His eyes flare with anger, but it doesn't affect me in the slightest.

"Let's go, Barkley. I won't say it again."

What is he, my dad? Giving him a look of pure hatred, I take a step closer to him, getting in his face. Well, as much as I can considering my face is at his chest.

"What are you going to do if don't, Monroe? Make me?" I wish I was as intimidating as I feel right now, but I know I'm not.

Holland gives me a devilish smirk, and I glower at him, daring him to try something.

"Damn right, I will."

"Listen, I-" Colton, who I forgot was even here, starts.

Holland's head snaps to him. "I thought I told you to go," he seethes. What is his issue tonight?

Colton holds his hands up in surrender, blowing out an exasperated breath before backing away and disappearing into the crowd.

Looking at Holland in disbelief, he peers down at me again. We're standing so close now that I can feel his heat. My irritation grows as he stands here, glaring at me as if I've done something wrong.

So much for having a good distraction. The alcohol in my system might as well have evaporated because I feel nothing but annoyance at this moment.

My head turns toward the table my friends are sitting at, and they're all so deep in conversation that they're not even looking at us. I was hoping one of them would come get this man away from me before I wrangle his neck.

"Are you ready to stop being a brat?" Holland asks, crossing his very large, very sculpted arms across his chest. Tearing my eyes away from the veins stick out along his forearms, I life my gaze to his face.

Holland clenches his jaw, and I can't help but find this a bit entertaining. One of my favorite pastimes is pissing him off.

"Fuck you," I say, and a smirk crosses his lips.

"You want to?" he inquires. My body stiffens slightly at the thought of his body and mine pressed together, him rocking into me, him on top of me.

No, Lainey. You cannot go there. You don't want to go there, not with him.

"You wish, you cretin."

Holland's eyes fill with heat, and I can tell he's having the same thoughts I'm having as his eyes shamelessly roam over my body. My cheeks heat, but I keep my gaze locked on his face.

"Well, now that you've ruined my night, I'm leaving," I tell him, sidestepping and moving toward our friends.

For a few long minutes, I really thought Holland was going to throw me over his shoulder to get me out of there. I was hell bent on staying right where I was just to piss him off, but since Colton left, there's no point. It isn't a fun game anymore.

All of a sudden, I feel hot and lightheaded. The room feels like it's spinning, and my heart is racing. I don't know if it's from the alcohol or the adrenaline from getting a rise out of Holland, but I have to get out of here.

When I reach the table, I bend in between Gwen and Ellie to let them know I'm leaving.

"Are you okay? Do you want us to come with you?" Gwen asks, her eyes full of worry. I shake my head, not wanting to ruin their night.

"No, I'm a big girl. I'll be fine," I tell her. "I'll see you guys later. You're staying with us tonight, right?"

Gwen nods. "Yes but are you sure you-" I cut her off before she can finish her sentence.

"I'm okay, Gwenny. I'm just over it for the night."

I give her a quick squeeze before do the same to Ellie, and Haley. Giving the boys a quick wave goodbye, I head for the door before anyone can ask any more questions.

I have no idea if Holland is following me, but I hope he has the sense to leave me the hell alone right now.

When the fresh air hits my face, my body finally seems to start to calm down. My stomach churns slightly, and for a moment, I think I'm going to puke.

Breathing through my nose, I swallow down the urge, pulling out my phone to order an Uber.

"You good, Barkley?" I hear the familiar voice ask from behind me. Rolling my eyes, I turn around to face Holland, who in fact did not have enough sense to fuck off.

His eyes search my face, as if he's concerned about my well-being. It pinches something in my chest. I hate when he's nice to me. It makes my brain think stupid, dangerous things, and my body yearn for more.

Why did he even follow me out here? He's the reason I'm leaving.

I cross my arms, the cold breeze sending shivers through my body even with my coat on. My hair flies around my face as I watch him slowly stalk toward me until he's right in front of me.

His blonde hair moves with the small gust of wind, and his blue eyes look remorseful. Shoving his hands into his pockets, he looks to the ground.

This is what happens almost every single time. He's a raging dick, and then he feels bad and comes to apologize.

Our relationship, or friendship, or whatever this is has always been weird. We've always had this dynamic where we're utter assholes to each other and then he apologizes.

In high school, Holland would constantly try to scare any guy that looked at me. I thought it was because he saw me as a sister, but there was a small part of me, and I mean a tiny, miniscule part of me that hoped it was because he was jealous.

That tiny part of me was stupid. That kind of thinking only ends in disaster, and I've had enough of that to last a lifetime.

Chapter 14

LAINEY

"**W**hat do you want?" I snap, watching Holland wince a bit. Good, he should feel like an asshole. That was so unnecessary.

Colton wasn't being obnoxious. He wasn't do anything against my will. I was having a good time with him. I swear, Holland picks and chooses which guys to be pissed about, and I've never understood how he decides which ones to screw with.

Holland's eyes meet mine. "I just wanted to check on you," he admits, shrugging. I scoff.

"Well, here I am. I'm leaving," I tell him, hoping he'll accept that and just go away. I'm over being around people today. I'm tapped out on my social battery today.

"I see that. How are you getting home?"

I hold up my phone, showing him my Uber app. He just nods, turning to look out at the road.

"I can take you," he offers. That is the last thing I want right now. Being stuck in a car with him while I'm drowning in weird fucking feelings. I'm pissed and irritated, but him being him and standing in front of me, all muscles and smelling like a sex god, is messing with my mind.

"No, I'm fine. The Uber is almost here. You can go back inside," I say, turning away from him and toward the road because if I keep looking at him, I might tell him yes.

"You can cancel it. Let me take you home, Barkley."

"Why would I do that?" I ask, turning back to him and waiting for him to give me some sort of convincing answer.

He just shrugs, looking to the building and then back to me.

"My sister would kill me if you got kidnapped or killed by a random driver," he smirks.

My eyebrow raises and I give him a 'what the hell are you talking about' kind of look.

"Really? Killed?"

Holland shifts from one foot to the other, looking like he's losing his patience.

"It happens. Come on, let's go," he holds out his arm, waiting for me to follow him to his car as the Uber pulls up to the curb.

Well fuck, what the hell do I do?

I look from Holland's outstretched arm to the Uber now waiting expectantly.

Take the Uber, Lainey. You don't want to be near Holland right now. Get in the Uber and go home.

Exhaling a shaky breath, I look between them once more. The driver rolls down the passenger side window, leaning down so his head is seen through the crack.

"Are you Winifred Ackley?" he calls out. I wince at the fake name I'd put in the app because I didn't want anyone to know my real name.

Holland cocks his head in question, raising an eyebrow, a smirk on his lips. "Winifred?"

I roll my eyes. "Shut up," I hiss.

"Come on, *Winifred*. Let me take you home," he urges. Fuck it.

"Fine."

Walking toward Holland, he swings his arm over my shoulders, walking us to the parking lot.

Oh, Lainey. You stupid, stupid girl.

When we get to Holland's Mustang, instead of opening the door for me, he walks to the driver's side and gets in. Rolling my eyes, I tug on the handle, but it's locked. Are you kidding me?

I knock on the window to get his attention, and he rolls it down slightly.

"What are you doing? Get in the car," he orders. Crossing my arms over my chest, I glare at him.

"I would if I could. It's locked, genius."

'Shit, sorry," Holland laughs, unlocking the door so I can finally get in. Is he seriously laughing at me right now? I am in no mood for his shit, and now I'm thinking taking the Uber may have been a better choice.

Pulling on my seatbelt, I look out the window, ignoring Holland completely. Well, I'm trying to, but his annoying ass keeps looking over at me like I'm some exhibit in a museum.

Huffing out a breath, I turn to look at him. "Do I need to tell you to take a picture because it'll last longer?"

Holland narrows his eyes, studying my face before shaking his head and turning back to the windshield.

As he pulls out of the parking lot and onto the road, I sink back into my seat.

"Is bitch your natural setting? Is there like, an off switch for that?" he asks, my eyes widening at the audacity.

"Excuse me?" I ask, shooting him the biggest death glare I can muster. Holland chuckles to himself, thinking he's so fucking funny. Well, he's not.

"You're so nice to everyone else, why are you so prickly with me?"

"Because I like other people. I don't like you," I shoot back, knowing that's a bullshit lie. I do like him. I think I like him a lot even though he annoys the shit out of me, and I want to hit him half the time.

He chuckles again, looking so carefree and unconcerned, and watching him now makes me think about when we were kids, and he would run around without a care in the world.

He had no idea that I was dying inside, no idea how much I yearned for a relationship with my parents like the relationship he had with his. No freaking clue that I was drowning in feelings I couldn't even comprehend at that age, feelings no child should ever have to endure.

But watching him, seeing how he never let anything bother him, that helped.

"Oh, come on, Lainey Bug. We both know that's not true. You're in love with me," he teases. My heart stops and a spark of anxious energy runs through me at his words.

I am *not* in love with him. I've never been in love with anyone. I don't believe that a love like that can exist. Everyone is out for themselves, and you can't trust anyone to love you enough to stick around when shit gets tough.

"You're delusional, and borderline insane," I hiss, trying not to sound as frazzled as that statement made me feel. "I am using you for a ride home and that's it. It doesn't require talking. So just… shut up."

"You can use me for a ride anytime, baby," he winks. "Whenever, wherever, and however."

I scoff, feeling a strange tingle in my core as I let that image fill my head for the briefest of seconds before coming back to reality.

"You are so gross," I say. "I should have taken the Uber," I mumble, resting my elbow on the window and leaning my head in my hand. We're almost home, and then I can get of this car that suddenly feels way too small and get into the shower to wash away the feelings I'm having right now.

When Holland pulls up in front of my campus house, I have a brief feeling of déjà vu as I unbuckle and step out of the car.

Before heading for the door, I turn around to thank him for the ride home, but he's out and rounding the car to stand in front of me. I stand frozen in place for a moment, letting me alcohol-soaked brain catch up to what's happening.

"W- what are you doing?" I stumble over my words. I blame it on the alcohol and not the fact that he's standing so close to me that I can smell the distinct vanilla and sandalwood scent of his cologne.

The tight, dark navy-blue shirt he's wearing under his coat shows every ridge and bump on his stomach, and his hair is contained by a black beanie. He looks so much more grown up that I have to remember he's not the same punk kid I grew up with.

His eyes roam over me once before landing on mine. I'm sure I look confused, because I am. Why did he get out of his car? He could have just left, but he's standing in front of me, looking like a sex god.

Oh god, Lainey. Shut up. That's your best friend's brother. No matter how much their mom tried to get us together when we were younger, Ellie would surely have something to say about it.

No matter how much you want to see what he must be packing under those jeans. I've seen the man shirtless, and it is a sight to behold. But never down below, and right now, my vagina wants to see.

Shut up, vagina. You don't get a say. You're not in charge here.

"Are you okay?" Holland asks, looking slightly concerned. It feels like a bucket of ice water was just poured on me. My eyes narrow and my arms cross over my chest like armor.

"Why wouldn't I be?" I ask, a bite to my tone. I'm fine. I'm perfect.

I'm not having confusing as fuck feelings about my best friend's brother, a guy I practically grew up with. I'm not worried about my parents and why I haven't heard anything from them in weeks. I'm just peachy.

"Well, you were pissed at me, so-" he begins.

"I'm always mad at you," I interject. Holland rolls his eyes.

"Yeah, okay. Anyway, you seemed pissed off and kind of upset and I just wanted to-"

"I'm fine, Holland. I'm great, honestly," I say, my voice a pitch higher than normal. I'm not sure if I'm trying to convince him or myself.

His brows furrow and he crosses his arms over his chest. Why won't he just leave?

"Have you heard from your-" I don't even let him finish that sentence. He knows the answer. It's the same almost every time someone asks.

"Thank you for driving me home. I have to go take a shower."

Turning away from him, I begin to head for the front door, but a hand grabs my wrist, stopping me from moving any further. My head falls back out of annoyance. I don't want to talk about this, especially not with him.

Holland and Ellie know more about me and my life than anyone, even Gwen. Gwen knows the gist of it, but she didn't grow up with me.

She didn't see the nights where I'd curl up in a ball and cry because I hadn't seen or heard from my parents in weeks. She didn't see me when I was sick and calling out for my 'mommy' because all I wanted was her comfort. Holland and Ellie did. They saw it all.

Their mother was the one that stepped in most of the time. My nanny wasn't very attentive, especially when I was sick, which left Mrs. Monroe to help, and thankfully she did. I don't know where I'd be without her.

Letting out an exasperated breath, I turn back to face him. He looks like he wants to say something, but he just looks down and shakes his head.

"Can you let me go? I have things to do," I tell him. I don't have anything to do but get away from him and erase all of the emotions I'm feeling right now.

He runs a rough hand through his hair and blows out a breath. If I weren't so irritated, I'd probably chuckle at the fact that he seems so uncomfortable. Holland doesn't get uncomfortable often, so this is entertaining to say the least.

His eyes burn into mine, filled with emotion and sincerity. His hand releases me and the loss of contact causes a shiver to run down my spine. My hand absentmindedly grabs for my now abandoned wrist and wraps around it.

"I'm sorry, okay?" he states, and he looks like he actually means that. Like he's actually sorry, but for what?

"Why?"

"For bringing up your-"

"It's fine," I say, not letting him continue. "Just… don't do it again. If I wanted to talk about it, I'd bring it up. Got it?" I tell him, hoping he just accepts that answer and doesn't ask any questions.

To my surprise, Holland nods. "Fine, okay. I won't bring it up again," he tells me, and I believe him.

Looking down at the sidewalk, I shift awkwardly. There's a weird kind of tension in the air and I'm not quite sure what it is or what it means.

"Okay. Thank you."

Turning around, I head for the porch before he can stop me to say anything else. Of course the sight of me shutting the door doesn't deter him from saying his last thought.

"Let my sister know I got you home safe. She's probably concerned I kidnapped you again," he chuckles to himself before heading back to his car and driving the rest of the way down the street to the Elite mansion.

Shit. Ellie, Gwen, and Haley are probably worried sick about how I got home. I'm sure Holland told them he was going to bring me, at least I hope he did.

Chapter 15

HOLLAND

I fucked up. I know I fucked up. Why the hell did I try to bring up her parents? Oh, I know why, because I'm a fucking idiot. Good going, Holland. Real nice job.

Who knows when the last time Lainey talked about her parents was. She hates even the mention of them, and I know this. She's always been like that, even when we were kids. Yet, my dumbass still brought it up.

I know it upset her. I could tell she was holding back, and she couldn't get away from me fast enough. But I needed her to know I was sorry for mentioning it.

I can't stand the thought of her sitting in her room or in her shower curled up and crying because I stupidly brought up something she probably wasn't even thinking about.

I should go back and make sure she's okay, right?

No, Holland. You're not her boyfriend, and she sure as hell doesn't want to see you right now. Give it up, man.

Running my hands through my hair, I walk into the empty kitchen and grab a water from the fridge. The guys are still out, and the rest of the house is quiet.

Deciding against watching a movie alone, I make my way to my bedroom. Setting the water bottle down on my bedside table, I faceplant onto my king-sized bed with a loud groan.

Lainey and I always joke, we always rib each other, that's our thing. I've always known where the line was. Never bring up her parents or her childhood.

Honestly, I think a lot of it is because she's embarrassed. She tried really hard to act as if it didn't bother her, but I knew better. Growing up without parents would be difficult for anyone. I can't imagine not having my mom at my side. I honestly don't have a clue where I'd be without her.

I'm sad for Lainey that she never got to experience that. When her parents were home, her mom barely paid attention to her. Her dad hardly acknowledged her existence.

I used to think it was really strange. What kind of parents left for weeks on end when their kid was at home with a nanny? What kind of mother would come home after a long trip and practically ignore her daughter.

My mom aways told Ellie and I that some people weren't meant to be parents. Mr. and Mrs. Barkley definitely fall under that category. Why'd they even have Lainey if they were going to ignore her?

I'm sure Lainey asks herself these questions daily, and that thought sends a surge of pain to gather in my chest. She doesn't deserve that.

Groaning loudly into my comforter, I finally move my head to breathe. A loud ping interrupts the angry thoughts in my brain.

Unlocking my lock screen, I see I have a text from Ellie. I scoff at the name she's created as her contact.

Best Sister Ever

Best Sister Ever

Thank you for bringing Lane home.

You did bring her home, correct? 😬

Me

No. I left her on the sidewalk to fend for herself. 👻

Best Sister Ever

😒 *Hilarious. I just texted her. Why does she sound pissed off?*

What did you do to her?

Fuck. Why does she always assume I've done something wrong?

Me

I didn't do anything, I was the perfect gentleman.

I avoid telling her the part about where I did the one thing we both know not to do. I already know I'm an idiot; I don't need Ellie reminding me.

Best Sister Ever

*Yeah, right. If I find out
you did anything to piss
her off or hurt her feelings
I'll hurt you.*

Better yet... I'll tell mom.

Me

You wouldn't.

But I know she would. She'd do anything to get me in trouble with our mother. My sister can do no wrong in our mother's eyes. Ellie is the perfect angel. Don't get me wrong, my mother loves us both equally, but Ellie is her baby girl.

Being twins, our mom made us do everything together growing up. If I wanted to play soccer, mom would sign Ellie up with me. When Ellie wanted to play an instrument, I was forced to play the viola.

When I decided to go to Ellington to follow in our father's footsteps, before I knew what a crook he was, of course, Ellie had to come too.

We had the same friends, the same circles, and the same feelings for the girl next door. Except, where Ellie wanted to help her friend by throwing her distractions, I wanted to burn down the world to take away her pain.

It's crazy to me that even when I was younger, I could tell the amount of pain Lainey hid behind her eyes. Behind her "don't care" façade. Behind the guys and the parties.

Lainey tries to act happy all of the time. She never shows her true feelings, and that bugs me because I don't know why she feels like she needs to hide.

Best Sister Ever

You know I will.

Shaking my head, I groan loudly as my body stretches out across my bed. I feel like I've been run over by a bus. Between practice, my time in the gym, and the tension that is still heavy between my father and I, my body is spent.

The thought of an upset Lainey replays in my mind as I enter the shower to wash the night down the drain.

My cock stands at attention as glimpses of Lainey being so pissed off at me that interrupted her time with Colton flood my mind.

Her pouty lips, the way her eyes narrowed, the way her jaw ticked as she held back the things she truly wanted to say.

God, that girl is fucking sexy when she's angry, especially when it's directed toward me. The tension between us is off the charts, and I know she feels it too.

It's even hotter that she tries to deny it. She really does try to act like she despises my very being, but we both know that's not the case.

The hot water rushes down my body as I try to distract myself from yet another jerk off session to thoughts of Barkley.

Tomorrow is Ryker's bachelor party. Logan and I planned this whole night out at this wicked exclusive club downtown.

I don't know where the girls are taking Gwen, but it can't be as cool as Flux. You need to know people to get in, and luckily, I do. So, it wasn't difficult to snag us entry.

Ryker gave Logan and I free reign to do whatever we wanted as long as it didn't involve strippers because Gwen would rip his dick off, and I believe she would. She may be small, but that girl is feisty. She would probably cut his dick off, and then mine and Logan's for planning it.

So, no strippers. Just a night of drinking expensive liquor and dancing the night away like drunken idiots. The Elite mansion had parties going on almost every single weekend, and we still do.

It's just different without Pat, Ryker, and Mason there to help plan and supervise.

We still have fun though, and Logan and I do a pretty damn good job taking care of everything if I do say so myself.

Ryker was kind of the leader of the Elite since his father was not only a legacy member, but he shoveled a shit ton of money into Ellington. Christ, the whole athletic complex is named after Robert Steele, Ryker's father.

His father might be an even bigger prick than mine is, which is crazy. But they both had their fair share of issues, and that's putting it lightly.

Shutting off the shower, I grab my towel off the rack and dry off, throwing my towel around my waist.

My heart stops and I swear my breath gets caught in my throat as I step out into my room.

"Holy fuck! What the hell are you doing here?"

My hand involuntarily tightens around the edge of my towel to keep it still.

"Sorry. Shit, I'm sorry. I didn't mean to freak you out," the brunette perched on my bed says, biting her bottom lip. Her eyes roam over my body slowly, from my face, down to my abs, and to the towel covering my dick that is hardening steadily.

Blue-grey eyes meet mine and my dick stands at full attention now. Fuck, why is she here? How did she even get in?

"You didn't think sitting in my room while I was in the shower would freak me out?" I ask, narrowing my eyes at her, and her cheeks turn a bright shade of pink.

"Well, I planned on storming in here and yelling at you, but you weren't in here. I heard the shower running, and I decided to wait until you got out," she shrugs, as if that's a valid excuse for her being in my room right now.

"You came to yell at me? You know they make phones for a reason, Barkley. You didn't have to come here to do it," I shrug, a smirk tugging at the corner of my lips at how uncomfortable she looks right now. "And let's not pretend you stayed to lecture me."

Lainey's face scrunches up as if she has absolutely no idea what I could be insinuating. The flush in her cheeks gives her away though.

"Why else would I have stayed?" she asks, crossing her arms as she abruptly stands from the bed. Her eyes hold mine as I step toward her. I'll give her credit, if she's nervous, she's not showing it.

When I'm standing right in front of her, I look down at her with a smirk. Her nostrils flare and she looks like she's trying so hard to look mad.

I take another small step into her, causing her to fall back onto the bed so that I'm towering over her even more than I was when she was standing.

I notice how her breath catches and how her eyes darken just a bit as she looks into mine.

"To see me come out all wet and dripping for you," I offer. I bring my hand up to rub my thumb over her bottom lip, but she smacks me away, huffing.

"You wish, you perv," she says, but she doesn't attempt to move away from me. Is she enjoying this as much as I am? This teasing and taunting?

I mean, I'm in a towel, and I'm standing above her. It would be so easy to rip those pajama pants and tank off her smooth skin. So easy to…

"You're staring," Lainey whispers in a sexy as fuck tone. Fuck, she's right. She's not wearing a bra, I can tell by the way her nipples are poking out from under her shirt.

"I know," I admit. No point in trying to deny it when she clearly caught me in the act. She moves slightly, causing my hard cock to brush against her leg.

Shit, this girl is going to drive me crazy, but for some reason, I can't back away.

Chapter 16

LAINEY

Why must this man be so infuriatingly attractive, and why must he smell so goddamn good?

He knows exactly what he's doing as he leans over my body, standing in nothing but a towel as water slowly drips off him.

When I marched myself over here in the cold night air, I planned on bursting in and yelling at Holland for making me think about my parents and how depressing it is that neither of them actually give a shit about me. For bringing up a forbidden topic.

I know he didn't do it on purpose. I know I act like it doesn't bother me. I can see it being hard to tell if it even bothers me from an outsider standpoint, I guess.

I feel like I do a great job at hiding the fact that some days, it actually crushes me. I've been told it would be beneficial to see a therapist, mainly by Mrs. Monroe who says that a therapist could help me "work through my feelings".

Honestly, it could help, although I hate the thought of talking to someone who is only there because I'm paying them to listen. Which is hilarious because I'm a psychology major. I'm just not sure if it's truly what I want to do with my life.

The fact that my parents act as if I don't exist and only contact me once in a blue moon doesn't exactly bother me twenty-four seven. I don't let it. If I did, it would destroy me.

When I was little, sure. I didn't know how to regulate my feelings, but now? I know how to push those feelings down and bottle them up. Until I'm reminded by a stupid boy that my life is pathetic.

This is why I turned to sex and drinking. It would help distract me from my reality.

My eyes meet Holland's green ones, which are no longer locked on my nipples. I mentally chastise myself for not putting on a bra before I walked over here in a fit of rage.

Then again, I didn't imagine I'd be getting this close to him. Why has he not moved? Do I even want him to move? I mean, I just felt his dick rub against my leg, and damn. That thing seems big.

Shit, Lainey. Don't think about his dick. This is Holland. This is Ellie's brother. Think with your head, Lane, not your vagina.

God, it's right there. All I'd have to do is push the towel down, and it would be free.

I have to physically keep my eyes from traveling south as I glare at him. He's smirking, as if he can read my mind, and I pray he can't because damn, that would be embarrassing.

Deciding that the temptation is too much, and that he'd never let me live it down if I made a move first, I push up on my elbows, causing him to back up. At first, I don't think he'll move, but he does, taking a step to the side to let me up.

Clearing my throat, I move toward the door. I no longer feel like yelling, and this whole thing was a waste of time. I should have just stayed home and wallowed, except I had to get the last word.

"Where are you going?" Holland asks, sitting down on the edge of the bed where I just vacated. He looks delicious, and I hate myself for thinking that.

"I'm leaving," I tell him, reaching for the doorknob. Before I twist it, Holland scoffs. I freeze before looking back at him with narrowed eyes. Did he just scoff at me? Really? "Something funny?"

Holland shakes his head, a cocky grin on his face as he looks down at the floor. His wet, dirty blonde hair drips as it falls over his face.

"Nothing," he shrugs and chuckles to himself without even looking up at me. My arms cross over my chest and my foot taps impatiently as I wait for him to tell me exactly what he thinks is funny.

Nothing about this situation is funny. Nothing about the sexual tension in the room that I know we both feel is funny. Nothing about the reason I even came over here in the first place is funny.

I know he can tell I'm uncomfortable, that much is obvious by the knowing smirk on his lips. I hate that he knows me so well, because he can read me like a freaking book.

Letting out a huff, I say, "Tell me, now."

Holland shakes his head as he leans back on his forearms, getting comfortable as he watches me. I'm really tempted to walk over there and slap his smug face.

"Why?" he asks. My blood begins to boil. He knows what he's doing, and I hate him for it.

"Because I want to know what you think is funny about this situation," I tell him, standing taller than before. I don't want him to know he's affecting me, even though I'm pretty sure he knows that he is.

Holland shrugs his shoulders, and I'm practically drooling at the sight of his abs contorting as he moves. God, why does he have to be so hot. He could have grown up to be ugly, but no.

"I don't think I'm gonna tell you," he taunts. I hold in a growl of frustration at his stupidity.

"Fine," I spit. My arms fall to my sides as I turn around and take a step back toward the door. If he doesn't want to tell me, fine. I'm not standing here like an idiot waiting for him to give me an answer.

Before I can open the door though, a hand slams on it from above me. The loud noise startles me a bit, but I don't show it. I can feel him behind me. I feel his body heat, and I smell his soap.

I almost feel the need to clench my thighs together for some friction, except that would be crazy because I can't be sexually attracted to this guy. Not this one.

Looking up at the strong arm above me, I watch the muscles cord as he applies pressure to the door so I can't open it. Oh lord. Who knew a forearm could be so damn attractive.

Holland's breath fans over the back of my neck as he leans down to whisper in my ear.

"Where ya going, Bug?" he asks in an almost taunting tone. The nickname makes my face heat, and I have to stop myself from pressing back against him.

The name would usually piss me off, however all I can think about is the way I can feel his breath on me and the heat radiating off of his body. I can't think clearly, and it's making me crazy because I'm not the kind of girl that gets crazy over guys.

Guys don't usually get me flustered, or nervous. I'm confident, and I'm good at acting like I don't care. It makes it easier that a lot of the time, I really don't. It's just a way to release tension or anger.

Maybe it's not the healthiest coping mechanism, but hey. I'm trying here.

My breathing picks up as Holland moves an inch closer to me, his front against my back, and the distinct feeling of something hard pressed against my ass. Oh my God.

Please tell me that's his phone and not his rock-hard erection against me right now. Please tell me my best friends' brother doesn't have a hard on for me at this very moment. For the love of everything holy, please tell me I'm not fucking turned on.

There is no way I am turned on. Not with Holland Monroe. He's a prick, a ladies' man. He's not what you're looking for, Lane. He's the opposite of everything you want, which is something easy and uncomplicated.

This whole thing would be so complicated and not at all easy. Ellie would find out, and I would have to explain to my best friend why I'm fucking her brother.

Personally, that doesn't sound that appealing to me, and I'd like to avoid having that conversation like the plague. So no, I cannot be turned on my Holland Charles Monroe. That can't happen.

So why can I feel the wetness between my thighs? Why is my breathing so crazy? Why do I have goosebumps?

"You wanna know what I think, Lainey Bug?" Holland whispers in a deep tone, causing a shiver to run down my spine. I shake my head.

"Not particularly."

I feel a puff of air as Holland chuckles softly. A large hand runs up my thigh, lifting my tank up slightly in the process.

The warmth of his fingertips against my skin makes me tremble. My breath hitches as he moves in closer, effectively trapping me between him and the door.

"I think you were about to give in to your urges. I think you got so worked up having me on top of you that you just couldn't take it anymore," he states as if everything he's saying is face rather than his assumptions.

To be fair, he's not completely wrong. I was having… *urges*. I would not have given in, even if I didn't get up.

Holland's finger draws light circles on my bare skin, and it makes me shiver. I bite the inside of my lip to stop the noise that was about to escape my mouth. Fuck him. He knows exactly what he's doing, and he's not going to win this.

"You want me, Barkley. Admit it."

Instead of barking out a laugh like I'd like to, I turn around so that I'm facing him. My back is against the cold door, and Holland's hand is still on the door next to my head. I have to look up to look him in the eyes.

Giving him my best sexy smile, I say, "and so what if I did, Monroe? What then?" I ask seductively. His eyes narrow and darken. He goes from looking teasing to looking hungry, his eyes falling from my face to my legs and back up again.

"We could definitely arrange something," Holland winks. Shaking my head, I scoff.

"You're so sure of yourself," I tell him. Tilting my head, my eyes lock with his. "What makes you think you're so irresistible?"

Holland's gaze darkens, his confidence shifting into something more primal. "Because I know what I'm doing," he murmurs, his voice dropping to a whisper. "And I know you've been thinking about it too."

He couldn't know that. I've never shown anything close to lust or want for him. Even knowing this, my breath hitches, and I force myself to stay in control. This is my game now.

Taking a step closer, my chest brushes against his as I lean in. "Prove it," I challenge, my voice barely above a whisper.

Holland's smirk falters for a moment, replaced by a hungry look that sends a shiver down my spine. He looks like he might call my bluff, but instead he reaches out, his fingers brushing the strap of my tank top, but I catch his hand before he can pull it down.

"Not so fast," I say, my voice sweet but firm. "If you're so sure I want you, then let me take the lead."

His eyes narrow, but he doesn't argue. Seeing the challenge in his gaze makes me want to make this even more difficult for him. Holland Monroe needs to be knocked down a peg or two, and I'm the one to do it.

Chapter 17

HOLLAND

Holy fuck.

I never actually thought Lainey and I would get to this place. I mean, yeah, we have a shit ton of sexual tension, but I never imagined she'd make a move. Now she's asking to take charge?

I've never really had a girl take charge, and I don't think my dick has ever been so hard. It is so fucking sexy, and it's even better because it's Lainey.

I'm not usually at a loss for words. I always have something to say, that's just who I am. Right now, all I can say is, "okay."

Lainey steps back, her movements deliberate as she begins to move around me, her body swaying to a rhythm only I can hear.

Watching her, my jaw clenches, and my chest rises and falls with my quickening breath.

She stops behind me, her hands resting lightly on my shoulders as she leans in, her lips brushing against my ear.

"You're so tense," she murmurs, her fingers digging into the muscles of my back. "Let me help you relax."

I let out a low, involuntary groan, my head falling back as her lips trail down my neck. Lainey smirks against my skin, her hands moving down my chest, her nails scraping lightly over my abs.

My mind is racing, and my body is responding to her touch in ways it shouldn't.

"You like that, don't you?" Lainey whispers, her lips hovering over my collarbone. I don't answer, afraid of what might come out of my mouth. I should tell her to stop. I shouldn't let this go any further.

I know I tease her, and I definitely talk the talk, but I didn't expect her to go along with it. This is bad, Holland. Stop her before it gets to a point where there is no turning back.

I can't. I can't get my body to cooperate with me. So, I just stand there, letting Lainey do whatever she wants to me.

Lainey's hands move lower, her fingers slipping down to the towel still tied around my waist. The towel that is now tented with my hard erection.

My breath hitches and my hands ball into fists at my sides. I can feel my heart pounding a million miles a minute, and my body is trembling with anticipation. Just as she's about to pull the towel loose, she stops.

What the hell? Why did she stop?

"What are you-" I start, my voice rough with need and probably a little bit of disappointment at the fact that she just halted all of her teasing. Lainey cuts me off with a soft laugh.

She pushes me away from the door and turns to leave with a mischievous look on her infuriatingly gorgeous face.

"Where are you going?" I ask, my voice tight. I'm trying not to sound too pissed off at the fact that she's seemingly leaving me with the worst case of blue balls the world has ever seen, although I'm not so sure I'm doing a great job.

Lainey pauses, her hand on the doorknob. "I'm going home. I'm like, really tired all of a sudden," she says, a smirk playing on her lips as she opens the door and walks out of my room and down the stairs.

My eyes widen, realization dawning me. She did that on purpose.

Leaning through the doorframe with my hands at the top, I watch her descend.

"You're playing with fire, Bug," I warn.

Lainey turns to face me once she hits the bottom level, her eyes sparkling with challenge. "And you're about to get burned," she replies simply, before turning the knob and slipping out of the house, leaving me hard, frustrated, and alone.

The door clicks shut behind her, the sound echoing in the silence. All I can do is stand here, my chest heaving, and my body throbbing with unfulfilled desire.

So that's how you want to play it, Barkley? Fine, I can play dirty too. I can play even dirtier. Lainey thinks she just won this round, but this dangerous game she just started is far from over. A slow, dangerous smile spreads across my face.

Lainey Barkley isn't going to be able to resist me after I'm done with her.

———————

It's been two days since what I'm calling the bedroom incident. I think I've been rock hard since Lainey left my room. I haven't been able to get her out of my head.

I haven't seen her since, not because I'm avoiding her, but because we've been busy with classes, and I had practice.

Tonight is Ryker and Gwen's bachelor and bachelorette parties. So I won't be seeing Lainey tonight either. Which is fine, because I'm not even sure how to act around her now.

I know she's attracted to me. I saw it in her eyes. She may have been messing with me, but she wanted me just as badly as I wanted her. She wasn't completely unaffected.

Tonight isn't about me or Lainey or our mutual attraction to each other. Tonight is about my best friend and giving him a night to remember.

Flux is packed tonight. The techno music is blaring through the speakers, and the smell of alcohol, sweat, and weed fill the air. You're not allowed to smoke in the building, but people definitely take a hit or two before they come in.

The bright lights flash, and the colorful dancefloor changes patterns to the beat of the music. This place is always full, but it never gets too rowdy. This crowd doesn't really do rowdy.

The guys and I are seated in a round booth toward the back of the lounge, sipping on our various choices of alcohol. Whiskey for Ryker and Logan, Mason's got some sort of rum concoction, I went with scotch, and Patrick isn't drinking because he's apparently completely sober now. Boring.

None of us have seen Pat in a while since he moved to California to be a freaking doctor. Don't ask me what kind of doctor because fuck if I know. What I do know is he's done well for himself. He got out of here as soon as he could, and I don't totally blame him.

After the take down of our fathers' company, we were the talk of the media for a while. Some of it good, a lot of it shitty. Campus was rough for a few weeks until everyone moved on to something new.

We'd told our fathers' that we'd keep the whole thing quiet from the tabloids and the police, but we never said anything about deterring rumors.

A lot of what was being said was rumors, but there was plenty of shit that was true. People they worked with really didn't like them, and they weren't afraid to turn on them.

"So, man, you're getting fucking married! Shit, I never thought this day would come," my idiot cousin says, patting Ryker on the shoulder.

Ryker takes a sip from his glass. "Yeah, yeah. I get it. It's a shock to all, including me, but fuck if Gwen didn't show up in my life and turn the whole damn thing upside down," he says, looking a bit nostalgic.

Ryker was Ellington University's most eligible bachelor. He was untouchable by all, even the professors. He had everyone in his pocket, and the girls? They'd fall at his feet.

Sure, Mason, Pat, Logan, and I are all Elite's too, however Ryker was the top dog. Everyone wanted him and he knew it. It made his college career a breeze.

He'd had a girlfriend once back in like, high school or something like that. After they broke up, he swore not to date again. So instead, he slept his way through campus.

Then he found Gwen, and she quite literally changed everything. I'd never seen Ryker so crazy for a girl, and he was crazy about Gwen. He still is.

I raise my half empty glass of scotch in the air as a toast and watch as the guys follow.

"To my brother, I am truly happy you've found someone that wants to deal with your crazy ass forever. Just remember, I was here first," I say, earning a few chuckles from the boys.

Ryker nods once before we all clink our glasses together. "Cheers, buddy," I say.

"Cheers," we all say in unison.

"Can I get you boys another round? Maybe something to eat?" a cute blonde woman with a skintight tank that says 'Flux' on it asks. Her tits practically spilling over the top of her tiny shirt.

The short as hell shorts she's wearing leave little to the imagination, and her makeup is a bit over the top, but she seems like a sweet girl.

"Another round would be great, sweetie. Maybe you can join us? We're celebrating my brother here's wedding," Mason drawls while he obviously checks the poor girl out. The blonde blushes before looking down at the notebook in her hands.

"Christ, Mason. Stop being a creep," Patrick scolds. Mason holds his hands up in surrender.

"Hey, I was just inviting her to hang with us," Mason states. I wish I could say he's being an ass because he's drunk, but that's just his personality.

"Sorry about our friend, here. He has this thing where he just can't shut up. We'll take another round, please," I politely tell the girl who quickly walks away from our table.

Ryker smacks the back of Mason's head, and Mason's hand flies up to sooth the ache. I chuckle to myself because I've missed this. These guys are my brothers, and we haven't been all together in months.

We probably wouldn't be if it weren't for the fact that Ryker's getting fucking married. It still blows my mind that he found someone he wants to settle down with.

The thought of settling down with someone for the rest of my life unnerves me. I mean, sure, I could see myself getting married one day, I guess. It would take one hell of a girl to make that happen.

A quick flash of Lainey pops into my mind, and I quickly shake it out as the waitress brings over our drinks and places them on the table.

Reaching for my glass, I down it all in one gulp. The burn feels good and it's a welcome distraction to the fact that I just thought of Lainey Barkley as the girl I would want to marry.

There is no way in hell Lainey and I would get married. Lainey isn't the type of girl who dreams of a white picket fence and a big house on a hill with six kids and a perfect husband. She's not the settling down type.

So why do I find myself wanting to make her that type of girl? Making her want to have that big house with all the kids and a big porch swing where we sit and sip our morning coffee together?

Why is it that the one girl I shouldn't want is the one girl I can't fucking get out of my head? Is it some kind of cruel joke? Is this karma for something I did? I don't get it.

"Uh oh. Here comes trouble, and she brought friends," Mason shouts over the blaring music. My eyes follow his line of sight and land on exactly what he's seeing.

A leggy brunette with curled hair that falls over her shoulders in a blue dress that ends mid-thigh and heels that make her at least 4 inches taller walks toward us. Lainey is followed by Gwen, Ellie, Hailey, and Gwen's best friend Damian.

The group doesn't look exactly thrilled to see us here, and honestly, I'm a little pissed as well. What the hell are they doing here? Clearly they didn't know we were here, considering the looks on their faces.

As they approach, I can't stop my mouth from watering, and I have to mentally will myself from getting out of my seat and throwing Lainey over my shoulder to get her away from all the male attention she's receiving.

I'm not usually a possessive guy, at least, I've never really had anything to be possessive about. But God damn, if I wouldn't throat punch every single dude in this place for looking at her wrong.

That includes my cousin who is ogling her like she's his next meal.

Reaching across the table, I slap Mason on the back of the head just like Ryker did, although this time he doesn't have a clue why he's being hit.

He shoots me a glare. "What the fuck, dude? What was that for?"

I just shake my head, not wanting to give away my reasoning. I won't hear the end of it from any of the guys if they find out I'm horny for my sister's best friend.

When they stop in front of our booth, Gwen and Ryker exchange a small smile. Lainey glares at me. What the hell did I do?

"What the hell are you doing here?" she spits, directing her question to me, and not the four other guys sitting at the table with me.

"What am I doing here? What are you doing here? It's reserved for us guys tonight. Take your girls club somewhere else," I reply just as harshly. How can she be mad at me for booking a popular, exclusive club for the bachelor party when she did the same thing for Gwen?

Lainey's eyes narrow, and she looks like she might explode until Gwen puts a hand on her shoulder, effectively distracting her from tearing my head off.

"It's okay, Lane. We can all hang out together," Gwen reasons. Ah, Gwen. Always the reasonable one. She has a temper too, don't get me wrong. There were plenty of times I heard her and Ryker going at it, but she's leveled out a bit.

Lainey on the other hand? I think she's filled with so much anger and rage that it all just bubbles to the surface when she's upset. She may act like nothing bothers her, but I know there are certain things that do.

Lainey's lips turn down into a pout, and my dick twitches in my pants because fuck, if that isn't the most adorable thing I've ever seen.

"This is supposed to be your bachelorette party. You're supposed to be living it up and getting shitfaced. Not hanging out with your fiancé," Lainey whines. Gwen laughs before scooching into the booth next to Ryker who throws his arm around her shoulders and kisses her temple.

"I wasn't going to get shitfaced anyway. This is perfect, just the way it is. I promise," Gwen tells Lainey, who still looks unsure of the whole situation.

Haley and Ellie grab chairs from a close by table and stick them at the end of our booth. Damian does the same, yet Lainey continues to stand.

"Come here, babe. I've got a great place for you to sit," I tease, winking at her as I gesture to my lap. Her face twists in disgust while chuckles fill the table.

"Ew, Holland. Stop being gross," Ellie squeals.

"I'd rather sit on burning coals than on your lap, you creep," Lainey says before turning back to look at Gwen. "I have to go the bathroom. I'll be back."

"Do you want me to come with you?" Ellie asks her, concern lacing her features. Lainey shakes her head.

"No, I just have to pee. I'll be quick."

As she begins to walk away, my eyes trail after her, focused on her ass as it sways back and forth to the beat of the music. My god does that woman have the perfect ass.

Before I know what I'm doing, I'm standing from the booth and about to follow her.

"Where are you going?" Pat asks, his brow furrowing.

Without taking my eyes off of Lainey through the crowd, I say "I'll be right back."

Where am I going? Well, I'm following Lainey to the bathroom like a fucking creep. Could I tell you why? No, no I couldn't. Here I am, standing outside the woman's bathroom, waiting for Lainey Barkley to exit.

I am so fucking screwed.

Chapter 18

LAINEY

Placing my hands on the edge of the sink in the women's restroom, I stare at myself in the mirror. My curls fall over my shoulders and the blue of the dress I'm wearing makes my blue-grey eyes pop.

I went with a more subtle makeup look tonight with a smokey eye, some light blush and mascara.

I'm not one of those girls that can spend hours on makeup, and I'm nowhere near as good as Haley or Ellie, but I do my best.

My attire for tonight is a nice, strapless royal blue dress that stops about mid-thigh, but doesn't make me nervous that my ass will fall out of it.

The four inch heels I'm wearing have straps that go up my shins a bit and tie into a cute little bow at the top.

I didn't want to go too overboard with the choice of outfit tonight, so this is a happy medium between what I'd normally wear to a club and what I think is mild.

Some would look at me and say this isn't 'mild,' but for me it is. This outfit is tame compared to some of the other things I've worn in the past.

When you've lived your whole life without parents telling you what to wear or where you can and can't go, it's easy not to care about what I wear.

I don't even do it for male attention. I mean, maybe when I was in high school going to parties and such I was, but now? Now I do it for myself because it makes me feel confident.

It feels good to put on a nice outfit, do my hair and makeup, and look in the mirror feeling good about myself. Of course, there's times when I look in the mirror and hate the way I look. Nonetheless, I always try to be positive about my looks.

The more confidence you exude, the more people you attract. Even if you're not feeling all that confident, fake it until you make it, baby. That's my mantra.

Taking a step back, I look over myself from head to toe.

Of course Holland chose the same club to bring Ryker to. Of freaking course. He just has to ruin everything. I know there wasn't a ton of planning on my part, and this was kind of a last-minute decision, but what are the odds.

Out of all the clubs downtown, including the string of nightclubs Holland and the other guys now own, he chooses Flux? The one club I didn't expect he'd choose.

How can we have a bachelorette party when the groom is sitting with us? This is supposed to be Gwen's night. We were supposed to get shit-faced and dance and scream and vent.

Now we're stuck with the guys for the night. It doesn't even feel like a bachelorette anymore. It just feels like our normal club nights.

I don't know. Maybe I'm making a bigger deal out of it than it needs to be. The guys don't seem too bothered that we crashed their party, and Ellie, Haley, and Gwen seem fine with joining them.

Maybe I just need to take a breath and have fun. We're still at the club together after all and I'm still pissed about it.

I don't know how long I've been in here, but I decide it's probably best if I go back to the table before reinforcements are sent in to make sure I didn't drown in a toilet.

Taking a deep breath, I look over myself one more time in the mirror before walking out of the bathroom and straight into a hard body.

Looking up, I find that the hard body belongs to none other than the guy I came in here to escape.

Being this close to him after the show I put on in his bedroom is causing a million butterflies to flutter in my stomach. When I saw him sitting there in that booth in his black, plain t-shirt with his muscles and his perfect jaw line, I swear to God I felt like the air had been sucked out of me.

I know he's hot, I've known that. Yet, I've never thought about fucking his brains out, and after what happened between us the other night, I can't stop thinking about it.

I tried my best to seem unaffected by him and by what I was doing. I didn't want him to know that by attempting to tease him and turn him on, I was getting turned on too.

When I got home, I had to use my vibrator to release the tension I was feeling after rubbing up against him for so long.

I mean, the guy is seriously sex personified. I don't know when it happened or how, but I am starting to see Holland Monroe as more than just my best friend's twin brother or the annoying boy next door.

Somehow, he's turned into this man with these muscles and this deep, sexy voice that for some reason makes me want to take all of my clothes off and jump him.

Holland's eyes roam up and down my body once before settling on my face. A small smirk forms on his lips, and I just know he's about to say something that'll piss me off.

"You should watch where you're going, Bug," he says in a taunting tone. I scowl at him, crossing my arms over my chest. Holland's eyes dart down to the ample amount of cleavage that is now noticeable.

"You shouldn't be in my way, Ball Boy," I shoot back. The smirk on his face grows wider.

"Ball Boy? That's a new one. Why Ball Boy?"

I shrug, because honestly, I don't know where that came from. It kind of popped into my head, and I just said it.

"I don't know. You play a sport with a ball. It makes sense," I explain. Holland chuckles, and it makes me want to laugh too. It is a ridiculous nickname, and a terrible logic.

"I play a sport with a ball, yes," Holland nods, and I can tell he's trying really hard not to burst out laughing. I don't know whether to be pissed off or amused.

I decide to go back to being pissed when I remember where we are.

"Why are you here?" I ask. Holland gives me a bewildered look, as if he has no idea why I would ask such a question.

"I was here first," he shrugs nonchalantly. Shaking my head, I glare at him.

"I don't mean why are you here at the club, I mean why are you standing outside of the bathroom waiting for me like a stalker?" I bite out. A laugh bursts out of him, startling and confusing me all at once. What was funny?

"Stalker? Seriously, Lainey Bug, that's a bit dramatic. Maybe I had to pee. You know, that's normally why people go to the restroom."

I feel my face heat as he looks down at me, and I feel kind of dumb for insinuating the stalker thing. Of course he isn't stalking me. He probably went to the bathroom, and I walked out when he did, causing me to bump into him.

Standing straighter, I try my best to look as confident as I possibly can.

"Whatever. Let's just get this night over with. Gwen deserves the best bachelorette party there ever was, and I won't let the fact that you're here ruin it."

As I walk past him, I purposely bump into him. He doesn't even move. Not even an inch, and that pisses me off even more for some reason.

The rest of the night went off without a hitch. The guys kept to themselves for the most part, except for when Ryker took Gwen to dance with him during a few songs.

Ellie, Haley, and I got way too drunk and danced our asses off while Holland, Patrick, and Mason did the same. It ended up being a great night, and I'm glad I didn't let the fact that Holland was there bother me.

Surprisingly, the only thing that did bother me was when some girl came over and starting flirting and touching Holland like she wanted to eat him.

I felt this twinge of jealousy and anger that she was touching him, feeling him, and making him laugh. He didn't look uncomfortable in the slightest, which pissed me off even more. I'm pretty sure he even looked over at me at some point to rub it in.

This whole sexual tension thing between us is really messing with my fucking head, and I hate it. I didn't anticipate this feeling with him, and I wasn't prepared for how much I'd crave him.

I know I can't go there with him. I know who he is, I know he's my best friend's brother, I know he's like forbidden fruit. Maybe that's why I want him so badly. Or maybe I haven't had sex in so long that my body is desperate for something.

I can't actually want Holland Monroe, can I?

Chapter 19

HOLLAND

"Man, have you even packed anything yet?" Logan asks as he stands against my wall, looking around my mess of a room. We leave for the wedding tomorrow, and I in fact have not even begun to pack.

I know, I should have probably started like, last week. I've been busy with practice and classes and just not wanting to do it.

I nod as I pull open my suitcase. "Yeah, I've started," I lie. Logan laughs sarcastically.

"You haven't, have you?"

I scoff. "Ye of little faith, my man. Of course I've started packing, we leave tomorrow."

Logan pushes off the wall, giving me a look that tells me he doesn't believe a thing I'm saying. Smart man.

"Bullshit. Your suitcase is empty," he motions toward the empty suitcase on my bed. I look down, trying to think of something else to say to save my ass.

"Maybe I already packed a bag, did you ever think of that?" I question. Logan raises an eyebrow, not looking convinced.

"Well, have you?" I nod. Logan takes a step toward me.

"Okay, let's see it then."

Fuck. "Okay fine, I haven't started packing. There, you happy?" I ask, throwing my arms in the air. "Jesus, what's with the third degree?"

"I just asked if you'd started to pack since you know, we leave first thing tomorrow morning to get on a plane to Italy for my brother, your best friend's, wedding."

"Well, I've been kind of busy, man. I'll get it done," I shrug, turning back to the empty suitcase in front of me. I fucking hate packing, and I severely hate traveling.

Flying scares the living shit out of me. The truth is, I've been putting off packing for a while now because I'm scared shitless to get on this damn flight tomorrow.

No one knows that I'm terrified of flying except Ellie and Mason. We went on a trip to Disney World when we were kids, and I cried the entire way to Florida. Every time the plane would jerk, I'd cry harder, gripping onto my mom's arm for dear life.

Ellie made fun of me for months, and I haven't flown since. That was when we were like, twelve. I have been petrified to fly ever since. I really didn't want anyone to know that.

Logan's right, this is my best friend's wedding. When Ryker told me he'd be getting married in Italy, I thought he was joking. Well, no such luck. He was serious as can be, and now I have to fly to fucking Italy.

Ellie is excited to go to another country and watch her best friend get married. Logan and Mason seem to be totally fine with the idea of getting on a metal death trap. Lainey hasn't mentioned being frightened or nervous about the flight.

Me? I'm already thinking of everything that can go wrong. What if the airline loses my luggage? What if I miss the flight while I'm taking a piss? What if the flight gets cancelled and I miss the damn wedding? What if the fucking plane goes down? Fuck.

My palms feel sweaty, and I can feel my breathing accelerating but I try my best to hold it together since Logan is still all up in my space.

Growling, I walk to my closet and pull some shirts off the hangers, tossing them haphazardly into the open suitcase on my bed.

I can feel Logan's intense gaze on me as I rummage through my dresser to pull out a few pairs of pants, briefs, socks, and a few pairs of pajamas. Lastly, I throw a couple pairs of shoes in and call it a day.

Cramming them all into the suitcase, it struggles a bit to zipper, but I eventually get it to stick.

"You good, man?" Logan asks, a hint of concern lacing his voice.

"Great," I bite back. "Can you fuck off now?"

Instead of leaving the room, Logan takes a step closer to me, causing my fists to clench at my sides. If he doesn't leave now, I might hit him.

It'll really suck when the best man shows up to the wedding with a huge black eye, but if he doesn't stop pushing, that's what's going to happen.

I'm already anxious, and I hate being anxious. I'm normally cool and collected. Even when all the shit went down with my father, I stayed rational. Right now, my skin is crawling, and I feel like I want to scream.

"What is your problem, Monroe?" Logan spits, clearly frustrated at my outburst. I don't blame him. I'm being a dick, right now I can't control it.

"Woah, what's going on, Shitheads? Familial dispute?" Mason asks, letting himself into my room that already feels way too cramped. Logan turns to my cousin who looks more entertained than he should.

"Your boy here's being an asshole," he explains, as if it isn't his fault that I'm being like this.

In all fairness, he probably doesn't even realize that he's the one that set me off.

Mason looks between me and Logan, then to the bed where my suitcase sits. Realization seems to hit him before he looks back to Logan who looks lost now.

"You finally got him to pack?" he asks Logan. Logan shrugs.

"I guess, but he turned into a dick, and I'm trying to figure out why."

Mason moves beside me, his hands landing on my shoulders and squeezing as if I'm about to enter a boxing ring.

"Well, that would be because my dear cousin here is-" I cut him off before he can finish.

"Fuck off, Mason," I snap, shrugging his hands off of my shoulders. Instead of backing off, Mason stays where he is, chuckling to himself.

"What?" Logan asks. Mason opens his mouth to finish his statement. I shoot him the strongest death glare I can. His smile just grows.

"Keep your mouth shut," I warn. Mason ignores the threat in my voice and continues.

"He's afraid of flying."

I'm going to kill him. I know a shit ton of people are afraid of flying. That doesn't mean I wanted it advertised that I'm a bitch about it.

I'm supposed to be this tough, rugby playing asshole that has no fear, and here I am, terrified of getting on a damn airplane. Pathetic.

Logan looks from Mason to me, confusion laced in his expression.

"That's why you weren't packed? Did you think if you didn't pack, you wouldn't have to get on the flight tomorrow?" he inquires. I don't know what I was thinking, honestly. I never put myself in these situations.

I don't travel, and when I do, I do it by roadway. Flying is never my first choice. Unfortunately, there's no other way to get to Italy by tomorrow morning. So plane it is.

I shrug. Logan chuckles, and I think he's going to give me shit about being a little bitch, but he doesn't.

"Tons of people are afraid to fly, Monroe. That's nothing to be ashamed of, it's pretty normal," he assures me, patting my shoulder. I let out a breath and nod.

"I know, I just don't need it broadcasted all over the place. I'd like to keep it between us three, got it?" I say in a slightly authoritative tone as I look between the guys. They both nod in understanding. Mason gives me one of his 'I'm going to do something stupid' grins on his face.

"I'm serious, Mase. This doesn't leave this room."

Mason holds his hands up in surrender. "Okay, okay. I won't tell anyone else," he agrees as he walks toward my door. "I won't need to. Everyone will already be able to tell by the way you cry like a little bitch when we get on."

Mason and Logan laugh at Mason's comment. I grab the closest thing to me, which happens to be a shoe I was going to pack sitting on my bed and chuck it at him.

"Fuck you, dude. Both of you get out of my fucking room."

The two of them laugh hysterically as they exit my room, and I want to do a lot more than just throw a shoe. Instead, I slam the door shut and throw myself onto my bed. Throwing my arm over my eyes, I let out a long breath.

Fuck them. Fuck this trip. Fuck Italy. And fuck flying.

Chapter 20

HOLLAND

JFK is packed to the brim with travellers going to all different places. Sounds of the airport fill my ears, and I can already feel the panic setting in. So many voices talking at once, the sound of luggage being wheeled across the floor, the loudspeaker announcing flights.

I can't seem to focus on anything. It feels like I'm in a trance, and I'm not in control of my body. I'm just blindly following Mason, Logan, and the girls to check our luggage.

I've been out of it since we pulled up to the airport and the Uber dropped us off. I don't know if anyone's tried to talk to me. All I know is that my heart is racing, and my skin feels like a bunch of tiny ants are crawling under it.

Not even the jeans that look like they're painted on to Lainey's skin are distracting me from the impending panic attack. I'm pretty positive I've looked normal so far, and I don't think anyone can tell I'm freaking the fuck out.

After we've checked our bags and went through TSA, which was literal hell, we finally sit down at our gate. We got here two hours early, so now we just have to wait to board.

Falling into a chair, I set my carry-on bag down and lean back, pulling the baseball cap I decided to wear this morning over my eyes and crossing my arms over my chest.

Just as I think I'm beginning to doze off, a body flops down in the seat beside me. I don't move, in hopes that whoever it is will leave me alone. No such luck.

Lifting my hat off my eyes, Lainey looks at me with a small smile. The blue in her greyish blue eyes stands out against her long, dark hair that has fallen in her face. She looks fucking gorgeous, even in her big baggy sweatshirt and jeans without a trace of makeup on her face.

I always thought she was naturally beautiful. I may not have let myself admit it, but I knew she was a pretty girl. She never even had to try.

"Are you sleeping?" she asks softly. I close my eyes again.

"I was," I lie.

"You've been really quiet ever since we got in the Uber. Are you alright?" Lainey asks, her brows furrowing. She's never really shown concern for me, or even asked me how I was, so this feels odd.

Without opening my eyes, I say, "I'm fine."

"You sure? You look kind of pale," she states, putting her hand on my forehead. What the hell is she doing? Why is she acting like she cares about how I'm feeling? Does she? Maybe she's finally giving in to her urges.

"I'm fine, Barkley. Give it a rest," I snap. I don't mean to be a dick, but when my anxiety gets bad, I get irritable. My eyes open, and I see the confused look on Lainey's face. She doesn't look hurt or upset that I snapped at her. She just looks suspicious, like she doesn't believe me.

The girl has a good reading on me I guess, because I'm not even close to being fine. I feel like I could vomit all over the floor right now or pass the fuck out. As the time gets closer to boarding, I can feel the panic rising.

"You're afraid of flying," she says matter-of-factly. My head snaps to her, and I can see the triumph in her eyes at the fact that she knows she's right. I scoff, trying to play it off.

"I'm not. Just impatient," I lie. She sees right through the bullshit. Lainey always knows when someone's lying, it's like her superpower. I've always hated it, the way she would always know when I was lying to her.

It made it extremely hard to play games as a kid or cheat a little when we played Monopoly.

She inches a bit closer, and her arm brushes mine, making me forget about the nausea in my stomach and direct my attention to my dick, willing it not to get hard from the simplest touch.

A brush of her arm against mine shouldn't make me want to fuck Lainey's brains out, but for some reason, it does.

As if she can hear her thoughts, she moves back just a little so that she's no longer touching me. The loss of touch sends a shiver down my spine. Fuck, I didn't want her to move.

Lainey's eyes wander over my face, searching for an honest answer that I'm refusing to give her. I don't want her to think I'm a bitch for being afraid to get on the damn plane. She's one hundred percent make fun of me for it.

That's what we do. We poke fun at each other and our fears and insecurities. It's wild that we're even still friends, if you can really call it that. I guess I could say she's friends with my sister, and I've just always been around.

I don't know if Lainey would have chosen to have me in her life if it weren't for Ellie. I don't know if I would have sought her out either. Knowing her reputation in high school, if I hadn't already known her, I would have steered clear.

I've never been one for drama, and Lainey Barkley is drama personified. At least, she was. She's definitely calmed down a lot since her wild teenage years, but she's still dealing with the same shit which is her shitty parents.

"I know there's something wrong. It's written all over your face. You're afraid of flying, aren't you?" she probes. Fucking hell.

"Go bother someone else with your incessant questions, Bug," I say lowly, sounding much more rude than I anticipated, but the questioning is making my anxiety worse.

My nerves are on fire and my entire body feels like it's in flight or fight mode. I'm trying my best to stay calm, using all the techniques I've used in the past. Breathing in through the nose and out through the mouth. Pinching my leg to feel something physical.

Refusing to sit here any longer and be berated with questions, I stand, grabbing my bag off of the floor and walk toward the bathrooms.

"Where are you going, man? Boarding's about to start," Logan tells me as I stroll past.

"Taking a piss. I'll be right back."

I don't turn around to see if anyone's following me. I head straight into the men's bathroom and set my back down so I can grip the sink in front of me.

Staring at my reflection in the mirror, I watch my complexion turn paler by the second.

Get it together, Holland. You're better than this. You can get on this plane and sleep until we're there. So what if people know you're a bit of a nervous flyer. Hundreds of people are terrified of flying.

Grow a pair, get on the damn plane, and go to your best friend's wedding in fucking Italy. Anyone else would be ecstatic. Take a breath, stand tall, and get on that fucking plane.

Splashing some water on my clammy face, I look at myself one more time before grabbing my bag and walking back to my friends.

Mason walks right up to me, placing both of his hands on each of my shoulders. He looks dead serious, which is weird for him because the dude's never been serious a day in his life.

"We're going to be fine. The chances of the plane crashing are slim to none, cousin. Chill," he tells me. His words of encouragement don't help even a little bit, but I nod. He's probably right. Everything's going to be just fine.

There is a noise over the loudspeaker before a sweet female voice comes through.

"We are now boarding flight 672, all passengers should make their way to the gate immediately."

Fuck, here we go. I can do this. I can do this.

Chapter 21

LAINEY

We've been in the air for almost two hours, and it's been a relatively smooth flight so far. I just finished reading my sappy romance novel, and I'm kicking myself for not bringing another book.

We have about six more hours to go before we land in Naples, and I am already going stir crazy. I hate sitting around doing nothing. I can barely stand watching movies since you have to sit so long.

I like to move, I like to jog, I like to be active. I never played a sport in high school, but I am on the dance team at Ellington. It gives me something to do so I'm not sitting at home all the time bored out of my mind.

If you ask Mrs. Monroe or Erica, I was always an active kid. I kept up more with Holland than I did with Ellie most days. We'd run around the yard for hours playing tag and tumbling to the ground.

Being cooped up in an airplane is not my ideal way to spend time. I don't mind flying. I've been flying since I was kid. The Monroe's would let me tag along on a lot of their family vacations since I was alone more than half of the time.

When I was lucky, my parents would bring me along on one of their glorious adventures, but the chances of that happening were slim to none by the time I was thirteen.

I texted mom before we boarded to let her know I was leaving the country and would be back in a week but got no reply. Shocker.

Truthfully, I wasn't expecting a reply, but it would be nice to know that my parents actually care where I'm at and what I'm doing. I guess that's too much to ask from Tatiana and Drake Barkley.

'Never expect anything, and you can never be disappointed,' my mother used to say to me. She'd said it once when I was upset that they had forgotten my birthday. It was my fifteenth birthday, and I was home alone yet again.

Erica made me a cake, and the Monroe's came over to celebrate with me. Mrs. Monroe got me a beautiful charm bracelet that I still wear to this day.

My fingers run over the bracelet around my wrist, and a small smile touches my lips. The Monroe family has always been there for me, and I couldn't be more grateful.

The night of my fifteenth birthday, after my mother had called to tell me that 'of course I didn't forget my only daughter's birthday. Your father and I had an event to attend,' Holland had come over.

I heard a faint knock on my bedroom window, and when I looked down, Holland was staring back at me with this huge, goofy grin on his face.

When I met him outside, he had his hands behind his back, and he looked mischievous as hell. Part of me always loved that side of him. The playful deviance. It was one of my favorite things about him.

"Happy birthday, Lainey Bug," he'd said as he handed me a small red velvet box. I'd stared at the box in his hand far longer than I should've before taking it from him.

My brows furrowed and my suspicion grew as I stared at the small box in my palm. Holland had never gotten me a birthday present before, and honestly it was a little out of character for him.

"Well, come on, open it, Barkley. It's not gonna open itself," he'd said, rolling his eyes with impatience.

When I opened the box, a small ladybug charm sat inside. It's red wings and black spots standing out against the white foam inside the box.

My breath caught in my throat as I stared at the small, meaningful gift. I looked up at him, trying to fight the tears that were begging to be let out. This boy that I've teased and mocked, who's tackled me to the ground and thrown mud at me, bought me a gift.

Not only a gift, but one that had meaning. One that didn't look like it was cheap.

"Get it? Because we call you Lainey Bug? So I got you a ladybug charm to put on the bracelet my mom got you," Holland had said with a smile. He looked so proud of himself, and it was honestly one of the sweetest things anyone had ever done for me.

"You're the only one that calls me that," I'd said with a quiet chuckle.

Playing with the small ladybug charm on my bracelet, I become aware of my present surroundings. I'd been so caught up in my memory that I'd forgotten I was on a plane, and sitting next to Ellie, who by the way still doesn't know that her brother got me the charm.

I wear it every day, but she's never asked about where it came from, and I never really felt the need to tell her. Not that I'm trying to hide it from her or anything. It just hasn't come up in conversation.

"You okay?" Ellie asks softly, her brows pinched. I nod, smiling.

"Yeah, of course. I'm fine," I tell her. She looks down at my lap where my finished novel sits.

"I told you you should've brought another book. You read too fast."

Tossing my book into my bag on the ground, I lean back in my seat and cross my legs.

"I don't recall you saying those words to me," I tease, knowing full well she said those exact words to me last night when I threw everything into my carry on bag.

Ellie rolls her eyes and puts her earbud back in, watching the screen on the seat in front of her.

With a heavy sigh, I get up out of my seat and head to the bathroom. I don't have to pee that bad, but I need to stretch my legs and freshen up.

The door is shut and locked, and it's like my bladder knows there's a toilet right there because I suddenly feel like I could pee my pants.

After waiting about five minutes for whoever is taking forever in the bathroom, I knock. The door opens right away, and a puffy faced Holland stares back at me. His eyes are watering, and he looks as pale as a ghost.

"Oh my god, are you okay?" I ask, even though it's a stupid question because he's obviously not okay, Lainey.

Holland's eyes search my face before he shakes his head, and the look on his face breaks my cold heart.

Pushing him back lightly, I squeeze my way into the small space and slide the door shut behind us. There's barely enough room for both of us in here, so we're chest to chest, and the smell of his cologne is intoxicating.

I place my hands on his chest awkwardly, not knowing where to keep them. I can feel his breath and the hurried beat of his heart against my palms. The way he looks right now is unrecognizable.

This very large, very muscular rugby playing man looks like a small child as he trembles beneath my touch.

"Holland, what's wrong?" I ask, worry laced in my tone. He doesn't say anything at first, just continues to take deep breaths.

"Holland?"

"I-I'm fine," he stutters. He's very clearly not fine. I shake my head, hoping he'll tell me what's wrong so I can at least try to help. I'm not good with feelings. I'm not good with comforting people, I can barely comfort myself.

I use sex to cope with my issues, and something tells me Holland is not going to be using that same strategy.

"Well, you don't exactly look fine…"

"Thanks," he mumbles, rolling his eyes. I chuckle softly, hoping I can distract him with a little humor.

"Hey, I keep it real. I wouldn't lie to you," I tease. A small hint of a smile appears on his lips, and I can tell I'm getting close. Holland nods.

"Yeah, you've always been pretty up front, haven't you?"

"It's a talent of mine, actually. Brutal honesty is my specialty."

Holland scoffs, and a real smile finally appears on his face, making me smile in return. The Holland I know is back, and I can finally breathe again.

The smile on his face fades quickly though, replaced with his worried expression again.

"I hate flying," he says softly. I know he's always had a weird thing with flying, but I've never seen him like this. Is he having a panic attack?

"Is that why you look like you've run a marathon and have puffy eyes?" I ask, grimacing.

"Yeah. I think I'm having a panic attack," he says quietly, almost as if he's embarrassed to admit it. I don't know why he'd be embarrassed. It's just me, and it's not like I don't know him.

Holland drops his head back and looks at the ceiling before letting out a big breath of air.

"I came in here to splash some water on my face, but then the plane shook and I freaked out. I know it was turbulence, but I thought…" he swallows as he looks back down at me.

The vulnerability in his eyes is killing me right now. I really don't like seeing him like this. Something in me wants to take away his worry, his pain. I want to help him, but I don't know how. We still have hours left on this plane. How is he going to last?

A bit of turbulence shakes the aircraft again and Holland's face loses any color that was left in it. He looks like he's going to vomit, and if he does, it will be right on me since I'm standing in front of the toilet and have no room to move.

"Shit," he hisses, grabbing the wall. When the plane evens out again, he takes a few deep breaths, but they're not strong. "Fuck, I need to get out of here."

"Hey, you're okay. We're okay, Holland," I urge, my hands cupping his cheek in a surprising gesture. What the hell am I doing?

Holland doesn't even seem to notice my hands as he closes his eyes and shakes with fear.

Before I know what I'm saying, the strangest thing falls off of my lips in a whisper.

"Holland, kiss me."

His eyes snap open, confusion replacing panic for a moment. "What?"

"Yeah, just kiss me," I repeat, my gaze steady. I don't know what the hell I'm doing, but I do know that I want to take his mind off of the flight and his anxiety. "Come on. It'll distract you."

He hesitates, watching me as if I grew two heads. In any other circumstance, this would probably never happen, but I don't know what else to do. This is what helps me, and it's all I have right now.

"Are you sure?" he asks, looking completely stuck between giving in and running for the hills. My eyes search him for a moment, trying to figure out what he's thinking, but I'm not a mind reader and I honestly hate that at this moment.

I nod, giving him the go ahead to do whatever he needs to distract himself. After a few awkward moments, he finally leans down, and my pulse races. Holy shit, is this really about to happen? Am I letting Holland Monroe kiss me?

His lips brush softly against mine. The kiss is tentative at first, a question more than an answer. But suddenly Holland isn't shy anymore. Maybe he's feeling relief or confusion?

To my surprise, he deepens the kiss. He pulls me closer to him, but I didn't need to move much. The bathroom is cramped, but the tightness feels comforting rather than suffocating.

My lips seem to part involuntarily, and Holland wastes no time as his tongue brushes against mine. The taste of him is intoxicating, a mix of mint and something uniquely him. He's a really good freaking kisser.

He groans softly, his hands moving to my hips, holding me steady. Thank God for that because I'm feeling a bit off kilter right now.

The kiss is frantic, desperate, a lifeline in the chaos that must be his mind.

But as quickly as it started, it comes to an abrupt end at the sound of a knock on the door.

Holland pulls back quickly, his breath ragged. He tries to back up, but he can't get far.

"Shit," he hisses, running a hand through his messed hair. I just stand there, looking between him and the door as another knock comes from the other side, and then a familiar voice calls out.

"Hey, I've really gotta go, can you hurry up in there?"

Holland blows out a breath and looks visibly more relaxed as I reach for the handle to slide open the door. I'm greeted by Mason's annoyed expression. Something tells me he's been waiting out here for a bit.

My cheeks heat as he looks from Holland to me, putting the pieces together. He needs to keep his mouth shut because I don't want Ellie finding out about this. Not yet.

"What… you guys…" Mason gestures between the two of us, his expression almost horrified. "You…" he points to Holland. "And you…" he says as he points at me. "Did you guys-"

I cut him off before he can even finish that sentence. "No! No, of course not. He just-"

Holland cuts me off before I can say anything more.

"We were planning a, uh… surprise. Yeah, a surprise for Ryker and Gwen. We wanted to keep it quiet until we were sure of our plan," Holland spouts out. What a ridiculous lie! Mason isn't that stupid; he'll never fall for…

"Oh sweet! So, what is it?" Mason asks, his face lit up with excitement. He looks between the two of us again and my pulse picks up speed. I am not good at lying, and here I am, trying to come up with a 'surprise' that wasn't even a thing until five seconds ago.

"What is what?" Holland asks. If I had enough room to maneuver myself enough to face palm, I would. He's kidding right?

"The surprise. What is it?"

"Oh, right. Well, I can't tell you because… well, because you're not really great with secrets, Mase," Holland says, his face crinkling. Mason's hand flies to his chest and his mouth falls open.

"What? I'm great with secrets. I could keep a secret forever if I had to," he defends. He looks genuinely offended, and I have to keep myself from laughing because he has to know how awful he is when it comes to keeping a secret.

Last year, we tried to throw a surprise party for Holland's birthday and Mason ruined it. He was in charge of getting Holland where he needed to be, and he let it slip that they had to be there right on time or it would ruin the surprise.

We were all so pissed we locked him out of the party, causing him to pout outside the entire time. It even started to downpour, and he still stood out there, pouting. He's never let us live it down, but we've never let the fact that he spoiled a surprise be forgotten either.

Hence Holland's comment about Mason not being good with surprises.

Mason is always acting like everyone is against him, but that's only because he's usually the one we have to worry about. He's the one that hits on anything with a pair of tits and a vagina.

He's the one that'll get us kicked out of a party because he hit on someone's girlfriend. That's just the way he is, and we love him for it.

"Oh, Mason," I placate, placing both my hands on either side of his face. He looks down at me with a bewildered expression. "You're horrible with secrets. But at least you're cute."

I pat his cheek and lightly push him so he moves out of the doorway.

When I get back to my seat, Ellie gives me a quizzical look, but she doesn't say anything. I give her a small smile before she turns back to reading her book.

Chapter 22

LAINEY

We landed in Naples hours ago, and as I sit on my hotel bed, all I can think about is Holland's hands on my body. How his lips tasted like mint and a little salty from sweat. How his strong chest felt against mine.

I keep finding myself tracing my lips, remembering the way his felt as he kissed me so deeply, so needy. It's like he's been wanting to do that forever.

I was only trying to distract him from his panic attack, but it felt like a lot more than that if I'm being completely honest. It felt like an explosion.

Not in a destructive kind of way, but in a 'holy shit, this is really happening and it's freaking amazing' kind of way. You know what I mean?

The kiss was hot, it was passionate, it was sexy, and it was only supposed to be a quick distraction. It turned into so much more so quickly and I didn't have the will to stop it. In fact, I would've probably gone further if Mason didn't interrupt.

In hindsight, it's probably best that nothing else happened. I already feel guilty about kissing my best friend's brother. I can't go and fuck him too, even though after that kiss, I can tell he's really good in bed.

Stop it, Lainey. That's Holland. Ellie's twin brother, your best friend's twin brother. The boy that used to tug on your pigtails and throw dirt at you. The kid who once tripped you in front of a whole group of majorly hot guys at a party, on purpose.

He's also the guy that sat there with me on my porch on my twelfth birthday while I cried for an hour about my parents canceling their trip home. The guy who punched some rando at a party for trying to touch me after I told him no. There's no doubt in my mind that Holland Monroe would kick anyone's ass for hurting me.

That's something I really respect about him. He's loyal and protective of everyone that's close to him. He'd never let anyone hurt his circle. Even though he annoys the shit out of me ninety nine percent of the time, I know he'd never let anything happen to me.

Groaning, I fall backward and spread out on the queen-sized bed. The white sheets are soft, and they smell like lavender. The hotel Gwen and Ryker booked for the wedding party is absolutely beautiful. The view from my room is something out of a freaking fairytale.

The grand hotel overlooks the crystal blue water of the Bay of Naples, its pale limestone façade glowing gold in the late afternoon sun. The terraces are draped in ivy and pink wild bougainvillea. It looks unreal, like it's a painting, and I can completely understand why Gwen and Ryker chose this as their wedding destination.

Inside, the lobby boasts high ceilings, beautiful old paintings and pictures on the walls. The marble floors are so clean, they reflect the light from the glass chandeliers.

The reception desk, which looks like it's carved from dark oak, stands beneath a massive oil painting of the Amalfi coast, the vibrant colors sticking out in the almost stark white interior.

From the outside, each room seems to have floor-to-ceiling windows that open onto private balconies.

It would be an amazing palace to sip a coffee in the morning and read a book while overlooking the bay. God, what I'd do to stay here forever.

I haven't been up to the rooftop yet, but according to what Gwen shared with us about the hotel, there's an infinity pool that looks as if it's a part of the sea, bordered by cream-colored loungers and shaded pergolas.

There are apparently some wild parties that happen up there at night, and I'd hate to know what's happened on the loungers and in the pool. God only knows the kind of shit that's gone down.

Needless to say, this place is incredible, and I almost wish we were staying for more than a week. There's so much to do and see, there's no way we'll be able to get it all done in seven days. I guess I'll just have to use mom and dad's credit card to come back. Not like they'll notice, or care anyways.

Deciding I need to move instead of lounging inside my hotel room, I jump out of bed and walk out onto the balcony. The sound of the water crashing below and the birds flying above is so serene. Things like this make me forget all about the fact that I'm all alone.

I know I have friends and people that care about me, but I don't have my own family and that's kind of shitty.

I swear I'm not depressed or anything like that. I can have fun and party. I'm not always thinking about my parents or how much I wish they were in my life. How much I want to feel wanted by them.

I'm the fun friend. The one that makes everyone laugh and cheers everyone on. I'm the one who keeps the party going and makes sure everyone is having a good time. I always have a smile on my face and I'm always up for a little adventure.

But sometimes it gets a little tiring always being the one that has to be strong. I know my friends would be there for me; they always are. I just don't like looking weak. When people know you have a weakness, they can exploit it.

They'll use that weakness to tear you down. They'll use it against you. I don't need anyone seeing that I'm not as tough as I make myself seem. It's my little secret, and I'll keep it hidden as long as I can.

Obviously, my closest friends like Ellie, Gwen, and Haley know about my past with my parents. They know when I'm feeling down about it, too. But I don't ever let myself cry about it.

I doubt my mother or father give a second thought about me except when they send the rare text asking how I am or if I'm still at school. They don't call or facetime, they send a text.

How pathetic is that? Poor little Lainey, her own parents don't even want her. God, I'm such a loser.

Letting my head fall forward, I close my eyes and listen to the noises and smell the scents wafting around me. The sun is warm on my skin and the light breeze feels amazing.

Fuck, Lainey. Get out of your damn head. You're in fucking Italy right now for your best friend's wedding.

The rehearsal dinner is tomorrow, and the wedding is Saturday. It's going to be beautiful and you're going to have a blast. You're going to--

My thoughts are interrupted with a loud knock on my door. Twirling around, I head for the door and look through the peephole to make sure it's not a stranger.

When I see its Gwen, I open the door and she barrels into the room, squeezing me so tight I lose the air in my lungs.

"Oh my god, you're here! I'm so excited!" Gwen squeals, pulling back to look at me. She's glowing, as always. Her brown hair is curled, and her skin looks sun kissed causing her blue eyes to pop.

She's grinning from ear to ear, and I don't think I've ever seen her so happy. Gwen was a bit of cynic, not as bad as I am, but she didn't totally believe in happily ever after, as much as she wanted to. I'm really happy she found hers, even if I am a little jealous.

The thought of attaching myself to someone forever scares the shit out of me, and the thought they could leave you at any moment scares me even more. I've been perfectly happy with my casual hookups and one-night stands. That is, until recently.

I've been feeling a bit lonely, and I don't normally feel that way, so this is new to me. Is that why I'm feeling this emotional attachment to Holland all of a sudden?

Am I so desperate and alone that I've gained an attraction to one of the most annoying men on the face of the planet? Although, seeing him so vulnerable on the plane made me feel a different type of way.

I wanted to help him. I felt this nagging feeling in my gut that made me feel like I had to make sure he was okay. I've never been that way, not even with Gwen or Ellie.

I'm the kind of friend they make memes about. The one where the friend is standing super far away and patting their friend on the back with a broom. That's me.

Comforting people isn't really my forte. Never really has been.

Speaking of Holland, the thought of him sends a shiver down my spine and Gwen obviously notices because the grin on her face slowly fades away, replaced with a look of concern.

Her head tilts in confusion and I know she's going to ask a million questions, but I don't want to talk about what I'm feeling or what happened on the plane. I know she'd keep it to herself, I just don't even know how I truly feel about the whole thing.

She wouldn't judge me, she never has. I just, I don't know. This is all so complicated and the look Gwen is giving me right now is making me want to curl up in a ball and hide.

"What's wrong? Are you okay?" she asks. Turning on my heel, I walk toward the bed and plop down.

"Yes, I'm great. We're in Italy and you're getting married and-"

Gwen cuts me off before I can continue rambling.

"You're full of shit. What happened?"

"Nothing happened, I'm okay!" I chuckle softly at the worried expression on her face. I swear she's like a mother, always worrying about everyone else and their feelings.

She rolls her eyes exaggeratedly. "Lainey Barkley, you tell me what the hell is wrong with you or so help me, I will uninvite you from my wedding," she demands, crossing her arms over her chest as she attempts to look threatening. I can't help but laugh.

"You're going to uninvite your maid of honor a day before the wedding?" I challenge, knowing she is absolutely not going to do that. Her lip juts out in a pout.

Falling onto the bed next to me, she places her hands on my legs, her tan skin making me look like a ghost.

"Please, just tell me. I can tell something is bothering you, and I'm only trying to-"

"Holland and I kissed," I blurt out, not even sure if I meant to say it or if it just forced itself out.

Gwen's eyes go wide, and she freezes. Shit, I shouldn't have said anything. She doesn't need to deal with this a day before she gets married. Damnit, I'm a horrible friend.

"Holland, Holland? Like, Ellie's brother Holland?" she asks, her eyes still wide, but she doesn't look like she's judging me.

I nod.

"You let him kiss you? Like on the lips?"

"Well, yeah, I guess. I mean, it was kind of like a mutual thing at the time but, yeah..." I say, cringing at the awkward feeling in the pit of my stomach.

Gwen squeals before jumping off the bed and dancing in her spot. "I knew it! I freaking knew it! I told Ryker something was going on between you two! The tension was so obvious," she exclaims. Okay, so this wasn't exactly the reaction I thought I'd be getting.

"What do you mean it was obvious? There was no tension, and there's nothing going on between Holland and I," I try to explain, but she's still jumping around like a lunatic.

"Bullshit. There is so something happening between the two of you. You like him, don't you? You think he's sexy," she drags out the end of the word sexy.

Rolling my eyes, I stand from my spot on the bed and begin to pace back and forth, hoping that will help the headache that is now building inside me.

"I do not. He was having some sort of panic attack, and I was just trying to distract him, and I didn't know how else to do it," I clarify. She can't honestly believe that I of all people would have a thing for Holland Monroe.

Except, do I have a thing for him? Do I think he's sexy? Do I want to see how good he is in bed? Yes, yes, I do. Fuck, I do have a thing for him. I am so screwed.

Chapter 23

HOLLAND

The large room is adorned with white and light blue decorations to match the color scheme of the wedding. White tablecloths cover the tables, and extravagant floral arrangements sit as the centerpieces on each.

A lit candle sits beside it, which almost seems like a fire hazard to me. An open flame next to flowers, on a flammable surface? That doesn't seem like a good idea, but that's just me.

Name tags sit at each place at the table, as if we're children and need assigned seats. Large crystal chandeliers hang from the tall ceilings, and there is a massive dance floor at the front of the space.

The ballroom in the hotel is the perfect place for a huge party, and that's exactly what it will be used for tomorrow after Gwen and Ryker tie the knot.

I haven't seen either of them all day. In fact, I haven't seen much of anyone all day other than Mason, who apparently made use of the hotel's spa this morning.

He's also made use of the large infinity pool that overlooks the water, and the hotel gym that is somehow bigger than the gym back at Ellington, and that's saying something because that gym is huge.

Leave it to Mason to be the one to use every single amenity there is to be offered. We've been here for less than twenty-four hours, and he's completely made himself at home.

After we landed in Naples, I immediately went to my room and took a long, hot shower. I needed to wash away the stress from the plane and the thoughts of Lainey's mouth on mine.

Fuck, was she a good kisser. I always had a feeling she'd be a good kisser. She's got those full pink lips, and I would love to see the way they look wrapped around my-

Woah, there, Holland. Slow down. It was a kiss, one kiss. Yes, it was an amazing kiss, and if we weren't interrupted by Mason, the fucking idiot, I'm not sure I would have been able to stop myself from touching her further.

The small space would have made it a bit difficult to do everything I want to do to her, but I would have found a way.

I know she wanted me too. I could tell by the way her kiss deepened when I lightly squeezed her hips and pulled her closer to me. It was the best distraction I could have asked for.

She told me to kiss her, and I was completely taken aback. She's always been pretty forward. Lainey Barkley is not a shy girl. She isn't afraid to tell you how she feels or make sure you know what's up.

But when she demanded that I kiss her, my whole world stopped. I thought I'd heard her wrong, because why would she tell me to kiss her? I don't even know if she considers us to be friends half of the time.

She completely shocked me, but I wasn't going to pass up the opportunity I'd been dreaming about for months. Maybe even years.

Lainey was right there in front of me, her petite body, curly brown hair, and blue grey eyes staring back at me, telling me to use her as a distraction, and I had never wanted anything more.

I don't know if I'll ever have that chance again, but I do know I need to at least try to make it possible. Now that I've had a small taste of her, there's no way I can go the rest of my life without having more. She's like a drug, and I'm not incredibly hooked.

"Why are you just standing there? You're in the way," a familiar feminine voice says from behind me, breaking me out of my trance like state.

Lainey walks past me, rolling her eyes. Her brown curls fall down her back, and the airy, sky blue, dress that falls to just above her knees makes my throat dry. She looks delectable, and I want to taste every single inch of her until I memorize her every curve.

"Hello? Earth to Ball Boy," she chides, waving her hand in front of my face. "Did you forget how to read? Can't find your name?"

Well, just like that, the moments gone. Instead of thinking about how much I want to taste her again, I'm now thinking of different ways I can shut her up.

Rolling my eyes, I stride past her, finding my spot and taking my seat. She and I are the first ones here, and the tension in the room is high.

Looking at the spot next to me, I check the name on the tag, smiling devilishly when I spot the name. Placed right next to me is none other than the little bug herself.

"Looks like you're right here, Lainey Bug. I grin, winking at her. She groans, rolling her eyes and making her way over to where I'm sitting.

As she sits, the scent of her fruity perfume and sweet shampoo surrounds me, and I wish I could bury my face in her neck and never leave.

She doesn't make eye contact with me, instead she looks down at her phone and stays silent until Haley and Ellie enter the room. I wanted to make a comment about what happened between us, but it'll have to wait until we're alone again, if she ever lets that happen.

Theres a weird tension between us for the rest of the night, like we both know how we feel and what we want but we're refusing to admit it. It's almost funny how Lainey tries to act as if I don't exist.

That is, until we're forced to practice our duties as the wedding party. Apparently, Gwen and Ryker thought it would be a great idea to have Lainey and I walk down the aisle together. Remind me to kick Ryker's ass later.

An hour later, the entire wedding party is in the ballroom, chatter and clanking of glasses filling the space. Gwen and Ryker sit at the front of the room at their own table. They smile and laugh, and I'm finding myself feeling a bit jealous that I don't have that.

I've never really thought about marriage or kids or having a family. I've never really been a playboy either. Yes, I've had one-night stands, what college student hasn't. But I've never been considered a player like Ryker was. He was Ellington's most eligible bachelor.

Hard to pin down, never staying with a woman for more than a month, and having the bad boy reputation, Ryker was every girl's wet dream. That is, until Gwen came along. Ryker made sure every girl, and guy, on campus knew she was his.

I'd never seen him so head over heels for a chick, and it was honestly a shock when we found out how serious he was about Gwen.

She's good for him. She's strong, and she doesn't take any of his shit. She'll set him straight if he needs it, and she won't hesitate to tell him when he's being an ass. They've got a good connection.

I've never had that. I haven't found someone that I connect with that deeply that I can imagine a life with them. Especially one that can handle the chaos of my life currently. With the takeover of my dad's company and the drama that comes along with the criminal world, no girl could handle being with me.

No one really knows about all that, but eventually it would come out. There's no way to hide that once you're with someone.

Lainey's laugh interrupts my thoughts, and the sound gives me butterflies. Hearing an honest, genuine laugh from this girl feels so good. She's always pretending, and I don't even know if she notices anymore.

She's been acting as if her life is perfect and that the fact that she hasn't spoken to her mother in weeks isn't bothering her. She's always been strong, one of the strongest women I know, but I wish she knew she didn't have to be that strong all of the time.

Lainey isn't one to talk about her feelings. In fact, she's pretty against feelings in general. She's always hidden how she feels, and she's never been good at comforting people when they're upset.

A thought occurs just then as I sit next to her, listening to her talk to my sister about who will get the drunkest tonight. I would take away Lainey's pain if I could, so that she would never feel unwanted or unloved.

Lainey Barkley is a lot of things, but she shouldn't have to be strong all of the time. It's going to consume her, and one day she will break. Of course, I'd be there for her when that day came, but I don't want it to. She doesn't deserve to feel that way.

"Can I have everyone's attention, please?" Ryker asks as he stands, lightly tapping his knife on his champagne glass. He doesn't look nervous or frazzled. In fact, he looks completely put together, like he has absolutely no doubts or worries at all.

I wonder what it's like to be that sure of how you feel about someone. Will I ever find out?

The room quiets and everyone turns to face the man of the hour.

"I just wanted to thank you all for coming to celebrate us. I know it was a long a trip, and some of us had to face some fears to get here," he chuckles softly, looking directly at me when he says that last part. I shrug, grinning.

"Listen, I got here, didn't I?" I respond, and everyone chuckles around me. A small sound even comes out of Lainey, who is watching Ryker intently.

Ryker nods, laughing. "That you did, my friend. Anyway, thank you all for being here with us, and we can't wait to see you all tomorrow when we finally say 'I do'."

Everyone claps and Mason whistles loudly, clapping his hands and giving Ryker a standing ovation.

I shake my head, chuckling under my breath. Catching sight of Lainey out of the corner of my eye, I find that, although she's clapping, instead of looking up at Ryker, she's looking at me.

Chapter 24

HOLLAND

The party is in full swing, and the energy in the big room is palpable. Everyone dances and signs along to the music as the DJ plays some absolute bangers.

Ryker and Gwen dance in the middle of the dance floor while the rest of the wedding party dances around them. Lainey, Ellie, and Haley dance together in one corner of the dancefloor, and they look like they're having the time of their lives.

I know they've all had quite a bit to drink already, and the party isn't close to over.

Lainey and Ellie began drinking as soon as they sat down at the dinner table. They started with the champagne that was given. When Haley joined in, that's when the shots began. Gwen even partook in some of the drinking fun, to which Ryker got a bit overprotective and cut her off.

I would've told Lainey to switch to water over an hour ago if I had any say in what she does, but I don't. So she's stumbling in her heels and dancing like she's Jello.

She probably doesn't even realize how much alcohol she's consumed in the short amount of time that has elapsed, but I've kept track. She's had three glasses of champagne, five shots of who knows what, and I haven't even seen her drink a sip of water since we arrived.

I've been drinking, too. I think I may have had a few too many beers to be honest, but I'm sober enough to make sure Lainey's safe.

The only thing keeping me from going over there and throwing her over my shoulder is the fact that she's dancing with my sister and her friends. I don't care what my sister thinks about us, but Lainey does.

I know that's one of the reasons she's holding back. It's obvious by the way she kissed me that she wants more, but I have to give her time to get acclimated with the feelings she's having.

She's the kind of girl that gets spooked by commitment, which usually wouldn't be a problem for me. However, since I realized that the feelings of annoyance were actually feelings of attraction, I haven't been able to get her out of my fucking head.

When the song begins to fade and a slow song comes on, Lainey and the girls stop dancing. Lainey leans over to say something in Ellie's ear and walks out of the room and into the hallway.

My curiosity spikes as I watch her leave, her dark curls bouncing as she walks. My eyes find her ass as her hips sway from side to side, and my god, she is stunning. If she'd let me, I'd devour her.

Before I can stop myself, I'm following after her. She's looking down at her phone, her brows pinched together as if she's just seen something upsetting.

Walking over to a small bench against the wall, she sits and stares at her blue painted toes. Her delicate features look so sad, and I wonder what could have made her mood shift so quickly.

I take a seat next her, and I can feel her body stiffen slightly. She doesn't do feelings, especially her own. She's going to act as if everything is just peachy when it's obviously not. That's when she starts making questionable decisions.

I'm not one to tell anyone what to do or how to deal with their shit because I have my own shit that I can't deal with, but Lainey has made some questionable decisions over the years to deal with her pain.

Instead of simply talking about her feelings, she bottles it up and eventually it explodes, and she does something reckless or crazy. Ellie's tried to talk to her in the past. She's tried to get Lainey to open up about how she's feeling, but the stubborn girl refuses to let anyone help her.

I wouldn't exactly consider Lainey and I to be friends per se, but we've known each other forever, and my sister would kill me if I knew Lainey was upset and drunk and I left her alone.

Honestly, I don't know if I'd even be able to walk away at this point. I don't think I'll ever be able to.

"Can you go?" Lainey asks without looking up, her voice soft but with a hint of annoyance.

I shrug, leaning back against the wall and crossing my ankles. "I like it here. It's… relaxing."

Lainey scoffs. "It was."

"What's wrong?" I ask, hopeful that she'll just tell me the truth, but knowing she won't.

"Nothing. Did you follow me out here?"

"Yep," I say, completely unashamed. She still hasn't lifted her head to look at me, and I have to stop myself from placing my finger under her chin and turning her to face me.

"Okay… well I came to be alone. So, leave," she demands, but I don't move, and I have no plans to. Not until I know what's going on with her.

Chuckling at her forwardness, I sit up a bit straighter and watch as she fiddles with a loose string on her gown.

"Damn Barkley. It's a public space," I tell her, gesturing to the empty hallway.

"Fine. I'll go," Lainey states, standing from her seat and wobbling slightly. As she begins to walk away, I reach out and grab her wrist. Her face twists in what looks like anger.

"Holland… let me go," she orders, trying to look intimidating, but I can't take her seriously with that red hot lipstick and her pouty expression.

"Tell me what's wrong."

Rolling her eyes, she shifts toward me, her knee hitting mine, and the small touch makes the hair on the back of my neck stand up.

"Why do you even care?" she inquires, her gaze narrowing on me as if I'm the last person she wants to be near right now.

"Believe it or not, Lainey Bug, I don't like seeing you hurt," I tell her, and I mean it. I don't know what happened or what's making her upset, but I do know I would do anything to take the pain away.

She scoffs, shifting her weight between each leg before looking down at me.

"You've never cared about my feelings before," she shrugs, and the tone of her voice makes it sound like she's challenging me. As if caring about her feelings is a new thing and I have some ulterior motive.

Standing, I step in toward her, and she takes a small step back. I didn't mean to get all up in her space, but now that I'm here, I don't want to back away. So instead, I take a step closer and her back hits the wall.

Lainey's breathing picks up slightly, and it's a bit shaky. I'm not sure if it's from the closeness of our bodies or the amount of alcohol she's consumed.

"Yeah well, some things change, Barkley," I say quietly, bringing my face closer to her ear and neck. Lainey stiffens, and I can feel her pulse start to race. She's nervous, and she never gets nervous. I love that I can make her feel this way.

"Nothing can change that much," she says breathily. I chuckle lowly before looking her directly in the eyes. She doesn't know how wrong she is.

Weeks ago, I wasn't planning on acting on my desire for her, but now, I'm ready to throw all inhibition out the fucking window to taste her again.

"You'd be surprised."

Her blue-grey eyes search mine as if she's trying to figure out what I could possibly mean. I wonder how she'd feel if I told her what I've been thinking about her recently. I wonder how she'd react if I tried to kiss her again, this time not as a distraction.

Every fiber of my being wants to try it to see what would happen, and the thought of it alone is making me harden in my slacks. If Lainey can feel it, she doesn't show it.

"I… I have to lie down. My head is spinning," she tells me, and I want to ask her if it's because she's so consumed with thoughts of me fucking her, but I know it's most likely from drinking all night.

"Okay, I'll walk you up," I say, and before she can refuse me, I back away from her, taking her hand and pulling her with me toward the elevator.

When the elevator doors open, Lainey stumbles in and leans her back against the wall, her eyes closing.

She looks breathtaking, and if she were mine, I'd take her right here in this elevator. God, the things I'd do to her, with her, for her.

The doors open on the third floor, and I follow Lainey down the hallway to the room she's staying in. She rummages through the tiny purse she holds and fumbles with the keycard, somehow managing to unlock the door and walk inside.

I follow, not really knowing if I should stay to make sure she's okay or leave and give her privacy.

The room is dim, the curtains drawn, and the air thick with the scent of perfume and alcohol. Lainey collapses onto the mattress, her body limp, her eyes half-closed. The blue dress she wears rides up slightly, showing off her long, tan legs.

My dick twitches and I wish more than anything that she wasn't drunk, and she would admit to herself that she's attracted to me.

I should go. I should really, really get out of here. But as I begin to back away, Lainey turns over, her dress moving just far enough off her shoulder that the pink of her taut nipple pokes out.

Fuck. Fuckkkk. God fucking damnit. Get out of here, Holland. Abort mission.

Lainey groans, opening her eyes and watching me as I stand there, trying not stare at her fucking nipple.

"Holland?" she says softly. Clearing my throat, I nod.

"Yeah, Lainey Bug?"

"My parents are in Italy," she tells me, and the reason for her being upset becomes abundantly clear.

Her parents, whom she hasn't seen in probably six or more months, who she barely speaks to, are in the same country she's in right now.

"Shit. How do you know?" I ask, rubbing the back of my neck awkwardly.

"My mother called. She said she'd meant to call for a while, but she got busy," Lainey explains.

Too busy for her own daughter? That's what I want to say, but I'm sure Lainey's already thinking that, and I don't want to make her feel worse, so instead I say, "Does she know you're here?"

Lainey nods, her face falling into a deeper frown.

"Yeah, she knows. I told her about Gwen's wedding and asked if they'd want to grab lunch while I'm here. She gave me some excuse about them being 'super busy' and that was it. She told me to have fun and then hung up. She barely acknowledged the fact that I was here. I haven't spoken to them in months, and she didn't even ask about my life or what I've been up to," she sits up, wobbling a bit, but continues her story.

"Why doesn't she care about me? Why don't my own parents want anything to do with me? What is so wrong with me that they can't even spare a few hours to see their own daughter?" she asks, tears welling in her eyes.

Lainey Barkley doesn't cry. She doesn't talk about her feelings, or her parents, or how she truly feels about the fucked-up situation.

The alcohol in her system must be taking over, because on a regular day, she'd rather be caught dead than talk about her feelings.

Moving toward her, I wait for her to object to me sitting on the bed next to her. When she doesn't, I lower myself down and grab her hand.

I hate that she's feeling this way. I hate that her own parents have made her feel so small, so insignificant. They're the reason she's so guarded. They're the reason she's afraid to let anyone in or get close to people.

I hate them. I hate them for making her feel like she's any less than amazing. I hate them for thinking that sending her money or expensive gifts would make up for the years of neglect and parental guidance. My dad may be a piece of shit, but at least he was around.

He was at every function, every party. He never let his shit get in the way of family. Which is probably why my mother let him get away with the shit he did for so long, and probably why we didn't see all of the illegal shit he was doing.

Regardless, he was there. Lainey's parents never were. I can't imagine how that must feel, to have parents but to never really know them. Never feel their love.

"Listen to me, Bug. There is nothing wrong with you. Nothing. Your parents are fucking idiots. They have no idea what they're missing. You're a badass, and they don't deserve you, you understand me? Fuck them," I say, meaning every single word and hoping she believes them.

Her teary eyes look up at me, and my heart constricts at the broken look on her face. The last time we had a talk like this was when we were kids. She's a grown woman now, and she's had plenty of time for these feelings to fester and build.

I wish she'd talk about it more. I wish she'd let me in, let someone in. She doesn't even talk to Ellie, Gwen, or Haley about this shit. She just lets it build and build, and now the dam is broken and it's all spilling out. I just hope I can help build her walls back up or at least patch them up the best I can.

Chapter 25

HOLLAND

Lainey sniffles, and my heart aches for her. I don't know how to make her realize that she's fucking perfect, and her parents are assholes. Nothing I say will make her understand that it has nothing to do with her and everything to do with them.

Honestly, she's probably not even going to remember any of this in the morning. I could tell her I was in the mob, and she wouldn't remember. She'll wake up in the morning and completely forget that she even spoke to her mother. So it doesn't matter what I tell her.

"You think I'm a badass?" she asks, wiping her nose with the back of her hand. Even tear streaked and snotty, she's beautiful.

Laughing softly, I say, "Hell yeah. You're freaking awesome. Tough as nails, and even a little scary at times," I tell her, and she smiles.

"I thought you found me annoying and bitchy," she shrugs, and I chuckle.

"You are, but that's okay," I say, and she nudges me with her shoulder, no longer crying. Thank fuck.

"Hey!" she shouts, and we both laugh. It's so nice to hear her laugh after seeing her cry. It feels good knowing I'm the one that put that smile on her face.

After a moment, her laughter dies down, and her face is back to serious. Shit, what happened? She was just fine.

Before I can ask what's wrong, Lainey maneuvers herself so that she's straddling me, pushing me down on the mattress and smashing her lips against mine.

It happens so fast, I don't even realize what's happening until her tongue is slipping into my mouth and her breasts rub against my chest. Oh, fuck. What the hell is happening right now?

Two seconds ago, she was crying, then laughing, and now she's on top of me, devouring me like I'm her last meal.

"Lainey," I try to say through kisses, but she doesn't let up. I have to physically pry her off of me in order to catch my breath and attempt to think rationally.

She doesn't know what she's doing. She's drunk. She's drunk and she's upset and she's doing what she does best. Distracting herself.

As much as I want this, I know we can't do this right now. Lainey doesn't want me, she wants a distraction from her thoughts and feelings. When this happens, I want it to be for real. I want it to be because she wants me, not just somebody to take away her pain.

"Lainey, stop. You're drunk, and you're upset. You don't want this," I try to explain, lifting her off of me and gently placing her back on the mattress. Fuck, I want her so bad. But I know this isn't how this should go. She's not thinking clearly.

"You should get some rest," I say softly, my voice gentle but firm. Lainey's bottom lip shoots out in a pout, and my god, if she isn't the sexiest thing I've ever seen.

"Come on, lie down, Lainey Bug. You've got maid of honor duties to fulfil tomorrow, and Gwen will kill you if you show up hungover to her wedding."

Lainey lies down on her back and watches me as I take her heels off of her feet, tossing them to the floor. I tuck her in and watch as she begins to tear up again. Oh, shit. What now?

"Why are you crying? What's wrong?" I ask, my voice sounding more urgent than I meant for it to. She shakes her head.

"My parents don't want me. You don't want me. Nobody wants me," she sobs, and my heart breaks. Fuck. She thinks I don't want her? Is she serious? If only she could hear the thoughts inside my head when I'm around her, then she'd know crazy that statement is.

"Trust me, Lainey," I begin, leaning down and touching her tear-stained cheek with my hand. "You couldn't be more wrong."

Looking up at me through her lashes, she sniffles.

"Then why won't you kiss me?" she asks, and the shake in her voice makes me want to do whatever she asks of me. Fuck, why is she making this so hard?

Chuckling softly, I push a strand of her curly hair behind her ear.

"I would absolutely devour you if the timing wasn't so shitty. You're drunk, Barkley."

Lainey shakes her head. "I'm not that drunk," she insists, and even though I'm pretty wasted, I'm not as bad as she is.

"Why don't you ask me tomorrow?" I ask, knowing she won't remember any of this in the morning.

Lainey's bottom lip juts out as she pouts. Huffing, she sinks into her pillow.

"Fine."

"Go to sleep," I order, hoping there won't be any more tears from her tonight. I don't think I could handle it.

"Don't go," she whispers, her voice thick with emotion. "Stay with me. Please."

Hesitating, my gaze flicks to her face. She's looking up at me, her eyes pleading, her lips slightly parted. There's something raw and desperate in her expression, something that tugs at my fucking heartstrings.

I know I shouldn't stay. I know this is a bad idea. But I also know I can't walk away from her like this.

"Alright," I nod, my voice barely above a whisper. "I'll stay. But just for a little while."

That's fine. I'll stay until she falls asleep, which should be fairly quick considering her eyes are already closed.

Sitting down on the edge of the bed, my back stiff, and my hands clasped in my lap, Lainey turns to face me, her body inching closer, her movements slow and deliberate.

A jolt of surprise hits me as her hand reaches out, brushing against my cheek. Her touch is warm, her fingers trembling slightly.

She doesn't say anything, just lays there, staring at me. It looks like she's got something to say, but she's not letting herself say it.

Is she feeling what I'm feeling? Does she want me as much as I want her? Does she wish she wasn't drunk so we could fulfil our desires?

About ten minutes later, Lainey's breathing evens out, becoming heavier. Instead of getting up and leaving, I close my eyes and replay the night in my head. Watching Lainey dance and have fun and let go, it was a sight to behold.

I wish she could be that way all the time, and all of sudden, that's my goal. Making sure Lainey gets to live the life she deserves, instead of being a shell of who she could be.

Sunlight pours in through the curtains, and my eyelids flutter open as my arm tightens around something warm. No, not something. Someone.

Shooting upward in the bed, I realize that someone is Lainey, and she's still snoring softly. Shit, I fell asleep. Shit, shit, shit balls.

<hr>

Okay, if I can just move softly and quietly, I can sneak out before she wakes up and realizes I'm still here. She probably doesn't recall last night's events, especially the part where she asked me to stay. Sober Lainey doesn't like me as much as drunk Lainey did.

Moving as slowly as I possibly can, I begin to maneuver off the bed. Instead of quietly making an exit, however, I roll off of the bed and land on my ass.

"Fuck," I hiss, staring up at the ceiling. Well, there's no sneaking out of here now.

Lainey shoots up in bed, looking over the edge and finding me star-fished on the floor. Her eyes widen at the sight, and she immediately covers herself with the sheet. She's still wearing last night's attire, but apparently it's different in the light of day.

"Holland?" she says softly.

Lying on the floor, I reply. "Yes?"

"Why are you on the floor?"

"It's much cooler down here. Plus, the floor feels great on my back," I say sarcastically.

"Right," she drawls. "Well, can you get up?"

Nodding, I decide that's probably best right now.

Pushing myself off the ground, I stand over the bed and watch as Lainey's eyes trail up and down my body.

Am I crazy, or did her cheeks brighten a bit when her eyes hit the bulge in my pants? There's no way, right? Well, even so, I can feel myself hardening.

Lainey's eyes meet mine, and I swear there's a heat in them that I'm not used to seeing aimed at me.

"I'm sorry about last night. You didn't have to stay and take care of me," she tells me, and I immediately shake my head.

"I did," is all I reply. I don't know what made me stay all night. I don't know if it's because she's Ellie's best friend, if it's because I feel a bit responsible for her or if it's because it's her and I think I'd do just about anything for her.

Something told me to stay and make sure she was alright, so I did.

Sitting upward, Lainey lets the sheet fall off her and watches my face for a reaction. I take a small intake of breath as I notice the peaked nipples underneath the thin fabric of her dress.

"Holland?" she practically whispers.

Without looking away, I say, "Yes?"

"I remember last night," she begins, and I don't know whether that's a good or bad thing.

I nod slowly. "Okay… what exactly do you remember?"

She shifts, almost uncomfortably, her eyes darting down to the bed as she plays with the white sheet in her hands.

"Everything," she says, peering up at me and looking like a god damn angel.

I swallow hard, knowing exactly what she's trying to say. She's referring to the kiss and my refusal to touch her while she was intoxicated.

"Okay…"

"You told me to ask you today, and now I am… asking you to kiss me," she says, biting her bottom lip and causing my fucking cock to spring to life. Is she serious? Does she know what she's asking for?

"You want me to kiss you? Me, Holland? The guy you practically despise?" I ask, because I don't want her doing anything she'll regret, or using this as a way to distract herself from her problems.

Lainey giggles, still biting that damn lip as her eyes search my face.

"I don't despise you, Monroe. You have your quirks, and you did used to annoy the shit out if me, but I don't know. I'm slightly less annoyed with your presence now," she shrugs. I bark out a laugh, not meaning for it to be so abrupt, but her explanation caught me off guard.

"Slightly less annoyed, huh?" I ask, running my hand through my messed-up hair. Lainey nods, smiling slightly.

"Yeah, I mean, you're still my best friend's brother. You're supposed to be a smidge annoying, right?"

"Right," I nod. We haven't taken our eyes off of each other, and I am physically holding myself back from attacking her and feasting on her body.

Taking a step forward, I stop right at the edge of the bed, right next to Lainey who has now moved over an inch to let me join her on the bed.

I take a seat, the bed dipping slightly under my weight. My arm brushes against hers and a spike of adrenaline rushes down my spine.

"You sure you want this?" I ask breathily. God, I hope she says yes, because at this point, I don't think I could pull myself away.

"Yes," she answers, sounding so sure.

"You're not worried about Ellie?" I ask, knowing Ellie was a big reason Lainey would never cross a line with me.

"I am, a bit. But I think she'd want me to be happy, and right now, this would make me happy."

"She would," I agree, licking my lips. Her eyes follow the movement, and I watch as goosebumps form on her small arms.

"Holland," she murmurs, her breath hot against my skin. "I'm scared," she says softly, looking down.

Placing my pointer finger under her chin, I bring her face up to look at me.

"Don't be," I tell her. "I'm not going to hurt you, Lane."

"You can't tell Ellie, not yet. I have to be the one to tell her, do you understand me?" she says sternly, and I can't help but smile a bit at the authority in her tone. She's not even a little intimidating, but I nod, agreeing with her.

"Okay, I won't say anything."

"I'm serious, Holland. I will cut your balls off and feed them to you if she finds out from anyone other than me," she warns.

"As fun as that sounds, I solemnly swear that I will not tell my sister anything until you have done so," I tell her, holding up my right hand.

"You have to promise me one thing," Lainey says, and her face is much softer now, more vulnerable. "Don't make me regret this, Monroe."

My heart squeezes, knowing this girl never lets anyone in and she's choosing to let me in. She's opening up to me, and that means more to me than I ever thought it would.

"Wouldn't dream of it, Barkley," I tell her, and mean it. I would never do anything to hurt her.

Lainey takes a deep breath before looking me in the eyes and saying, "Okay, then kiss me."

Chapter 26

LAINEY

My heart pounds in my chest, my mind a whirlwind of conflicting thoughts. A part of me knows I shouldn't give in. I know this is probably going to be a mistake. I know I will probably get hurt in the end, but I don't want to wonder anymore.

I don't want to have to wonder what it would be like to be with him. I don't want to keep these feelings bottled up anymore. I can't, or I'll go insane.

Even if this is just a one-time thing, I need to try. I need to do this for me, so I can stop questioning what's going on between us.

Holland is obviously as attracted to me as I am to him, and we're both adults. We can do this and not make a big deal about it.

I am slightly concerned about what will happen when I tell Ellie, and I will tell her. I just don't know when. I can't tell her today, definitely not. It's Gwen's wedding day, and we all have other things to worry about.

She probably won't even care. She might even cheer and think it's amazing. Who knows? All I do know is that this is not the day to be dropping a bomb like this.

I don't think I've always had feelings for Holland. I've thought he was a pain in the ass, I've thought he was a dick, I've thought he was a good friend, and I've thought he was annoying. Granted, I still think that.

Now, I think he's freaking sexy, and I want to climb him like a tree. I don't know if I can even deny that anymore, and why deny it? Why not just do something about it?

He's right here, and he's been so sweet, and he helped me last night. I don't think I could stop myself from jumping him even if I tried.

He's still in his suit from last night, and he looks hot as hell. I swear, when I walked into the ballroom and saw him standing there, my panties almost dropped on their own. Like, how is it even possible for someone to be so effortlessly attractive?

Before I can stop myself, I lean in, my lips brushing against his. The kiss is soft at first, tentative, as if we're both testing the waters. But it quickly deepens, our lips pressing together with a hunger that surprises me. My hands tangle in his hair, pulling him closer, my body pressing against his.

It's as if Holland's resolve crumbles as he wraps his arms around me, his hands roaming over my back, my waist, my hips. He's warm and hard, and I can feel his heart racing, his breath coming in short, ragged gasps. I'm not even thinking about the fact that neither of us have brushed our teeth yet today.

Okay, well now I am.

"Lainey," he groans, his voice thick with desire. "Are you sure…"

But I cut him off with another kiss, my lips silencing him. My hands move lower, slipping under his shirt, my fingers tracing patterns on hot, smooth skin.

He shivers at my touch, his body responding seeming to react instinctively.

With steady hands, he begins to undress me, his fingers feeling like fire against my skin as he pulls down the straps of my dress.

I'm never self-conscious being naked around a man, but for some reason, I'm feeling like I want to hide. Holland pauses for a moment when my breasts fall out of the fabric, my nipples hard peaks. He seems to be drinking in the sight of me, his breath catching in his throat.

"You're beautiful," he whispers, his voice hoarse with longing.

A small smile takes over my face at his compliment, and I can feel my cheeks heat. I've never been complimented like that before sex. So intimately and honestly. Usually it's sexy or hot. But hearing Holland tell me he thinks I'm beautiful when I'm at my most vulnerable does something to me.

My eyes search his fort a moment before his lips descend on mine once more, his hands roaming over my body, exploring every curve, every dip.

I moan into his mouth, my hands gripping his shoulders, my nails digging into his skin. The room fills with the sounds heavy breathing, soft moans, and the rustle of fabric as we tear each other's clothes off.

Discarding Holland's shirt on the floor, my hands roam over his chest, his abs, his hips. He's hard and smooth, and when he presses his lower half against mine, I can feel his hard cock pressing against the fabric of his pants.

My eyes widen slightly as I shakily reach for the button of his jeans.

I expect him to stop me, to make sure I'm okay with this one more time, because that's just who he is, but he doesn't. Instead, his kisses grow harder and more urgent, begging me to take it further. So I do.

My heart is pounding in my chest, and every thought imaginable rushes through my head as I begin to tug at his waistline and pull his pants down along with his boxers.

This is wrong. This is a mistake. This is going to backfire so hard and I'm the one that's going to be hurt in the end. If Ellie doesn't approve, I lose her. If Holland hurts me, I lose him too, and possibly my entire friend group if they take Ellie's side.

Fuck, Lainey. What the hell are you doing? I know being reckless is your MO but come on. Sleeping with your best friend's brother? A guy you can barely stand to be around for more than an hour? What can go wrong?

But in this moment, with Holland's lips on mine, his hands on my body, and his hard dick jutting out and rubbing against me, I just can't bring myself to care about the repercussions. Consequences be damned.

With a swift motion, Holland kicks off his pants, his eyes darkening with desire as he takes in the sight of my naked body. My hands reach out to trace the length of his cock, and he hisses at my touch, his head falling back as I begin to stroke him, teasing and tormenting.

"Lainey," he groans, his voice a plea. "Fuck."

The sound of my name in that sexy, needy voice makes my pussy clench. Holy shit, he's so hot.

He's thick, his shaft pulsing with need, his tip glistening with pre-cum. My mouth waters as I sit up, pushing him backward and moving up his body until my face hovers over his cock. His breathing picks up as my tongue darts out to taste him.

Holland's breath hitches as my lips close around him, my tongue swirling around his tip. I suck him in, my lips moving up and down his length, my hands gripping his hips to steady him.

He tastes so fucking good. I cannot believe this is actually happening right now. I am sucking Holland Monroe's dick, and I just said he tastes good. Who am I?

Groaning, his hands tangle in my hair, his body tense with pleasure.

"Fuck, Lainey," he mutters, his voice thick with desire. "You're going to make me cum."

I don't stop. I want him to cum. I need to taste him, and I have this desire to make him feel good.

Humming in response, I continue to tease and torment him, driving him wild. His hips bucking slightly, and his breathing accelerating.

With a loud groan, he pulls away, his body trembling with unspent desire. I look down at him, disappointed that he stopped me because I really wanted to continue. He smiles, a crooked, lopsided grin that makes my heart flutter.

"Your turn," he says, his voice low and husky.

Wait, what?

Without giving me any time to think, he pushes me backward, my head hitting the pillow. He climbs over me and my body trembles with anticipation as I lie here, my legs spreading slightly, and my body on full display.

Holland's eyes darken as he leans down, hovering over my clit. Without warning, his tongue darts out and he begins to ravage me. He groans, his tongue delving deeper, his lips pressing against me, his hands gripping my thighs to hold me open.

I moan, probably louder than I should, my hands tangling in his blonde hair, my body arching off the bed as he eats me out, his tongue relentless in its pursuit of my pleasure.

"Holland," I gasp, my voice a breathy whisper. "Oh God, yes."

He smiles against me, his tongue never stopping its rhythmic motion.

With a final, lingering lick, he pulls away, his body hovering over mine. Fuck, why did he stop? I was so close. If he'd kept going for another few seconds, I would have cum.

My eyes lock on his, his expression hungry, and my body trembles with anticipation and a bit of disappointment at the fact that he just stopped. But then he says, "Ready?"

Ready for what? For him to continue? To-

Holland lines himself up at my entrance, and every thought flies out the window. Oh shit. He's so freaking big and I'm so ready to feel him inside me.

Nodding slowly, my breaths coming in short, ragged gasps, I reply.

"Fuck me, Holland. Please."

"Shit, Barkley. I never thought I'd hear you say those words," he chuckles softly, shaking his head. Rolling my eyes, I nudge his arm.

"I never thought I'd say them. Now do something before I come to my senses and change my mind," I tell him. I don't think I could change my mind even if I wanted to. With him naked on top of me, the way he's looking at me, the way he smells like vanilla and bourbon, I don't think I'm capable of stopping what's about to happen.

"Wait, fuck," he groans, and I want to cry because the need I'm feeling right now is painful.

"What? What's wrong?" I ask, a bit concerned that he's about to change his mind and tell me he can't do this.

Holland looks down at me, his expression disappointed. No, no, no. Do not do this to me now.

"I don't have a condom," he tells me. Oh, thank God, that's all it is.

"It's okay, I'm on the pill," I assure him, hoping he'll take that and continue.

He lets out a sigh of relief before his eyes search mine.

"Thank god, because I've been wanting to do this for a long fucking time."

With a swift motion, his tip presses against me, teasing, tormenting. I almost groan with impatience as my body tenses with anticipation.

"Holland," I warn, trying my best not to sound so needy and desperate.

With a small chuckle, Holland thrusts forward, his cock sinking into me. He groans with pleasure and his head falls back. Holy shit. Oh my god, he feels so good.

He pulls back, then thrusts forward again, his hips moving in a steady rhythm.

"Fuck, baby. You feel so good."

An involuntary moan leaves me at the way he called me baby and it didn't repulse me. I've been called baby before during sex, but every time it made me cringe. But coming from Holland, I think I just got ten times wetter.

My body begins moving with his, my hands gripping his back, my nails digging into his skin. The room is filled with the sounds of our skin slapping together, the wetness of our bodies, and our ragged breaths and soft moans.

Holland quickens his pace, his body driving into mine with a ferocity that I would have never imagined from him. He's like a completely different person and I think I'm loving it.

He normally gives me golden retriever vibes, but right now? I'm feeling the complete opposite. It's like he's starved, and he knows exactly what he wants and it's me.

Wrapping my legs around his waist, my heels digging into his back, I meet his thrusts with equal fervor. The bed creaks beneath us, and the headboard bangs against the wall, but I at this moment, I don't care if the whole world hears us.

"Holland," I gasp when the familiar feeling of an impending orgasm begins to take over my body. "I'm close."

He growls, his body tensing with anticipation. "Cum for me, Lainey. Let me feel it."

Fuck, I'm a goner.

My body tightens around him, and I cry out, my orgasm washing over me in waves of pleasure. Holland groans, his body thrusting into mine with renewed urgency.

"Fuck, Lainey," he mutters, his voice a rough whisper. "I'm going to cum."

I nod quickly, my body still trembling with aftershocks, my hands still gripping his back. "Please," I whisper.

With a final, powerful thrust, he pulls out of me quickly, his body tensing as he cums on the bare skin of my stomach. I let out a soft moan, loving the feeling of him on me.

When he's done, he collapses onto the bed next to me, his breaths coming in short, ragged gasps. My heart pounds as I begin to come down from the high.

Holland rolls onto his side, pulling me into his arms, his body still trembling.

Well, this is new. Cuddling after sex is definitely not something I'm used to. I either get cleaned up and leave right after, or the guy does. I'm not usually one for intimacy. It's easier that way. No feelings involved, just a good old-fashioned fucking and that's it. That way no one gets hurt.

The room is silent, the only sound is our heavy breathing and my thoughts that are now running wild. What the fuck did we just do?

LAINEY

We haven't said a word since we finished. We've just laid here in silence, and I wonder if he's feeling the same way I am right now.

A loud knocking on the door startles me as I lay tangled in Holland's arms. I shoot up, knocking his arms off of my naked body.

I look down at him when the knocking stops, and both our heads shoot right back to the door when Ellie's voice comes from the other side.

"Lainey Barkley! You better be up and getting ready!" Ellie shouts through the door.

"Shit. Shit, shit, shit! What time is it?" I ask, panic clear in my voice as I scramble around looking for my phone. Holland calmly hands it to me with a smirk on his face. Why is he smirking? Why is he not panicking like I am? His sister is literally right outside the door.

"It's nine thirty," he tells me, completely nonchalant and in absolutely no rush.

Fumbling out of bed, I rush to put on some shorts and a tank so I'm not naked when I answer the door. Finding Holland's clothes scattered around the floor, I pick each article up and toss them at him on the bed.

"What are you doing? Get up!" I whisper squeal. His lack of urgency is really beginning to piss me off.

Holland chuckles, and the urge to punch him in the face begins to overwhelm me. Is he serious right now?

"What is so funny?" I ask, whipping my curly hair on top of my head in a quick, messy bun.

"You, running around like a chicken with its head cut off," he shrugs, his eyes glimmering with humor. I hate him.

Another knock comes, this time it's Haley's voice.

"Lainey Elizabeth Barkley. If your ass is still in bed I'm seriously going to come in there and drag you out myself."

Looking at the door and back to Holland, I watch as he continues to chuckle and seem to have the time of his life as he takes his sweet old time getting dressed.

Oh my god, I'm going to kill him.

Murder is wrong. Murder is illegal. Murder is bad. Do I really want to spend the rest of my life in prison over this man? No, no I do not.

So, murder isn't an option, but I can definitely throw something at his stupid face.

The door handle begins to rattle, and even though I know they can't get in without a key, my heart rate spikes at the thought of them walking in and finding Holland in my room.

I'm not ready to tell anyone yet. I haven't even accepted that it happened myself yet.

"Lane? Are you okay? I can hear you moving around in there," Ellie says, concern in her soft voice.

Shit, okay.

"Hide," I demand, watching the smirk fall from Holland's face.

"What? Where?" he asks, looking around the small room, clearly finding the same problem I'm noticing. There aren't many places to hide.

"I don't know. On the balcony, in the shower, under the bed. I don't care. Just go somewhere they can't see you," I screech softly, throwing my arms up in the air.

Holland holds is hands up, looking equal parts afraid and entertained. He may not care if anyone finds out about us, but I do.

"Fine!" he replies, heading toward the balcony and hiding behind the wall. I rush over, closing the curtains, praying to god that Ellie and Haley don't decide to try to open them.

Rubbing my face in frustration, I mentally prepare myself for what's about to come before walking to the door and opening it slowly.

Ellie and Haley stand in front of me, Ellie holding two coffee cups and Haley holding a white paper bag out for me to grab.

"Blueberry muffin, your favorite," Haley winks, walking past me into my room. Ellie gently hands me one of the coffee's and follows Haley into the room.

Groaning, I shut the door and walk over to my bed, plopping down and taking a long sip of the warm coffee. Oh god, I needed this.

Haley watches me carefully, a curious but knowing look in her eyes. There's no possible way she knows anything. I don't think anyone saw us come up here, but then again, I was a bit out of it.

Her eyes follow as I bring the coffee cup back up to my lips. I take a slow sip before setting the cup down on the bedside table.

"Where is he?" Haley asks, crossing her arms.

My heart drops into my stomach and the room instantly becomes hot. Trying to keep my composure as to not give myself away, I straighten slightly.

"Where is who?" I ask, attempting not to sound like I'm guilty.

"The guy. Where is he?"

"What guy? There's no guy," I tell her, a bit too fast. She rolls her eyes as Ellie looks around the room, confused.

My pulse is racing, and my throat dries up. What the hell does she know?

"The guy you slept with. Your cheeks are rosy, and your sheets are half off the bed. You look entirely too content to not have just had sex," she explains. Although she has a good point, I can't believe she was able to deduce that just by those clues.

"I have no idea what you're talking about. I didn't have sex with anyone," I lie, hopefully pretty convincingly.

Haley's eyes narrow on me, clearly not believing what I'm saying. Ellie looks between us before clearing her throat.

"You did take quite a long time to answer the door," she says. I shrug, doing my best to look nonchalant and completely innocent.

"You just woke me up, I was sleeping."

Ellie looks down at her watch before looking back at me.

"You hate sleeping in. You say it's like wasting half your day away," she explains, and I'm cursing how well she knows me because she might be able to figure me out.

Standing from the bed, I set my coffee down on the end table and walk toward the bathroom to get their focus on something else.

Starting the shower, I turn around to see Haley and Ellie still staring at me suspiciously.

"It's so dark in here. You should open the curtains," Haley drawls, walking toward the balcony. My heart stops, and I fly out of the bathroom before she can open them.

"No!" I say, a bit to panicky. Clearing my throat, I hurriedly correct myself. "I have the worst hangover headache. I need it dark." It's not a complete lie, I do have a headache, and I'm pretty sure I have a slight hangover, but that's not the reason I don't want her to peel back the curtains.

"Are you going to be okay for the wedding today?" Ellie inquires, her motherly concern showing. I nod, hoping that she'll believe me, and they'll leave so I can get Holland the hell out of here and I can get ready.

"Of course, I'll be fine. I'll take some meds and be good as new. Now can you guys go so I can get ready? I'll meet you in the bridal suite in a bit?"

"Just make sure you're there by ten thirty. Gwen wants us there early so we can start our hair and makeup," Ellie explains.

Nodding, I walk back toward the bathroom. "I'll be there, Ellie Bear," I coo. She rolls her eyes, finally heading for the door, followed by Haley.

"Don't call me that, Lainey Bug," she taunts.

"You didn't," I say, my hand flying to my chest in mock offense.

Ellie shrugs, "I did," she smiles devilishly.

"You guys, I want a stupid nickname," Haley whines.

"You have one, Haley Boo Boo," I tell her, coming up with a name on the fly. It's the best I could come up with in the few seconds I had to respond.

Haley cringes. "Yeah, I don't like that one."

Shrugging, I say, "Oh well, you wanted a name. That's what you get. Now get out."

"Fine! Just hurry up," she says before opening the door and walking out. Ellie follows her out, the door shutting behind them.

For the first time in fifteen minutes, I feel like I can finally breathe. I fall back on the door, letting out a long, deep breath.

Staring at the closed curtains, I take another deep breath before heading over and opening them. Sliding up the door, I peer around the wall to see Holland standing there, watching me.

"Bad hangover, huh?" Holland asks teasingly.

"I will push you over that railing," I tell him, narrowing my eyes. He chuckles, clearly thinking he's funny.

"You're the worst liar," he says matter-of-factly.

"I am not!" I exclaim, my hands flying to my hips.

Holland shakes his head, chuckling lowly.

"Whatever you say, Lainey Bug."

A blonde curl falls in his face as he looks down at me, waiting for my response. His godlike smile makes my vagina yearn for more of him, and I have to maneuver myself so I can alleviate the feeling.

Oh hell, Lainey. You're in it now.

Chapter 28

HOLLAND

The light breeze feels good as I stand in my suit with the sun beating down on my back. I can feel the sweat on my back as I listen to the soft music, watching the last of the crowd take their seats.

The hotel has the entire back area completely set up for the wedding. It looks incredible, honestly. I don't think I've ever seen anything like it.

The white chairs are lined up in rows, draped with tulle and flowers attached to the backs.

The alter stands under a floral archway, and you can't beat the view of clear blue water and colorful buildings in the background.

Ryker really outdid himself with this one. This is the craziest wedding I've ever been to, although I haven't been to many. This has to be insanely expensive, but if anyone can afford it, it's Ryker and his family.

My family is really wealthy, but Ryker's family makes us look poor. His dad may be a dick, but he made a shit ton of money. Granted, a lot of it was probably due to illegal activity.

Standing up here, in front of Ryker and Gwen's family and friends, in fucking Italy of all places is actually crazy, but I feel good. I'm not feeling nervous like I thought I would. At least, not about standing in front of hundreds of people.

I'm more nervous that Lainey is standing on the other side of the aisle in a floor length, blue gown that makes her body look crazy good. Now that I know what's underneath that dress, I need more of it.

Her long, brown hair curls over her shoulders, and the blue and white bouquet she holds matches her dress perfectly.

After I left her room this morning, I went back to mine and got ready. I sat in the shower for twenty minutes replaying our time together over and over again.

I feel like a freaking sap. Lainey was everything I expected and more. It was like finally being able to catch my breath.

Jesus, I sound like a fucking ass. I am so screwed. There is no reason I'm this obsessed with this girl. I've never been this crazy about any other chick before. Why her? Why Lainey Barkley of all women in the world?

My mom will literally cut my balls off if I hurt her. She loves Lainey like her own daughter. If I even so much as make her cry once, my mother might disown me.

Lainey fucking Barkley. Who would have thought? Definitely not me.

Yeah, she's always been attractive. Yeah, I've always wanted to see what she'd be like in bed. Sure, I've thought about what we could be if she'd open up and allow herself to have more than one-night stands and broken hearts.

But did I ever think she'd actually sleep with me? Hell no! I still don't even know if it actually happened or if it was just a dream.

The music stops suddenly and changes to a soft melody and every voice halts.

Gwen appears at the other end of the aisle, her extravagant white gown hugs her body, a long, shear train following behind as her father slowly walks her down the aisle toward us.

Ryker stiffens slightly beside me, and I watch as a lone tear falls down his cheek. Damn, I can't wait to make fun of him for crying later.

Gwen looks stunning, and her and Ryker do look good together. I'm glad he found someone, and I'm glad I was there to witness the downfall of his fuckboy days.

As the two recite their vows, I find myself watching Lainey. The girl who never cries has tears streaming down her cheeks as she watches her best friend kiss mine, sealing their fates.

I've never really thought about marriage, at least, not until I saw Ryker and Gwen planning theirs, and even then, it seemed like more of a chore than anything.

But seeing Lainey standing here in that dress and knowing what she feels like in my arms and how it feels to be inside her… I'm starting to think about this marriage thing a bit more.

The wedding was beautiful. I mean, I don't think anyone expected anything less from a wedding in Italy. The reception is already in full swing, and I am already feeling a bit buzzed from the cocktail hour earlier.

I watch from my table as my friends dance to the upbeat music, taking slow sips of my beer. My sister, Lainey, Gwen, and Haley dance in a small circle, laughing and having a blast. Mason, Pat, Ryker, and Logan dance like idiots beside them.

When a slow song begins, Pat and Mason find some girls, Ryker and Gwen pair off, and Logan and Ellie, to my surprise, begin to slow dance.

I make a mental note to grill Logan later about putting his grubby little hands on my sister. But right now, Lainey is making her way back to the table I've been residing at, plopping down in her chair, and taking a sip of her cocktail.

She's definitely tipsy, or maybe even more than tipsy. She's no worse off than she was the other night, and I don't plan on letting her get to that point again.

I don't exactly know how I'll stop her from getting more drinks, but I'll find a way to intercept every attempt she makes at getting another fix.

Taking out her phone from her clutch, the screen lights up her face when she touches the screen. I watch her facial expression change from a smile, to… disappointment? Or maybe, it's anger. Or maybe it's a little bit of both.

She slams the phone down, screen first, and takes a giant sip of her drink, finishing it off.

Oh yeah, she's pissed.

My nosy ass wants to know exactly what changed her mood so quickly, but I know Lainey. The more that I push the subject, the more she'll pull away. So instead of outright asking her what happened, I say,

"All good over there?" That's casual enough. I'm not prying or pushing too much. Just asking a simple question.

Lainey slowly looks over at me before rolling her eyes and looking back to the dance floor.

"Peachy," she says sarcastically, picking at something nonexistent on her dress.

Nodding, I look to where she's watching. My gaze lands on Gwen and Ryker who have never looked happier. A small smile tugs at my lips at the sight.

"I hate slow songs," Lainey states, shaking her head and looking back down at her hands in her lap.

Looking back at her, I study her expression. I can't quite make out what she's feeling right now. It looks like a mixture of sadness and disgust.

I know she's happy for her best friend, so she can't be upset or disgusted with the sight of her friend dancing with her new husband.

"You wanna dance, Barkley?" I ask before I can stop myself. Why the hell I just asked her if she wants to dance is beyond me, but it's done now. It clearly threw her off guard too, because she looks like I just asked her if she wants to elope.

"With you?" she questions, a comical expression on her face. She looks completely unsure of how she should feel about dancing with me, even though we just saw each other naked hours ago.

Chuckling, I say, "yes, with me."

Standing from my seat, I extend my hand out for her to take. She stares at me like I have two heads. Like dancing with me is the craziest thing she'll ever do.

"Come on, Lainey Bug. Let's dance," I tell her. She hesitantly lays her small hand in mine, and I tug her up and over to the dance floor.

A new song begins, just as slow as the one before. My hands slowly wrap around her waist, landing on the small of her back. The fact that the dress she's wearing is backless is not lost on me. My finger slowly traces the edge of the fabric that falls low on her hips.

Lainey's hands slowly make their way up my arms and around my neck. Having her this close to me again is making my dick twitch in my pants. I have to remind myself where we are before I tear the thin fabric off of her and take her right here and now.

Looking behind her, Lainey searches for something before turning back around to face me.

"They're watching," she says softly. I look above her head and find that our friends are all watching us curiously, all except Gwen and Haley. The two of them seem to not find anything odd about the display.

Ellie looks a bit confused but it doesn't seem to be a major concern at the moment. Thank god, because I don't think I'd be able to let Lainey go now that she's in my arms.

Shrugging, I look down at her. "Let them watch," I say, winking. She knows what I meant, but she rolls her eyes anyway.

"You know I don't want anyone to know anything. Not yet, at least… not until we know what this is," Lainey explains. I understand why that's what she wants, but I don't care if anyone knows. If anyone has a problem with it, they can kiss my ass.

"It's just a dance, Barkley," I tell her, trying to ease some of her worry. She nods and seems to relax into my arms a bit more.

Pulling her a bit tighter to me, I lean down to her ear. "You clean up nice," I whisper, leaning close enough that I can smell the fresh scent of her coconut shampoo mixed with the champagne she's been drinking all night.

I can feel the goosebumps that break out over her soft skin, and I smirk.

"Thank you. So do you," Lainey says, her voice quiet. I pull back a little so I can see her face.

"Wait a minute, was that a compliment, miss Barkley?" I ask in mock shock.

Lainey shakes her head, chuckling softly. "Shut up, or I'll take it back."

"You wouldn't dare," I tease, and I love the way a smile begins to take over her face. How rare it is to see a genuine smile from this girl, and I've been lucky enough to see it multiple times in the last twenty-four hours.

We sway, the bustle of the reception fading into a soft blur around us. Lainey's head lays on my chest as I hold her close. I could stay like this forever with her. I wish we never had to go back to Ellington. I wish we could stay here, in this little bubble we've created, and never leave.

But in just a couple days, we will have to head back to reality and the truth is, I'm really fucking afraid that Lainey's going to completely back away and leave everything that happened here in her past.

The problem with that is, I won't be leaving anything behind.

Chapter 29

LAINEY

Well, shit. It's official. I am so screwed. Holland Monroe has slowly taken over my every thought. Every fiber of my being is telling me to run away now and never turn back.

To leave what happened between us, what's happening between us, in the past. I'm going to get hurt. I'm going to be the one that looks like an idiot at the end of this. I cannot let that happen.

People leave. Everyone leaves. Nobody cares about anyone but themselves, and once you let someone in, it's your funeral.

One thing I learned from watching my parents up and abandon me every chance they get since I was a baby is that even the people that are supposed to love you can leave you behind.

Maybe it's cynical, and maybe I'm being dramatic. But is what I'm feeling for Holland worth what I feel every time my parents leave again to go on some extravagant trip without me?

I don't know. I don't think it is. All I know is I don't want to feel like I'm a second option, or a burden, or like I'm being put on the back burner.

Holland makes me feel like I'm important. Like I matter, and what I do and say matters. That's how I've wanted to feel for so long, and this man that I've known practically my entire life is making me feel that.

When I received the text back at the table, I knew I should back off. I knew I shouldn't put my heart out there and let someone have a piece of it.

My mom had texted to let me know that they will not be coming home anytime soon. In fact, she told me they'd be away for the rest of the year on 'business'. She let me know that I was free to use the house whenever I wanted though. As if it's not my home and I need permission to be there.

Am I surprised that she sent a text and didn't bother to call to let me know? No, I'm not. Nothing they do shocks me anymore because I know them. They aren't meant to be parents, they never were. I just thought they'd be able to grow up and maybe realize that their daughter might need them.

But I don't need them. I've been doing life pretty much on my own my whole life, and I've done a pretty good job at it. I may not be a straight A student or a perfect role model, but who cares?

I've done the best I could under the circumstances, and I had Mrs. Monroe and Erica, and occasionally Gwen's mom to help me grow up and show me the ropes.

Who needs parents anyway?

I do often wonder what I would be like if I'd been brought up normally. If I'd had my parents there to raise me and nurture me. Would I be who I am today? Using sex and drinking to cope with my loneliness.

I've never really admitted it before, but I am lonely. Yes, I have my friends, and I have the Monroe's, but not having the two people that should be in my life has taken a toll on me. I'd never tell anyone that, but it does bother me.

Holland is the only one to ever question if I'm really okay. He's the only one that has ever noticed that I'm not really this party girl that everyone thinks I am. He's the only person that's ever called me out on my bullshit, and I think that's why we've always butted heads.

He is the only one that's seen the real me. The me that not even Gwen, Ellie, or Haley know. The vulnerable, sad, weak me that I've tried my hardest to keep hidden, and I hate him for it. But I also love him for it, because I'd probably be completely drowning if someone hadn't come to save me.

Wait a minute. What the hell did I just say? Did I just say I love him?

No, I do not love Holland Monroe. He is like an annoying dog that won't stop sniffing you and won't leave you alone no matter how hard you try to push it away.

I just need to forget this whole week didn't even happen. I need to forget about the amazing, mind-blowing orgasm he gave me the other night. I need to forget about the way he felt inside me, and the feeling of his body on mine.

Covering my head with a pillow, I groan loudly. I got back to my room two hours ago and I've been lying in bed, my mind racing and my body on fire after dancing with Holland all night.

The wedding was absolutely beautiful, and Gwen looked stunning in her wedding dress. The whole ordeal was elegant and magical, just like I knew it would be. Gwen deserves nothing short of a fairytale wedding.

When the slow songs came on, Holland forced me to dance with him. Well, I guess he didn't really have to force me, because I went willingly. It was stupid. It was a bad idea. Everyone saw us dancing together, and I can only imagine what everyone is thinking. I didn't want to make a scene, especially on Gwen's wedding night.

Holland doesn't care if anyone knows. In fact, I think he'd love to shout it from the rooftops, which I guess should make me feel good about myself, but I just don't want to jinx it.

I know everyone would be shocked, because up until a couple of weeks ago, it seemed like we hated each other. I also know that my friends want me to be happy, and if Holland makes me happy, they'd want that for me. Even Ellie, who I'm most nervous about finding out because it's her twin brother.

I won't know if I never try though, right? Maybe it is time for something good to happen for me. Maybe I do deserve to be happy, and maybe it's my time now.

I'm being given the chance to be happy. To have something good for myself, and I should take advantage of it.

I mean, Holland is sexy. He's smart, in a dumb, cute kind of way. He's funny, and we have fun together. We can joke around with each other without hurting the others feelings, and the tension between us is like nothing I've ever felt.

The way I feel like my entire body is on fire when I'm near him. The way my pulse races and adrenaline starts pumping through my veins. The excitement I feel whenever he's near because I never know what's going to happen between us.

Lying sprawled across the bed, my bare legs tangled in the rumpled cotton, I feel the faintest ache between my thighs at the reminder of Holland and the feelings I get when he's near.

My fingers trace idle patterns over the fabric, following the dips and creases where Holland's weight had pressed the mattress down, where his hands had gripped the sheets like he was trying to anchor himself to the earth.

Closing my eyes, I can still feel the ghost of his touch—rough palms skimming up my inner thighs, his breath hot against my neck as he whispered things that I never imagined coming out of his mouth.

A slow, deep pulse throbs between my legs, my nipples tightening beneath the thin tank top I'd thrown on when I got back to my room.

God, I shouldn't be thinking about it. Him. Not like this. Not with my fingers drifting lower, teasing the waistband of my panties, my breath already hitching before I've even touched myself.

But God, the way he looked at me this morning—the way he looked at me tonight, like I was the only thing in the world worth hunger, worth sin.

His mouth had been everywhere, his words filthier than anything I'd ever let myself imagine coming from the boy I grew up with, and I'd taken it all, arching into him, begging for more without shame.

A sharp buzz from my phone jolts me out of the haze. Who is texting me this early in the morning? It's three in the morning, and everyone I know is in this hotel.

Reaching for it blindly, my heart kicks up a notch when I see Holland's name flash across the screen.

Satan's Spawn 😾

Satan's Spawn 😾

Still thinking about how tight you were around my fingers.

My breath catches. The screen blurs for a second as my thumb hovers over the keys, my body reacting before my brain can catch up—my pussy clenching, a fresh wave of heat pooling low in my belly.

Holy fuck. He's thinking about it too?

I should ignore it, right? I should be good and just let this thing fizzle out because I know it can't lead to anything good.

Yes, that's what I should I do. Rolling my eyes, I toss the phone aside, pretending like I wasn't already half a second from slipping my hand into my panties and finishing what he's started.

But the memory of his voice, rough and dark in her ear…

"You're such a good girl when you're dripping for me…"

My thighs press together, and before I can stop myself, I'm snatching up my phone, my fingers flying over the keys.

Satan's Spawn 😈

Me

Oh, are you?

Satan's Spawn 😈

You have no idea. I've been thinking about your pussy all night. The way it felt around my fingers and my cock. The little noises you made… Do you remember?

Me

I remember. I remember you being all talk until I had to show you how it's done.

The response was instant, like he'd been waiting.

Satan's Spawn 😼

Oh, baby, you're gonna pay for that.

His next message followed so fast it might as well have been one.

Satan's Spawn 😼

I can still taste you on my tongue. Sweet little cunt, so desperate you were riding my face like you owned it. Bet you're wet just reading this.

Oh man is he right. My free hand fists in the sheets, my nails digging into my palm. I can hear his voice in the words, that low, smug drawl that makes my skin prickle. My thumb brushes over my clit through the damp fabric of my panties, a whimper escaping my lips before I can bite it back.

Me

Maybe I am. What are you gonna do about it?

The dots dance on the screen for what feels like the longest minute of my life before his message pops up.

Satan's Spawn 😼

I'm gonna make you come so hard you forget your own name. Then I'm gonna fuck that smart mouth of yours until you're choking on my cock, tears running down your face while you take it like the greedy little slut you are.

A broken sound tears from my throat, my back arching off the bed. Okay, what the fuck was that? I've never heard him speak that way, and holy fuck was it the hottest shit I've ever heard.

Chapter 30

LAINEY

My fingers slide inside my panties, two of them sliding easily into me, my clit already swollen and throbbing.

Circling it once, twice, my breath comes in sharp little gasps as I imagine his hands on me, his weight pinning me down, his cock thick and heavy against my stomach as he whispers every filthy promise into my ear.

Me
Fuck, you're an asshole.

Satan's Spawn 😾

*And you love it. Admit it.
You're touching yourself right
now, aren't you? Thinking
about how I stretched you
open, how you screamed
when I finally gave you what
you begged for.*

I am. God, I am. My fingers move faster, my hips lifting off the bed as my fingers move in and out, my other hand squeezing my breast hard enough to bruise. The phone buzzes again.

Satan's Spawn 😾

*Send me a picture. Let me see
that pretty pussy, all wet and
messy for me.*

My breath hitches. I should say no. I should tell him to go to hell. But the idea of him seeing me like this—spread open, glistening, my fingers buried inside myself—makes me whimper.

Oh, for the love of God. I can't believe I'm actually considering this. Not only considering, but I'm doing it.

Propping my phone up against the pillow, angling it just right, I hike my tank top up to expose my breasts, my nipples pink and stiff. I spread my thighs wide, my fingers still working their magic, and snap the shot before I can second-guess it.

My heart pounds as my thumb hovers over the send button. Am I really going to send him a picture if me like this? It's a terrible idea, and I know it. I've never sent a nude, not even in high school. I've seen too many horror stories of women whose nudes end up on the internet without their consent. I do not want to be part of that statistic.

But here I am. About to do something I've never done for this man. Who the hell am I?

My eyes squeeze shut as a press send. The response is immediate. Not just a text, but a phone call.

Holland's name flashes across the screen, and I answer on the first ring, my voice thick.

"You're a fucking tease," he growls, his voice rough. "Look at you. All pink and swollen, just begging for my cock."

A moan escapes my lips. My fingers continue their movement. "Then come get it."

There's a beat of silence. Then…

"Open your door."

My heart freezes its rapid beating, and my breath stutters. "What?"

"I'm outside your room, Lainey. Let me in before I kick the fucking thing down."

Holy shit, he came to my room?

My phone clatters to the bed as I scramble up toward the door. I don't even bother fixing my shirt or anything.

When I reach the door, I hesitate for a moment before taking a deep breath and slowly opening the door to reveal Holland standing there, his dark eyes burning as they rake over me, lingering on the way my panties are still twisted to the side, my fingers glistening.

He's already hard, the outline of his cock straining against his jeans, his jaw tight with restraint.

"Fuck," he breathes, and then he's on me. His mouth crashes into mine, his tongue forcing its way past my lips, tasting like mint and sin.

I gasp into the kiss, my hands flying to his hair, gripping tight as he backs me into the room, his body pressing mine against the wall. His hands are everywhere, palming my breasts, pinching my nipples through the thin fabric, then sliding down to grip my thighs, his fingers digging in hard enough to leave marks.

"You're a fucking menace," he growls against my lips, his hips grinding against mine, the thick ridge of his cock rubbing against my stomach. "Sending me pictures like that. You trying to kill me?"

"You asked for it," I say breathily. His grin is almost intimidating.

"You're right, I did," Holland groans, his teeth sinking into my bottom lip before he pulls back just enough to meet my gaze.

He lifts me, his hands under my ass, my legs wrapping around his waist as he carries me to the bed, tossing me down onto the mattress. I bounce once, my breath leaving me in a rush as he follows me down, his body covering mine, his weight delicious and heavy.

Tugging at his shirt, I whine, "take this off, now."

Holland smirks, but he doesn't argue. He strips his shirt over his head, his muscles flexing with the movement, then pops the button on his jeans, shoving them down along with his boxers. His cock springs free, thick and flushed, the tip already wet, and I swear my mouth waters.

"*Fuck,*" I breathe, reaching for him.

He bats my hand away, his eyes dark with promise. "Not yet."

His fingers hook into the waistband of my panties, yanking them down my legs before tossing them aside. Then his hands are on my thighs, spreading me wide, his breath hot against my skin as he leans in.

"I am gonna eat this pretty pussy until you're sobbing, baby. Then I'm gonna fuck you so hard you won't walk straight for a week."

"Please, God," I moan as my back arches off the bed. His tongue drags over me, slow and deliberate, before circling my clit. My hands fly to his hair, my hips jerking up as pleasure lances through me.

"Holland, fuck—"

He chuckles against me, the vibration making me whimper, before his mouth seals over me, his tongue working in deep, relentless strokes. Two fingers press inside me, curling just right, making me cry out, my thighs trembling around his head.

"That's it," he murmurs, pulling back just enough to speak. "Take it, baby. You're mine, aren't you? This tight little cunt is all mine."

"Yes—god, yes—" I can't even believe the words coming out of this man right now.

His fingers crook harder, his thumb pressing against my clit, and I fucking shatter, my orgasm crashing over me in waves, my nails raking down his back as I ride his face, my moans filling the room.

Holland doesn't give me time to recover. He crawls up my body, his cock dragging through my wetness, before notching at my entrance.

"You ready for me, baby?" he growls, his voice rough with obvious restraint.

I meet his gaze, my lips parted and chest heaving. "Fuck me."

And then he's inside me in one thick, relentless thrust that stretches me open, filling me so completely I swear I see stars.

We both groan, Holland's forehead dropping to mine as he bottoms out, his breath ragged.

"Fuck, you feel so fucking good," he gasps, his hips already rolling, each thrust deep and measured, like he's savoring the way my body clenches around him. "So tight. So fucking perfect."

I wrap my legs around his waist, my heels digging into his ass as I pulled him deeper, my nails scoring down his back.

"Holland," I say breathlessly, my voice a broken whine. "Fuck me harder."

He doesn't need to be told twice.

His pace turns brutal, his cock pounding into me with a force that has the bed creaking, the headboard slamming against the wall. Every thrust hits that spot inside me that makes me see white, my moans turning to sobs as pleasure coils tight in my belly, my body winding tighter and tighter.

"Come for me," Holland growls, his hand slipping between my legs to rub my clit in rough, demanding circles. "Now, Lainey. Come on my cock like a good girl."

And I do.

My second orgasm rips through me, my back bowing off the bed as I scream out, my pussy clamping down around him so tight Holland groans, his thrusts turning erratic as he chases his own release.

"Fuck. Fuck, baby-"

He buries himself to the hilt, his cock pulsing as he comes, filling me in hot, thick spurts, his breath ragged against my neck.

For a long moment, there's nothing but the sound of our combined panting, the slick, obscene noises of our bodies still moving together in slow, lazy rolls.

Holland's lips find mine, his kiss softer now, almost tender, before he pulls back just enough to meet my gaze.

His expression is unreadable. Something dark and hungry lurks beneath the surface, but also something else. Something that makes my chest tighten. Then he rolls off me, his cock slipping free, and the moment shatters.

The air between us shifts, thick with the weight of what just happened and what might come next. Holland lies on his back, one arm slung over his eyes, his chest rising and falling in slow, steady breaths.

Propping myself up on one elbow, my fingers trace idle patterns over his stomach, my mind racing.

Was this just another night? Another stolen moment before we go back to pretending we're nothing? Or is it the start of something more?

Holland's hand finds mine, his fingers intertwining with mine before he brings my knuckles to his lips, pressing a kiss to my skin.

The problem with pretending is it never lasts. You can only pretend for so long, and eventually, the truth comes out. And the truth is, I am falling for the boy next door. I am falling for my best friend's brother. I am falling… for Holland Monroe.

Chapter 31

LAINEY

The midday sun casts a golden glow over the cobbled streets of Rome as our group weaves through tourists and street vendors. The city is absolutely breathtaking, and the food is even better.

The train ride here took about an hour and a half, and the sights were unbelievable. I can't believe that places like this actually exist. Holland and Mason really wanted to go to Venice, but that would have been way too far to travel and we only have one day left here.

Being in Rome is like a fever dream. I can't believe we're actually here. My best friend got married, and now we're walking the streets of Italy. How freaking cool is that?

It's been difficult trying to keep up this ruse between Holland and me. I don't know what we are or what we're doing. I do know I don't want anyone to be suspicious, so I've been keeping my distance. If anyone will somehow notice something's off between us, it'll be Haley or Gwen, and Gwen already knows about the airplane kiss. I don't need her to think anything else is going on.

Nothing else is going on, right? It's just some innocent fun. Okay, maybe not so innocent.

Gwen and Ryker walk hand-in-hand ahead of Ellie, Haley, and I, glowing with their gross newlywed joy. Holland, Mason, and Patrick walk in front of the group, leading the way and laughing about something, probably something stupid.

I don't even know where we're going. Holland mentioned something he wanted to see and he's been using the GPS on his phone to lead the way, but I don't think he knows where he's going honestly.

It's chilly out, the slight breeze making me shiver. I guess I should've worn a bigger sweatshirt, but I didn't want to overheat.

"You know, for someone who supposedly speaks fluent Italian, your directions suck," I call up to Holland who looks at his phone cluelessly.

"He definitely knows no Italian," Ellie says, rolling her eyes.

"Clearly," Haley says.

"It's called scenic detouring. Sorry if your sense of adventure expired with your last overpriced espresso."

"It was so worth it, though," I say, smiling as I remember the taste. God, Italy knows coffee.

"Seriously, Holly. Are we there yet?" Mason asks in a whiny voice.

"In due time, my friend. In due time."

He has absolutely no idea where he is.

"Ah, there!" he shouts, pointing at a huge building with magnificent statues and a fountain attached.

"The Trevi Fountain."

"Finally! I feel like we've been walking for days," Mason says dramatically as he leans over the railing.

"Oh my god, it's beautiful!" Gwen exclaims, walking up to the water and taking in the beauty of it. Turning back to Ryker, she gives him a huge smile. "Do you have a coin?"

"Why would you waste a perfectly good coin by throwing it into a fountain?" Mason asks.

Haley rolls her eyes, and I stifle a laugh. I mean, he's got a point.

"Because, when you throw a coin into the fountain, it ensures that you'll visit Rome again one day," Gwen explains. "The coins get collected and are donated to charity."

"That's dumb. Anyway, when are we eating?" Mason asks, slapping a hand down on Holland's shoulders. Holland shrugs him off.

"We just had Gelato," Haley remarks.

"Your point? A man can't be hungry?"

Ignoring their little bicker session, I walk up to the edge of the fountain and watch as tourists throw coins and take pictures. It's stunning, and the more I stare at it, the more amazing it gets. The fact that this was fountain was built so long ago astounds me.

"Beautiful, isn't it?" Holland asks. I hadn't even realized he was next to me; I was so distracted by the architecture.

"It is," I agree without taking my eyes off the fountain.

I can feel his eyes on me as he stares, making my cheeks heat. His arm brushes against my shoulder, and that little amount of contact sends a bolt of electricity through my veins. Stepping away, I watch Ryker take a picture of Gwen in front of the fountain. She's glowing, and I couldn't be happier for my friend. She's living her best life.

"You look perfect. Better than the fountain," Ryker tells her. Gwen blushes, smiling at her husband.

"There's no way anything could be more perfect than this," she replies, placing a chaste kiss on his lips.

"You literally look like a princess, Gwen," Ellie tells her, beaming at the couple.

"Gag. Can you two go be happy somewhere else? I'm trying to enjoy the sights," Haley comments, rolling her eyes. We all chuckle at her attitude. She's worse than me when it comes to relationships and love. I didn't think it was possible, but apparently it is.

"Let them be happy, Haley. It's their wedding week," Ellie scolds.

"Yeah. Put that sour look away and try to smile for once," I say, causing her to shoot me a death glare.

"You mean the look you had this morning when you couldn't find your shoe?"

"Well, maybe if someone didn't throw it off the balcony—" I say sharply, glaring at the culprit.

"I thought I saw a bug. I was saving you. You should be a little more grateful, honestly," Holland says, rolling his eyes.

"Grateful? You lost my shoe! Those were my favorite shoes, too."

"My bad for trying to help," he replies, throwing his hands up in mock surrender.

"You could have just thrown it at the wall. You didn't have to shoot it out the freaking window!"

"So my aim was a little off, sue me."

"Yeah, well your aim's as bad as your sense of direction," I tell him, crossing my arms over my chest. Our friends have now gathered around us and are looking at us as if we have three heads. I don't blame them; this argument is ridiculous.

"Did I not get us here?" he asks, gesturing to the fountain.

"Okay," Ryker cuts in with a laugh, trying to diffuse the moment. "Let's all remember we're in the Eternal City. Can we be... less eternal enemies?"

I step past Holland, bumping his shoulder harder than necessary.

"You're right. I can't argue with him. His brain is too small to understand anything anyway."

Holland's eyes narrow, his lips twitching.

"You know what?" Holland growls, stepping forward suddenly and pushes me, causing me to stumble back. Before I can catch myself, I'm splashing into the fountain.

With a grin and absolutely no remorse, Holland breaks into a cackle. Ellie and Gwen are looking on in horror, while Mason laughs hysterically and Haley looks like this is the most excitement she's had on this entire trip.

"Well, so much for that," Ryker says.

"I am going to kill you!" I shriek, water dripping off of me as I clamber out of the water. My clothes cling to me like saran wrap. "Are you insane?!"

"You were overheating. Thought you could use a cool down."

Dripping, I walk over to Holland who is still laughing as if he is the most hilarious person on the planet. I am seriously going to murder him. Did he think this was going to make me want him more? What exactly did he think he was going to accomplish by pushing me into a freaking fountain?!

"This," I say, water dripping down my face as I shove my finger into Holland's chest, "is war."

Holland grins. "Looking forward to it."

Chapter 32

HOLLAND

Okay, so maybe I shouldn't have pushed her into the fountain. That was probably not the best thing to do. I'm man enough to admit my wrongdoings. However, I wasn't exactly thinking when I did it.

She just looked so hot while she argued with me and I was so fucking turned on that I needed to get her away from me before I took her right there in front of everyone. It was like I couldn't control myself. She was there and I saw the fountain and my brain said 'push her', so I did.

Looking back at it, that was probably a mistake. Okay, it was a mistake. Except, the way she's looking at me as we walk toward the Spanish Steps is making me think it wasn't. How can she be so fucking sexy when she's this pissed off?

Lainey squelches with every step as she stomps angrily beside me.

Swallowing my pride, I decide that apologizing might be the best course of action here.

"Look, Barkley. I-"

"Seriously, are you twelve?" she hisses.

"You look great, by the way," I say with a shrug, walking backwards with my hands in my pockets so I can face her. "Really makes your eyes pop."

"I hate you," she spits, but I know she doesn't mean it.

Gwen links arms with Lainey while hiding her laughter behind her hand. "You two are exhausting," she says. "And also, possibly in love. Or hate. It's hard to tell," she whispers so no one else but us can hear.

"I vote hate," Lainey mutters quietly, wringing out her hair.

"Sure," Ryker scoffs. Lainey shoots him a death glare.

"Do you want to be next in the fountain, *groomzilla*?"

Ryker raises his hands in surrender. "Alright, alright. Truce."

Honestly, this is too much fun. Why apologize when I can get her all worked up?

Leaning over to Gwen, under my breath, I say, "For the record, she started it."

Gwen rolls her eyes. "You literally pushed her into a public fountain."

"Details."

"Alright, can we head back now? I'm starving," Mason calls out.

"Shut up!" we all say in unison.

"Damn, guys. Chill," he says.

As we all make our way back to the train station, everyone is looking around at the sights and famous landmarks, but I can't keep my eyes off of Lainey.

Lainey hasn't spoken to me since we arrived back at the hotel. I guess I can't really blame her, but I did think she'd be over it by now. There's no way she's actually still pissed about it. She's just trying to prove a point.

I'm not going to let her be pissed at me anymore, though. She's had enough time to stew in her anger, but it's been long enough.

As I stand outside her hotel room door, I take one final deep breath before knocking on the door. She may be extremely sexy when she's angry, but she still kind of scares me.

"Gwen, if you brought another espresso martini, I swear I—"

"It's not Gwen," I call back, chuckling quietly. "Let me in."

I hear her pause just behind the door before she opens it halfway, only to find me leaning in the doorway. Her eyes narrow.

She's changed into a soft rust-colored slip dress, her bare shoulders kissed with sun, but her jaw is tight.

"Come to shove me into another body of water?" she asks coolly.

"Not unless there's a pool in this room."

"Then why are you here?"

I step forward, causing Lainey to take a step back.

"To call a truce."

She arches a brow, arms crossed. "Really? That doesn't sound like you."

"Well, that's why I'm here."

I take a step closer, entering her space. She doesn't move this time, and I can hear her breath catch as she watches me.

"Come on, Bug. Forgive me," I plead. She rolls her eyes.

"Why should I?" she asks, shifting her weight from one leg to the other.

Reaching up, I play with the thin strap of her dress on her shoulder. Her pulse is racing, and her face is flush. I know she's having just as much trouble as I am trying to control her urges. She wants to give in.

"Because…" I start, leaning down so that I'm next to her ear. "I'll give you the best orgasm you've ever had if you do," I whisper.

Her body stiffens in response. My hand traces down her arm, to her side, and down her thigh, landing on the hem of her dress. I begin to pull it up slightly, but before I can get too far, we're interrupted.

"Dinner's in ten…" Gwen stutters softly, looking between the two of us before fleeing the crime scene.

"Shit," Lainey grits out, turning back into the room. I follow her in, watching as she grabs her small purse off the bed and applies lipstick in the mirror.

"Should we be worried she's going to tell Ellie?" I ask. I mean, I'm not really worried about it. If Ellie finds out, so fucking what.

Lainey shakes her head, putting the lipstick back in her purse and walking toward the door.

"No, she won't say anything. Let's just... go to dinner," she says, walking out of the room.

Just like that, I'm left standing alone.

A while later, we all sit at a long stone table stretched under a canopy of vines and hanging lights, the soft glow reflecting off half-filled wine glasses and polished plates.

Lainey sits across from me, our eyes meeting every once in a while. The tension between us is palpable, and right now I'm wishing more than anything that we weren't sitting at a table right now full of our friends.

"I'm just saying," Ryker says, waving a forkful of pasta. "If anyone was gonna cause an international incident on this trip, it was gonna be Holland."

I raise my glass. "Thank you. I take that as a compliment."

Gwen smirks from Ryker's side. "Oh please, Lainey has been just as chaotic lately."

Lainey's jaw ticks.

"I'm sorry. I'm not the one who made a scene at the Trevi Fountain." She takes a sip of wine before crossing her arms.

"You're the one who got thrown into the Trevi Fountain," Mason adds, grinning. "Which was honestly iconic."

"I didn't get thrown; I was—"

"Gently placed," I interrupt, swirling my wine. "Like a water nymph returning to her natural habitat."

Lainey glares at me from across the table.

"I hope you choke on your gnocchi."

"These gnocchi?" I poke one with a fork and hold it up dramatically. "Lainey. You wound me."

The whole table cracks up, except for Lainey, who sips her wine with the same energy someone might use to sharpen a knife.

Beside her, Gwen leans in and whispers, "You know you two are *the* show, right?"

"What show?" Lainey asks, feigning innocence.

"The hot-mess enemies-to-lovers slow burn."

"Gwen, we're not-"

"Okay! Group toast before dessert," Gwen announces, standing abruptly with her wine glass in hand.

Everyone gets quiet as Ryker joins her.

"To all of you, our chosen family. Thank you for making this the most beautiful week of our lives. And to Italy—for the pasta, the wine, and the extremely entertaining drama."

Cheers erupt around the table. My eyes meet Lainey's as we raise our glasses. When we sit back down, my foot brushes lightly against hers, and she sips on her wine slowly, almost…seductively.

I don't care what she says. She might be scared of love, or getting close to people, but I am determined to make her realize that she is supposed to be with me. I'm determined to make this work, even if it's the last thing I do.

Chapter 33

HOLLAND

It's been a week. A whole week since we've been back at Ellington. Lainey and I have spent almost every night together. Mostly at my place since Ellie is at hers.

I don't know what Lainey's been telling Haley and Ellie every night about where she's been, but I know she hasn't told them who she's been with.

We've been doing a pretty good job at hiding whatever this is between us since we got back.

I'm pretty positive no one has caught on. Except for maybe Haley, because every time I see that girl, she gives me a weird ass look like she knows something.

Haley also has a resting bitch face, so that could have something to do with it.

Either way, I don't know how much more sneaking around I can do. I mean, don't get me wrong. The sneaking around is sexy as hell, and it adds a bit of a thrill to it. But I don't want to hide anymore. I want everyone to know that Lainey is mine.

Although, she isn't really mine. Not officially at least. Not yet. But she will be. I will make sure of it.

Lainey stirs next to me, her eyes fluttering open slowly as she wakes. It's six in the morning and I haven't been able to sleep since I woke up around four.

My mind has been racing with thoughts about school, Lainey, rugby, and the clubs. I've put work on the back burner for weeks, especially with the semester starting back up again, the wedding, and practice.

I know Ryker and Pat have a lot of that shit handled since they're out of school. I, however, still have to worry about school shit which is annoying as hell, and I cannot wait to be done with this crap.

"You're up," Lainey says sleepily. God, she's beautiful. Even when she's just waking up and her hair is an absolute disaster.

She stretches, her arms reaching over to wrap around my torso, her head leaning on my bare chest. My arm wraps around her and I kiss the top of her head lightly.

"I am," I say. Lainey looks to the alarm clock on the end table before groaning.

"It's only six. Why are you up? You don't have class, and practice isn't until noon."

I love that she knows my schedule.

"Couldn't sleep," I shrug. She pulls herself up so she's looking down at me, her expression mixed with confusion and what looks like a bit of concern. I tuck a piece of stray hair behind her ear.

"Why not? Have you been up long?" she asks sitting up, her bare chest staring back at me. My god, if she isn't the prettiest thing I've ever seen. I mean, I've seen tits, but Lainey's are out of this world.

Everything she does is out of this world. I don't know how I never realized it before, but Lainey Barkley is perfection. She's everything I need and more.

"A few minutes," I lie. I don't want her to worry about me and certainly don't want to talk about all of the shit on my mind right now. It's too early to talk about feelings and shit. Especially because miss psychology major will want to analyze my every feeling.

She gives me a look like she doesn't believe me, but before she can question it, I wrap my arms around her waist and flip her onto her back so I'm hovering over her.

Lainey squeals and laughs before my mouth crashes onto hers. Her body relaxes instantly, and mine lowers so that my hard dick rubs against her warm center. She lets out a soft moan as she kisses me back with fervor.

This wasn't exactly my plan this morning, but I'm not complaining. My tongue dives into her mouth, hers fighting for dominance, but she should know she won't win that fight.

I've always had a more domineering side when it comes to sex. I've been told I can get a bit too into it by some women who couldn't handle it, but Lainey? She seems to love it, and I love that.

My fingers trace idle patterns just above the waistband of Lainey's panties. I feel the faintest tremor run through Lainey's body, the way her muscles tense just slightly at the touch. A smirk tugs at the corner of my mouth as I continue to kiss her.

I absolutely love the way Lainey's body reacts to mine.

Pulling away, I begin to kiss beneath her ear, feeling the flutter of her heartbeat against my mouth. The kiss is soft at first, barely there, just the brush of my lips and the faintest graze of teeth.

Lainey exhales sharply, her fingers flexing against the mattress before her hand finds my hip, her nails digging in just enough to urge me closer.

She moans softly, and my dick twitches at the sound. Fuck I need to be inside her. But that's not my goal right now. My goal is to make her feel good.

My hand slides lower, palm flattening against the soft swell of Lainey's belly before dipping between her thighs. She's already warm and wet, the heat of her pussy radiating against my fingertips.

Lainey's breath hitches, her back arching off the mattress as my middle finger teases through her slit, gathering the slickness before circling her clit in slow, deliberate strokes.

"Fuck," Lainey hisses, her free hand tangling in my hair, yanking just hard enough to make my scalp prickle.

"Yeah, baby. You love it?" I murmur, my mouth trailing down the column of her throat, my teeth nipping at the sensitive skin where her neck meets her shoulder.

I taste the salt on her skin and something sweet, Lainey's perfume, maybe, or just the taste of her skin after hours of being pressed together.

My fingers keep moving, lazy at first, then firmer as Lainey's hips began to rock into the touch, her thighs falling open in silent invitation.

Shifting lower, my lips follow the path my hand had taken just moments ago, kissing over the swell of Lainey's breasts, my tongue flicking over one stiff nipple before moving to the other.

Lainey's gasp is sharp, her fingers tightening in my hair as I take the peak between my teeth, biting down just enough to make her whimper.

"God, yes—just like that." Her voice is breathy, needy, the kind of sound that makes my cock twitch with need.

I keep descending, kissing over the soft dip of her navel, the flare of her hips, the sharp jut of her hipbones. The scent of her is intoxicating, musky and rich, the kind of aroma that makes my fucking head spin.

Finally, I make it down to the spot I've been waiting to taste. When my tongue finally drags over Lainey's wetness, she lets out a broken moan, her thighs clamping around my shoulders.

"Fuck, Holland…please."

Shit, I love to hear her beg. I chuckle against her.

"Such a greedy girl," I murmur. "Already dripping for me."

My fingers join my mouth, two of them sliding inside her with ease, curling just right to make her breath stutter. My tongue swirls around her clit, slow and teasing at first, then faster as Lainey's hips begin to jerk, her body chasing the friction.

"More," Lainey begs, her voice raw. "I need…fuck…"

Her words dissolve into a cry as my fingers crook deeper, my mouth pressing down on her clit, sucking hard. Lainey's fingers twist in the sheets, her other hand still fisted in my hair, holding me right where she needs me. The sounds spilling from her lips are filth pleas and curses and my name, repeated like a prayer.

I can feel her getting closer by the way her inner walls begin to flutter around my fingers, her thighs trembling.

Pulling back slightly, I growl, "Come on, baby. Let me taste you."

Then my mouth is on her again, relentless, my tongue working in tight, fast circles while my fingers fuck her deep and hard. Lainey's orgasm crashes over her with a broken sob, her body locking up before she melts into the mattress, her pussy pulsing around my fingers as she comes in hot, messy waves.

Fuck, I'll never get tired of seeing her like this. All hot and bothered for me. God, it's intoxicating.

For a long moment, the only sounds in the room are Lainey's ragged breathing and the wet noises my fingers make as I slow my thrusts, drawing out the last of her shudders.

Her eyes open slowly, taking me in before giving me a small smile. She looks blissful, and I love that I was able to make her feel that way.

My cock hurts with how hard it is, but I didn't do this for anything in return. I did this for Lainey, and because I am obsessed with her and her body.

She reaches up, her arms wrapping around the back of my neck, and before I can react, Lainey pulls me down, flipping me onto my back, straddling my hips with a smirk that makes my heart fucking stutter.

"My turn," she purrs, her fingers wrapping around my cock.

Jesus, fuck.

I'm already leaking precum, my dick pulsating as Lainey strokes me once, twice, her thumb swiping over the slick crown before she leans down, her lips brushing the underside.

"I kind of wanna see you beg for it."

Oh lord, if she continues that I'm going to come right now before she even starts.

"You want me to beg, Barkley?" I ask, my voice deep with desire and need.

Lainey nods with a mischievous smile.

She runs her hand over my length a few more times and I'm about ready to do anything this woman asks of me.

"Fuck, Lainey, please," my voice cracks on the word, my hands flying to her hair, fingers tangling in the dark strands. Lainey's tongue flicks out, tracing the thick vein that runs along the length of my dick before she takes the head into her mouth, her lips sealing tight around the ridge.

Groaning, my head falls back against the pillows.

"That's it, just like that…fuck…" my hips roll up, feeding more of my length into Lainey's mouth, and she takes it eagerly, her throat opening around me as she swallowed me down.

Her tongue presses flat against the underside, her lips stretching around my girth. My fingers tighten in her hair, my breath coming in sharp, uneven gasps.

"You look so good with my cock in your mouth, baby. Such a pretty little slut for me."

Lainey moans around me, the vibration making my toes curl. She pulls back just enough to lap at the slick head, her hand working the base in tight, twisting strokes.

"You like that?" she asks, her breath ghosting over the wet skin.

"Yes…fuck…" my voice is weak, my hips snapping up helplessly. "Need you to…don't stop…"

She doesn't. She takes me deep again, her nose pressing into the base of my cock, her throat fluttering around the tip.

My body tenses, my muscles locking up as pleasure coils tight in my gut.

"Fuck, Lainey. I'm gonna come," I gasp, my warning lost in the wet sounds of Lainey's unrelenting mouth.

But she doesn't pull away. No, she takes me in deeper, her hand cupping my balls, her fingers squeezing gently as my orgasm tears through me. Groaning, my cock jerks between Lainey's lips as she swallows every drop, her throat working around me.

My fucking God. She is incredible. The pleasure is almost blinding, and I swear I died and went to Heaven because there is no way this girl is real.

Finally, Lainey pulls off me with a wet pop, licking her lips as she crawls up my body. My dick continues to twitch, my chest heaving as I try to catch my breath. I'm sensitive and oversaturated, but the way Lainey grinds her hips down against me sends a fresh spark of arousal through my veins. I never knew sex could be this addicting.

"You're insatiable," I tell her, her forehead leaning against mine, our hands intertwined with one another.

"Yeah, well," Lainey shrugs, her lips turning up into a sexy smirk.

Yeah, it's official. I'm a sap. This woman is without a doubt the most perfect woman on the planet, and I don't know how I went this long without being able to be with her like this. Being able to taste her, being able to see this side of her that not everyone is lucky enough to see.

Lainey leans down slowly as I push a strand of hair behind her ear. When her lips touch mine again, I let out a low moan.

"I wish I didn't have practice today. I'd stay here with you and do this all day," I say lowly.

Lainey nods, her bottom lip jutting out in the cutest pout. "I know. Do you have to go?"

"Unfortunately, yes. I missed a week, and the guys will kill me if I miss any more. We've got that game against Concoran next weekend."

I fucking hate Concoran. They're from Rhode Island, and the guys on their team are fucking dicks. They play like assholes and they're always little bitches when they lose.

Lainey sits up, throwing her curly hair up on the top of her head and climbing off the bed. I watch as she makes her way over to my bathroom and shuts the door behind her.

"You know you guys will kick their asses, right?" she calls from behind the door. I chuckle.

"Yeah, well, you'll be there, right?"

The door clicks open, and Lainey walks out with a toothbrush in her mouth. "Duh."

"Hey Lainey," I begin. She walks back into the bathroom, spits in the sink and comes back out, her hands on her hips.

"Holland," she urges, a small smile on her face, and I feel bad because I know what I'm about to say is going to make the smile disappear.

"You know people are going to find out about us sooner than later, and it'll be better if they find out from us," I shrug, and just like I predicted, her face falls.

Pulling one of my shirts over her head, she picks her shorts up off the floor and tugs them on.

"We don't even know what we are. How are we going to tell people about us if we don't even know what we're doing?"

I know what I'm doing. I want her, and only her. All the other girls, all the other bullshit, I don't want any of it. All I want is her. But how the hell do I convince the girl that's terrified of trusting anyone to trust me with something she's been guarding her entire life?

Chapter 34

LAINEY

The cold breeze sends chills down my spine as I walk to Café Grind to get my fix of hot tea. I have all of my work so I'm able to get some homework done while I'm out. I've been really slacking on school since I got back from Italy.

I haven't felt that motivated to do schoolwork honestly. I've been a bit preoccupied lately.

I guess that's one good thing about having completely absent parents. They can't get on my ass if my grades are slipping.

I do care about my grades, don't get me wrong, but I've been spending so much time with Holland that I've fallen a bit behind.

Okay, maybe a little more than a bit. I got an email from my English professor that I'm practically failing, and I need these three credits to graduate.

The last time we saw each other, Holland practically begged me to put a label on us, and I just said that we didn't know what we were doing.

Except, I don't think I'm confused. I know what I'm feeling.

What I feel for Holland is unlike any feeling I've ever felt before. It's real and vulnerable, it's scary and consuming. It's… unexpected. Completely and utterly unexpected. I don't understand what it is about that man that has made me want him so badly.

The café is packed, and the line is practically out the door which annoys me because all I wanted to do was get my tea and sit down in a nice comfy booth to do my work. I guess that's not going to happen since apparently everyone had the same idea at three o'clock on a Thursday.

"Hey, Stranger," a familiar voice says from behind me. Why is that voice familiar?

Turning around slowly, I realize why the voice is familiar. My stomach does a weird flip thing, like when you're nervous or scared. Archer, the guy from the party, the guy I turned down at the game.

I smile shyly. I know, weird for me, but I'm feeling a bit reserved. "Hey, Archer. How've you been?"

I don't know why I feel so awkward. He's just a guy, and I'm the one that turned him down, not the other way around. Is this what guilt feels like? And if it's guilt, why do I feel guilty? I've turned down plenty of guys before. Why does this one feel different?

Archer smiles, and he looks just as awkward as I feel.

"I've been okay. You know, just been busy with school and all. What about you? I haven't seen you around in a bit," he shifts from one foot to the other uncomfortably. At least I'm not alone in feeling weird.

Shrugging, I smile. "I've been good. I just recently went to Italy for a friend's wedding, so I was gone for a hot minute. But I'm back now," I explain, mentally face palming myself because no shit, I'm back. I'm standing in front of him.

Chuckling, Archer smirks. "I see that. How was Italy?"

"Amazing," I say, pictures of Holland and I naked together in bed flashing in my head like a movie.

I know the things I'm feeling aren't just going to go away any time soon, which is incredibly frustrating for someone who's never felt these kinds of things before, and never really planned to.

"That's good. I'm glad you had a good time," Archer drawls, waking me up from the highly inappropriate daydreams I'm having.

"Yeah, thanks," I smile politely, hoping this awkward encounter is about to end.

"I don't suppose you've changed your stance on the whole dating thing, have you?" he asks, and if I'd been drinking, it would have been spit out at the unexpected question.

"I don't suppose she has," another familiar voice says from behind me. *Holland.*

Again, drink, all over the place if I'd been drinking anything. Where the hell did he come from?

Holland's strong arm wraps around my waist, and I can feel my face get hot as Archer's eyes wander over where Holland's hand rests on my hip.

What the hell is he doing, and why do I find it kind of sexy? Like he's being possessive over me, even though we aren't official. I should hate it, right? I should tell him that I'm not some prize to be won, or a mailbox he can piss on to claim his territory.

But here I am, thinking that it's actually hot that he's claiming me in front of another guy.

"Holland, right?" Archer asks, pointing at Holland. Holland nods curtly.

"Yep, and you're the guy from the party," he acknowledges, and I can't believe he remembers that. I didn't think he was really paying attention. Apparently, I was wrong.

Archer nods, looking kind of nervous but also attempting to keep his cool. It's obvious that Archer isn't comfortable with any sort of confrontation.

Chuckling nervously, Archer says, "that would be me. I'm sorry, I didn't realize you guys were a thing."

His eyes dart between both of us, watching as Hollands hand moves over my hip and up to my waist protectively, possessively.

I can feel the goosebumps rise on my skin from the sensation, but I try my best not to show that the small touch affects me.

"Oh we're-" I begin, but Holland's reply cuts me off.

"Yeah, well, we are. So you can go now," he tells Archer, and I can't believe how rude he's being. I mean, I can be a bitch, but only to people that deserve it. Archer hasn't done anything to warrant Holland's nastiness.

Archer looks at me again, this time with a bit of disappointment. I feel a small pang in my chest as I watch his body deflate.

"Right, okay. I guess I'll see you around, Lainey," he says as he shoves his hands in his pockets and begins to walk away.

When he's out the door, I whip around to face the jerk who just broke that poor man's heart.

Slapping his arm, Holland's face contorts in pain as he grabs the spot I just assaulted.

"What the hell was that?" I ask, trying my best to act more annoyed than turned on. I mean, he could've been a bit nicer to the guy, but it was seriously hot seeing him get so territorial over me.

"What the hell was *that*," he asks, rubbing his injury. I shake my head in disbelief.

"You deserved it! What the hell was that macho, tough guy, possessive shit?"

Holland smirks, and damn it, my panties might just melt right off. Crossing his arms across his broad chest, Holland stands a bit taller.

"That was me claiming what's mine," he tells me, matter-of-factly.

I scoff. "What's yours, huh?"

Holland nods, taking a step closer until he's completely in my space. His index finger slides under my chin and lifts my face slowly so that my eyes meet his.

"Yes, what's mine. You're mine, now, Barkley. Not his, not anyone else's. *Mine*."

Holy. Fucking. Shit.

The way he says 'mine' makes my pussy pulse with need, and I swear to God, I'm soaked. Like I need to change. He hasn't even touched me yet and I'm about to combust.

No one has ever claimed me as theirs. Not even my own parents claim me as theirs, and here's this boy, this man. This man I've known practically my entire life telling me I'm his and only his.

I'd say this is something Holland's probably said to hundreds of women, but I know him. He's only had one serious relationship, and the rest were just hookups. He didn't usually repeat either.

Yeah, I know he has somewhat of a reputation, even if he claims he doesn't. But it's nowhere near as bad as mine. Or Ryker's for that matter.

"And what if I don't want to be yours?" I challenge, knowing full well that will get him going.

Holland scoffs knowingly.

"Well, Lainey Bug, the way you were sucking my cock the other night tells me otherwise."

Oh my god.

He laughs at my horrified expression. I cannot believe he just said that in public. My cheeks heat as I look around the busy café to see if anyone is watching our interaction. No one seems to be paying attention in the slightest, thank God.

"Do I need to prove to you just how mine you are, Barkley?" With a gulp, I nod. Yes, please Lord, yes.

Holland grabs my hand and pulls me toward the door of the café. Once we're outside in the cold air, he lets go and halts his steps. My eyes follow his line of sight and land on what made him freeze.

Ellie and Haley walk side by side, bundled in their winter attire and heading straight toward us. Oh shit, did they see us? Did they see Holland's hand in mine?

Looking up at Holland, I try to read his expression to see if he's freaking out as much as I am internally. It's no surprise that he's as cool as a cucumber.

As Ellie and Haley approach, I feel myself stiffen a bit, and I hate that I feel like I'm hiding this huge secret from my best friends. Except, you are hiding a secret from them, Lainey.

God, sometimes I wish my conscious would just shut the fuck up.

"Lane, you left without me this morning," Ellie pouts, a bit of her blonde hair sticking out of her knit blue hat.

"Shit, I know," I say, cringing inwardly. I may be avoiding her just a little bit. I know, I'm a terrible best friend. But it's easier to avoid her than come out and say, *'hey, so I'm fucking your brother and I'm pretty sure I'm falling in love with him even though I told myself that I'd never fall in love because no one ever actually stays, and I'm probably going to end up self-sabotaging the whole thing and watching it blow up in my face. But anyway, can I have your blessing?'*

"I'm sorry. I got up early and was craving a hot tea, so I came to the café," I lie. I mean, technically, it isn't really a lie. I did get up early, and I was craving tea. But I didn't need to leave without her. I could've waited until she was ready to go, but I'm a coward.

Ellie smiles softly, almost as if she can tell I'm full of shit. Instead of calling me out on it though, she just nods.

"So what's he doing here?" Haley asks, looking at Holland. My head whips to the side to see if Holland will answer and save me from whatever terrible lie is about to come out of my mouth. I can't lie for shit.

"I needed a coffee before I went to practice, and ran into Barkley here," he shrugs.

Nodding, I chuckle. "Jump scare," I say, automatically regretting it because even though it was intended to be funny, it came out more awkward than anything. Wow, I hate myself.

I receive three very questioning looks, causing my cheeks to heat. I look down at the ground before I can say anything else.

"Anyway, I have to get to practice. Lainey, did you need a ride?" he asks, and I thank him silently for helping get me out of this situation.

"Yeah, thanks."

Ellie hugs me before pulling back and walking toward the café.

"You're still coming to the game tonight, right?" she inquires. Well, yeah. I don't think captain possessive would let me miss it even if I wanted to.

"Of course. I'll see you guys later," I tell her before she turns around and heads into the café. As I begin to follow Holland, Haley grabs my arm.

"You have to tell her," she states, and I know my face is as pale as a ghost. How the hell?

"What?" I play dumb, hoping Haley can't tell, but Haley is smart, and she picks up on everything.

"You have to tell her that you're screwing her brother. You can't hide that from her."

Oh god, how in the hell does she know? I didn't think we were obvious at all.

"What… what are you talking about?"

Haley rolls her eyes. Haley isn't a bitch, but she tells it like it is. If she has something on her mind, she's going to say it. We're a lot alike in that regard. Except, I do sometimes care about people's feelings, whereas Haley does not.

"I saw the way you guys were looking at each other back in Italy. I know you guys slept together. I'm sure that's the reason you hadn't been sleeping at home until two weeks ago, right? Look, I don't care. You're my friend and I want you to be happy, but Ellie's my friend too. If you don't tell her and she finds out, she'll never forgive you," Haley explains, and God damnit she's right. I know she's right.

I need to tell Ellie. I need to stop pretending like I don't have feelings for Holland. I need to accept the fact that what I'm feeling for him clearly isn't going away any time soon. I need to tell Ellie before she finds out on her own somehow and she hates me forever. I'd rather her find out from me than some rando.

Groaning, I nod. "I know, okay? I know. I just… what if she hates me? I mean, it's her brother, Haley."

Haley's grip on my arm softens and the expression on her face turns to one of empathy and understanding.

"It's Ellie, Lane. She could never hate you. You've been friends forever, and she just wants you to be happy. But she will be pissed if it's not you that tells her," Haley shrugs and begins to walk in the direction of the café. "I'd do it soon too, because it looks like things are getting cozier between you two," she winks, then disappears through the doors of the café.

Well, fuck. This situation just got a whole lot more difficult.

Chapter 35

LAINEY

Holland watches from the edge of his bed as I pace back and forth across his room. I haven't stopped stressing about what I'm going to tell Ellie and when. Haley's right, I do need to tell her. I just can't figure out the best way to do it.

I don't really know what I'm so afraid of. I don't know if I'm more afraid of telling Ellie and having her hate me for it, or the fact that telling Ellie makes everything seem so much more real.

Making it more real means that there's an actual chance of this not working out and me getting hurt, proving myself right. I don't want to prove myself right. I want to be wrong. I want Holland to prove to me that people can and will stay.

But what if I'm right? What if I'm not worth loving or staying for? What if I'm destined to be completely alone for the rest of my life?

I don't know if I could handle losing Holland. I've known him my whole life, and if he left, I don't know what I'd do.

Who am I kidding? I know exactly what I'd do. I'd pull myself up by my bootstraps and handle it, just like I always have. Except, my version of handling it usually involves several bottles of liquor and a new man in my bed every night.

"Would you sit down? You're making me dizzy," Holland says. I glare at him and halt in my tracks.

"Why are you not more worried about this?" I ask, my voice higher than usual.

"Because I don't care what anyone thinks. Neither should you. So what if my sister doesn't approve. She can't stop us from being together," he shrugs nonchalantly.

I don't understand how he can just not care about what Ellie will say. Maybe because she's related to him and will be forced to see him at family functions even if she's pissed at him.

Me on the other hand, I may have grown up with them, and they may be like family to me, but I'm not blood. Ellie could turn on me and decide she never wants to see me again.

"We're not together, though. We're screwing. There's a difference."

Holland clearly doesn't like that answer because his face darkens and I don't think I've ever seen him look so possessive.

The words he said to me back at the café replay in my head. *'You're mine.'*

Without a word, Holland stands, his presence commanding the space around us. My breath catches as he reaches out, his large hands gripping my waist. His eyes bounce between mine as his breathing picks up slightly.

"No matter what, you're mine now, Lainey," he growls, his voice low and rough. "Stop worrying about her." His words are a command, not a suggestion, and a shiver runs down my spine at the forcefulness.

I feel the heat of his body against mine, his scent enveloping me, musk and something distinctly him.

Holland's hands move deliberately, his fingers brushing against the hem of my t-shirt. Leaning down, his lips kiss my neck.

"Say it," he demands.

My heart pounds in my chest, my stress dissolving into desire that coils low in my belly. I open my mouth to speak, but nothing but a small squeak comes out as Holland brings my shirt over my head slowly, the fabric sliding to the floor in a forgotten heap.

His touch is urgent and deliberate, as if he has all the time in the world, yet he can't bear to wait another second.

His mouth trails over my collarbone, his teeth grazing my skin in a way that makes my nipples hard and my body shiver.

I can't bring myself to say the words. The words he wants me to say mean that I'm committing to being his. Do I want to do that? Do I want to be Holland's?

I don't get to finish that thought before his lips are on mine, demanding and hungry. My hands fist in his shirt, nails digging into his back as he pushes me back onto the bed. The mattress dips beneath me as I crawl back toward the headboard.

He inches toward me slowly, like a lion stalking his prey, his movements confident and commanding. If he's trying to intimidate me, it's working, and that's saying something because I'm not easily intimidated.

His hands roam my body, his fingers tracing the curves of my breasts as his thumbs brush over my nipples.

I arch into him, a soft moan escaping my lips as his head dips and his mouth captures one peak, sucking gently. His tongue swirls, causing my head to fall back as my hands tangle in his hair.

"You're so fucking beautiful," he murmurs against me as he trails his kisses down my stomach. His hands slide lower, his fingers hooking into the waistband of my jeans. Lifting my hips, I allow him to pull them off, the denim sliding down her legs and pooling on the floor.

My breath comes in short pants as Holland's gaze takes me in, and he looks hungry.

Just then, his face moves between my legs, his hands gripping my thighs as he spreads them apart.

My cheeks burn and my pussy throbs with need. Fuck, I want him inside me.

"You're mine," he reiterates, his voice a promise. "Every inch of you."

His mouth descends, his lips pressing against the lace of my panties. My hips buck involuntarily as a take a sharp inhale at the feeling of his warm breath against me. Tauntingly slow, he pulls down my panties, tossing them aside and leaving me completely exposed.

His breath ghosts over my pussy, and I can't help the small whimper that comes out of me as my hands grip the sheets.

Thank God, he doesn't make me wait long because I'm about to combust. His tongue is on me in an instant, hot and wet, sliding between my folds with deliberate slowness. I squirm, but his hands hold my hips firmly, keeping me still as he explores me with his tongue.

Holland devours me with a hunger that leaves me breathless. His fingers delve deeper, his thumb pressing against my clit as his tongue flicks and sucks, driving me closer to the edge.

"Oh my God, Holland," I gasp, my tone begging, but he only growls in response, his touch intensifying.

I'm right there. I'm right on the freaking edge of the cliff, and I am so ready for the intense orgasm that I am about to have. Except, the feeling dissipates when Holland pulls away.

"What the fuck?" I spit. Why the actual hell did he stop? I was right fucking there! His eyes darken, and a devilish smirk crosses his lips.

"What, baby? Something wrong?" he asks mockingly. Oh, I'm going to throat punch him. There's no way.

"I swear to-,"

"Shhh," he brushes his thumb over my cheek, moving a loose hair out of my face. He's being so gentle, and it's odd considering how roughly he was just eating me. "Say it."

Oh, you've got to be freaking kidding me! He cannot be serious right now. He's withholding my orgasm because he wants me to cave? To tell him I'm his?

Come on, Lainey. Don't be so stubborn. Just say it, and then he'll continue.

Fuck.

"I'm…" I begin, but the rest of the words die at the tip of my tongue. Shit.

Holland's wicked grin grows wider as he enjoys my struggle. "Come on, Barkley. Tell me you're mine."

Rolling my eyes, I take a deep breath and exhale loudly.

"I'm…yours," I murmur softly.

"What was that? I couldn't quite hear you," he taunts. I hate him. I actually think I might punch him in the face.

"Suck a dick," I tell him, and his grin grows even bigger.

"You will be soon. Now say it again or I won't make this pretty little pussy come," he threatens.

"I'm yours," I say, a bit louder this time so he can actually hear me.

"There you go. Now was that so hard?" he asks, chuckling to himself since apparently, he thinks he's so funny.

"Debilitating, actually."

"Aw, you're cute. Now lay back down so I can finish my dinner," he demands, pushing my shoulders back so I fall back onto the bed. My head flies back as his tongue goes back to continue its torture.

Within seconds, I'm writhing beneath him, coming so hard I see stars. Holy fucking shit.

Pulling back, Holland hovers over me, smiling down at me cockily.

Moving quickly, he sheds his clothes, tossing everything onto the floor. When he's naked, he crawls back over me, his muscles flexing with every movement. My gaze finds its way down his rock-hard body to his large erection and my mouth waters at the sight.

Holland smirks as he reaches for me, his hands guiding my legs over his shoulders.

"You ready for me, Lainey Bug?" he asks, his voice a low purr.

Oh, God yes.

I nod, my breath hitching as he positions himself at my entrance. His eyes lock with mine, his expression fierce and possessive as he thrusts into me in one smooth motion. I cry out, my nails digging into his shoulders as he fills me completely.

Holland's growl is primal as his hands grip my hips and he begins to move, his strokes deep and relentless.

The bed creaks beneath us, and I don't even care if anyone hears us at this point because I'm on cloud fucking nine.

Holland's mouth finds mine, his kisses bruising and hungry, his tongue tangling with mine as he claims me again and again. My hips meet his thrusts, my body responding to his with a desperation that I've never felt before.

The intensity builds and Holland's movements become more urgent, his moans turning into ragged breaths. My cries of pleasure grow louder as my body tightens around him

"Holland…" I pant. "I'm going to-"

Holland's hands grip me tighter, his gaze never leaving mine, his expression fierce.

"Tell me you're mine again. Say it again," he urges. I don't even argue. I don't have the energy, and I really want to come again.

"I'm yours. I'm all yours," I tell him breathlessly. That seems to satisfy him because he begins to move faster, rougher.

"Cum for me, baby," he commands, his voice a rough whisper. "Cum on my fucking cock."

My second orgasm rips through me, my body shaking as I cry out his name. Holland follows moments later, his thrusts stuttering as he buries himself deep, his growl vibrating through me.

"Fucking shit, Lainey. You feel so fucking good," he pants.

When he's done, he collapses on top of me, his weight heavy but comforting, and his breath hot against my neck.

For a moment, the world is still, the only sound in the room is our ragged breathing. Holland's lips brush against my shoulder as his hands stroke my back in slow, soothing motions. My heart is still racing, and my mind is a blur of pleasure and confusion.

Although, I don't think I'm really confused anymore. I think deep down, I know what I want, and I just need to admit it to myself. I deserve to be happy, right?

Holland kisses my forehead gently and I can't help but smile at his gentle touch after being so rough and carnal.

"You're perfect," he whispers, his head nudging my shoulder.

Damnit, I want him. Not just in a sexual way, but in a real, I have feelings for him, type of way.

Oh God. I have feelings for Holland. Actual, real feelings. Feelings that I've never had for anyone else and told myself didn't really exist.

I think I might even love him. Can I love him? I don't know, I've never been in love. But this feels like a lot more than just some little crush.

Well, that's it then. I love Holland Monroe. I am in love with my best friend's brother.

I… am royally fucked.

Chapter 36

HOLLAND

One thing that wasn't on my life bucket list? Falling for Lainey Barkley. Try telling ten-year-old me that I'd eventually fall in love with the girl next door and I would have laughed in your face. There's absolutely no way I could have ever seen this coming.

I mean, my mom used to tell us that we fought like an old married couple, but like, I never took it to heart. I don't even know where to go from here, but I do know that now that I have her, I'm not letting her go anywhere.

I don't care what anybody says, especially Ellie. If she has a problem with it, she can fuck off. I love my sister, but I love Lainey. I won't let her, or anyone else stand in the way of us.

Honestly, I can't believe I got her to say it. She finally said she's mine. I never thought in a million years that she'd say those words out loud.

Hearing them almost knocked the wind out of me. It was like I was dreaming, except I wasn't. She was there, with me. She was real, and she was saying she was mine. Lainey Barkley is mine.

A large hand lands on my back hard, making me jump. The thoughts of Lainey and everything that happened between us the other day disappear as Mason's face pops into view.

"You ready, dumbass?" he asks, chuckling to himself as if he's the funniest guy in the world.

It's game day, and instead of getting my head in the game, I've been imagining Lainey's naked body on top of mine, riding my dick until we're both screaming out each other's names.

I'm not excited about this game tonight. Concoran State's guys are assholes who think their shit doesn't stink, and I can't stand them. Okay, I can't stand one of them in particular. One of the guys, Caleb Walker, dated Ellie a while back. They were pretty serious, and then one day, he ended it.

Not that big a deal, right? Wrong. Turns out the asshole had been cheating on her for months, got the other girl pregnant, panicked, and left. We didn't find out until a few months later when Ellie saw a picture someone shared on social media.

What a fucking tool. Everything about that guy pisses me off. All I want out of tonight is a win for us, and if I happen to get a hit or two in on Walker, I'm good with that too.

"You're the dumbass," I tell Mason, and his face falls into a pout.

"Hey, no need for hostility, bro," he says as he holds his hands up in surrender. I roll my eyes and finish lacing up my cleats.

"Let's just get out there and get this over with, okay?"

Standing from the bench, I walk toward the door to the field and Mason follows close behind. I don't normally want to get games over with, but tonight I do. Maybe it's because of who we're playing, or maybe it's because after the game I get to see my girl.

My girl. That sounds really nice. Lainey Barkley is *my* girl. Okay, Holland. Snap out of it and focus on the game.

When I open the door, the roar of the crowd fills my ears. It's a full house tonight, due to the rivalry between the schools. Everybody's hoping for a fight or two to break out, but if that happens, we get disqualified, and coach will have our asses.

My team follows behind as I walk onto the field. The stands are full of fans sporting Ellington green and white. On the other half of the stadium, blue and orange fills the stands as Concoran fans cheer for their team.

Across the field, Concoran State gets into position, their players slapping shoulders and shouting. I spot him right away. Caleb Walker. That cocky son of a bitch trying to look all tough and shit. No such luck, my guy.

Playing with my mouthguard between my teeth, my eyes lock on the enemy line. I take a deep breath, pushing everything else out of my mind and focusing in on what's important right now. Winning this game.

The whistle screams and the ball soars upward, spinning against the gray-black sky, and the game has officially begun.

"Bind! Set!" the ref barks, circling like a hawk. Our teams crash together, a tangle of legs and arms and raw power.

I send the ball flying down the pitch, and a few of my guys head for enemy territory. The crowd is insane as we run down the pitch, rain starting to fall from the sky, making it much muddier and a lot more slick.

I make the mistake of looking into the crowd, and I immediately spot her. The most beautiful girl I've ever laid eyes on. My girl. She sits with my sister and Haley who are sharing a box of popcorn.

Damnit, I wish I hadn't noticed her because now I'm going to be distracted as hell. I mean, I knew she would be here. She doesn't ever miss a game. I just wish I didn't see where she was sitting.

She's sitting there, looking perfect, with her Ellington U hat on her head and her green and white scarf around her neck, her long, dark hair in a braid over her shoulder.

Our gazes meet, and everything else, the noise, the mud, the crush of bodies, it all just falls away. My heart pounds in my chest from the adrenaline of the game and seeing her.

And then I'm on the ground.

Fucking shit! What the hell just happened?

"Better watch what you're doing, Monroe. It's a dangerous game. You could get hurt out here if you're not paying attention," Caleb Walker taunts as he stands over me, looking down at my sprawled-out body. The rain continues to fall, soaking through my clothes.

This fucking tool. He's really going to pick a fight this early in the game?

Standing, I rolled my neck, feeling the crackle of tension in my muscles. He caught me off guard, but that's only going to happen once.

I take one last look at Lainey, who's wearing a worried expression. I give her a small smile before turning back to Walker and refocusing on the game.

My fingers twitch at my sides, the callouses on my palms rough against my skin. It's taking everything in me right now not to knock the guys front teeth out.

Mason appears next to me, placing his hand on my shoulder.

"Fella's, fella's. Let's just play the game, yeah?" he says casually. Walker gives Mason a cocky grin, then begins to back off.

"Yeah, let's play the game, Monroe," he says as he turns away and runs back to his team. He's the one that hurt my sister. He's the dick. He deserved the last time I punched him in his ugly face. Now he wants to act all tough?

"Dude, keep it together. Don't let the guy bother you," Mason tells me, his hair a wet mop on the top of his head, his face covered in dirt. I know he's right. I shouldn't let it affect me.

The referee's whistle cuts through the all the noise, and I follow Mason back onto the pitch. The crowd cheers as we take our positions, and my adrenaline spikes. I love this feeling. This rush I feel when the crowd roars and the whistle blows.

Keeping my gaze straight ahead, I focus on the team in front of me. I watch their body language and facial expressions to try and determine what their next play is going to be. Walker leans over to his guy on the right of him and seems to say something. The other dude shakes his head, and a devilish smirk appears on his face. My stomach tightens. I know that look. That's the look that says they have a plan, it's not good.

Looking back into the stands, I watch Lainey as her hands grip the railing in front of her. She's watching me intently, waiting for my next move. I want to know what she's thinking. What's going through her head?

Her brows are furrowed, and she looks like she's studying me. Like she's taking in everything she sees and trying to piece some sort of puzzle together. Lainey says something to Ellie, and my sister nods before looking back at the field.

"Holland, go!" a voice next to me yells. Fuck, I'd almost forgotten where I was. When I'm looking at her, all the noise, the pressure, the weight of the game... it all fades. There's only her. That's fucking terrifying.

One of Concoran's guys is suddenly right in front of me, and I feel the impact shudder up his spine, the grind of muscle against muscle as the ball shoots back, clean and fast, and then we're running.

My lungs burn, but I don't slow down. I feint left, then burst right, my legs pumping as hard as they can. Walker lunges at me, but I'm already past him, the wind rushing in my ears as I charge toward the try line. I can hear him closing in, but I'm faster.

When I can feel his presence right on me, I sidestep, twisting and slamming the ball down over the line. The stadium erupts in cheers and applause. I watch as Caleb Walker stands in the middle of the pitch with his fists at his side. He looks absolutely pissed, and I'm loving every second of it. Smug prick.

With five minutes left, we're up by seven. The Concoran scrumhalf kicks deep, the ball arcing into the sky. My eyes never leave its spin as I call for the mark, my voice rough, and catch it with little effort. Bursting into a run, my teammates fan out around me.

Walker runs at me head-on, and I brace myself for the impact. There's no time to move out of the way before we collide into each other, each of us falling to the ground. The wind is knocked out of me as I stare into the dark, starless sky. A sharp pain radiates through my shoulder as I push myself back up. I wince at the pain but grit my teeth to keep from showing any weakness.

The final whistle blows.

For a second, there's silence. The crowd seems to have not caught up with the quick succession of events.

Moments later, cheers, stomping, and the music from the band fill my ears.

We did it. We fucking did it. We beat Concoran, and even though it was a hell of a game, we pushed through and worked our asses off.

When I look up, I find Lainey in the crowd as she claps and jumps up and down with my sister, her smile bright and her cheeks reddened from the cold. I don't think she's ever looked more beautiful.

She's wearing a genuine smile, and she seems to have forgotten about everything else in the world. She's here, in the moment, and I think knowing that is better than the feeling of winning tonight's game.

What Lainey doesn't understand is that she may be my biggest fan, but I'm hers. I will root for her, I will cheer her on, and I will make sure she knows she has someone in her corner every single day. I used to live to annoy the shit out of her, to push her buttons and piss her off. I never understood why I felt the need to do that, but now, I think I get it.

It's because whenever she's fired up, when she's pissed off or annoyed, she's showing real emotion. That's something she doesn't do very often. Lainey's a closed book, and she always has been. But I'd like to think I know her better than even Ellie knows her.

She may think that no one's really paying attention, but I am. I always have, and I always will.

Chapter 37

LAINEY

Seeing Holland play will never not be one of the sexiest things I've ever seen. The way he takes over the field, the way his team listens to him. It's like he was born to play, he was born to lead.

I admire that he has something that he loves to do so much. I feel the same way about dance. I love the dance team, and I'm really good at it.

Even with being so good at dance, I don't think I've ever felt that passionate about it. I wish I could have that drive, that passion for something. I've been too focused on other things like school and partying and guys to really ever find something that I loved to do.

The psychology student in me would say that I'm letting my past trauma take over my future. I need to let go of the fact that I won't ever have a normal family. I'll never have a relationship with my parents like some kids do.

My mom won't ask me how school's been or about the boy I like. My dad won't show me how to fix my car if it breaks down. I won't ever know what it's like to be tucked in at night by parents who love you more than life itself.

I have to be okay with that. I have to move past that and appreciate the things I do have, like friends who would do anything for me, and a family who may not be blood, but have always taken care of me as if they were. That's what I need to focus on.

It can be hard to focus on the good things in your life when there's bad things happening too. It's easier to let yourself feel down and depressed.

The thing is, though, that when I'm with Holland, none of that stuff matters. I'm not the girl with the broken home. I'm the prettiest girl in the world. God, I sound ridiculous. I've never been romantic. I was never one of those girls that watched romance movies and read novels of prince charming.

But somehow, Holland has changed my outlook on everything. I don't know if I should be grateful or if I should hate him for it.

Except, when I think about him, I don't feel hate at all. I don't feel rage or jealousy. It's like, all of those feelings have dissipated and have been replaced by one feeling. One aching, longing, disturbing feeling that I never thought I was capable of feeling. That four-letter word that can cause so much pain and destruction.

How do I tell him that I'm in love with him? I mean, does he even feel the same? What if he doesn't? He says I'm his, but what if that's just something he says until he's had enough?

More importantly, how am I supposed to tell his sister? Ellie is my oldest friend, and I don't want her to disapprove. If she does, I don't know what I'd do. Do I keep going with whatever this is between Holland and I, or do I stop seeing him to save our friendship. Would she really make me choose between her and her brother?

I just need to talk to her. I need to tell her what's going on and get this weight off my chest. Obviously, the feelings I'm having aren't going to go away any time soon, and I know I can't keep hiding this.

Okay, I'll tell her tonight. When she gets home from her theatre practice, I'll have an actual adult conversation with her about the fact that I am in love with her brother, and because she loves me and wants me to be happy, she will approve, and everything will be peachy.

With a heavy sigh, I fall back onto my mattress and stare up at the ceiling. When did life get so complicated? I miss when things didn't seem so serious. Things weren't life or death.

Now, it seems like every little decision that you make can shape your life for the worse or the better. You have to calculate everything you do to make sure you're staying in the right direction. And if you fuck up, well you're shit out of luck.

God, have I always been this cynical? I'm only twenty-two for crying out loud. I should be partying it up and not giving a damn. But here I am, lying in bed on a Saturday night, contemplating every decision I've made up until this point.

Is this what your twenties are supposed to feel like? Like all hope is lost?

The sound of a knock on the door has me jolting upright so quickly my head spins.

Who the hell is that? Haley is spending the night at a guy's house and Ellie should still be at practice. Holland should be at the club tonight. He has a ton of work to catch up on, and I wasn't really up for clubbing.

Did someone break in? Shit, do I need a weapon? Wait, I don't have a weapon. I guess I could use my lamp and-

Another knock makes me jump, and I am fully prepared to knock whoever it is out with a bedside lamp if it comes to that.

"Lainey, open up. It's me," the familiar voice calls out. Breathing out a huge sigh of relief, I decide that I'm going to kill Holland for scaring the piss out of me.

Swinging open the door a bit too aggressively, I have to stop myself from drooling as Holland leans against the door frame in his black V-neck and dark jeans. His dirty blonde hair is wavy, and a stray piece sits in his face.

The muscles on his biceps and forearms bulge as he stands with his arms crossed over his perfectly chiselled chest. Pull it together, Lainey.

"Jesus Christ, you scared the shit out of me! What the hell are you doing here?" I scold, hitting him in the shoulder.

Holland chuckles lightly before stepping around me and into my room, landing on the edge of my bed.

"Nice to see you too," he says as he leans back on his arms. I groan inwardly as I watch his muscles flex under his shirt with the movement.

Rolling my eyes, I try my best to seem cool and collected.

"You're supposed to be at the club," I tell him, as if he doesn't know that.

"I got done early. Wanted to see my girl. Is that okay with you?" Swoon. Okay, ew, who am I?

"No, it's not. I almost hit you with a lamp!"

Holland guffaws. "A lamp?"

"Yes!" I exclaim, annoyed that he's not taking this seriously. "A lamp. I thought you were a freaking burglar or something! What is wrong with you?"

He shakes his head and continues to laugh, which only annoys me more because what the hell? I seriously could have hurt him.

"You couldn't find anything other than a lamp?" he asks, and I think he's being completely serious right now.

"Seriously? That's what you got out of that?"

"No, I mean, there's just plenty of other things you could have used. Like the pepper spray I got you last Christmas," he explains, shrugging. Okay, I'll be honest. I totally forgot about the pepper spray. But that's beside the point.

"Listen, Ball Boy. Don't just show up here unannounced. What if Ellie was home? How would you explain that?" I ask, because it's just dawned on me that this could have ended terribly if my best friend had been home.

Holland sits up straight, watching me intently as I pace back and forth.

"I would've figured something out. But I knew she was at rehearsal," he nods toward me. "Come here."

I stop dead in my tracks at his command. He thinks he can just show up here, scare the shit out of me, and then make demands? Oh, hell no. Not happening.

"No, I'm pissed at you!" I say, and he smirks. Without warning, he grabs my wrist and tugs me to him so I'm standing in between his legs, looking down at him on my bed.

"Look at you, all fired up. It's kind of… adorable." His lips curve into a mischievous smile. I go to push him, but he grabs both of my wrists and holds tight. The gesture makes my stomach flip. Oh, no, Lainey. Do not get turned on by this. Not right now. You're mad at him, remember?

My vagina doesn't seem to get the memo, because I can already feel myself getting wet at the feeling of Hollands strong hands around my wrists.

"Shut up," I tell him through gritted teeth. He chuckles smugly, as if he can see the effect he's having on me, and I hate that I'm so transparent.

"Make me," he challenges, and ugh! I want to slap his stupid, gorgeous face.

I roll my eyes, and his hand comes under my chin, grabbing me and forcing me to look at him.

"Don't roll your eyes at me, gorgeous. You know that turns me on."

Fuck. I'm done for.

His hands snake around my back and make their way down to my ass, where he rests his hands before squeezing tightly. I supress a moan.

"Be a good girl, for once, and get on the bed," he demands, and I think my ovaries explode. God damn.

I do as I'm told, if only for the fact that if I don't, I think he might pick me up and throw me on the bed.

Once I'm sitting down, he stands and releases me. Leaning down, he moves close to my face, his breath ghosting over my lips. My heart pounds in my chest, my anger warring with the heat pooling in my belly.

I'm speechless as Holland's lips brush mine in a soft, teasing kiss. It's fleeting, but it's enough to send a jolt of electricity through me. I'm weak. I'm a weak, stupid girl, and I don't care.

Holland seems to sense my surrender as his hands move down to rest on my thighs. His kisses grow more insistent, his lips pressing firmly against mine, his tongue teasing the seam of my mouth.

My hands find their way up to tangle in his hair, my fingers gripping tightly as I kiss him back with just as much passion.

"I hate you," I say breathily, but he silences me with another kiss.

"No, you don't," his teasing tone is gone, replaced by a low, husky murmur that sends shivers down my spine. "I think we both know that."

Man, I wish he couldn't read me so well. I wish he didn't know me better than I know myself.

"You're beautiful when you're angry," he whispers against my lips, his breath warm and inviting.

My frustration is slowly becoming a distant memory, drowned out by the rush of desire coursing through my veins. I wrap my arms around Holland's neck, my body lifting off the bed slightly to meet him, the tension between us shifting from anger to something… unidentifiable.

Holland hovers above me, his hands moving to the hem of my shirt, pulling it over my head with practiced ease. My bra follows, and Holland's pupils dilate.

He pauses for a moment, his eyes raking over me with an intensity that makes my breath catch. I love the way he looks at me. Like I'm the only girl he wants. The only girl he needs.

"You're so fucking sexy, Lainey," he growls, his voice rough with need. "I mean, seriously. I don't know how I went so long without seeing you like this. If I knew this is what I'd been missing, I would've made a move a long time ago."

I chuckle, shaking my head. "I probably would have hit you if you tried," I shrug. Holland nods, laughing at my remark.

"Yeah, you're probably right." His thumb brushes over my already hard nipple, and I shiver. I feel my cheeks flush as he reaches for my pants and begins to push them down.

I'm down to just my panties and Holland is still fully clothed. I'm not self-conscious, but I would like to see him. Holland's body is unbelievable. He looks like he was created by a god. Like, serious muscles and an amazing set of abs.

Don't even get me started on his dick. I know I shouldn't objectify him, but holy shit does he have a nice penis.

"Are you going to take those off?" I ask, motioning to his clothes.

"You want them off, baby? Then take them off," he demands.

My hands immediately move to the hem of his shirt, pulling the black material over his head and tossing it on the floor. My eyes roam over his chest, so lean and muscular, and I can't resist pressing my lips to his skin, kissing a path down his torso.

Holland hisses as my hand slides down to the waistband of his jeans.

I watch as his eyes darken with desire as I unbuckle his belt and push his jeans down his muscular thighs. His briefs go with them into a pile on the floor. I take in the sight of him, naked and absolutely freaking perfect in front of me.

Hovering over me once again, Holland's hand moves to my hip, squeezing firmly. His other hand caresses my cheek before he leans down, and his lips are on mine. Our kisses become more urgent, his tongue delving into my mouth as his hand slowly makes its way down to where my panties cover me.

I let out a soft moan as he pulls the fabric to the side and runs his thumb softly over my clit. My nails dig into his shoulders as my back arches, my body responding to his touch.

He breaks away from my lips and moves to trailing kisses down my neck, pausing at the hollow of my throat.

"You taste so good," he murmurs, his teeth grazing my skin gently before he continues to move lower, his lips lightly brushing over my breasts, his tongue swirling around my nipples, making me gasp and squirm beneath him.

My hands grip the sheets, my body tense with anticipation as Holland continues to move down my naked body. I know what's coming and I know it's going to be so good, and so does my vagina. I'm so wet, it's actually kind of embarrassing.

I know Holland can tell that I'm growing impatient because he's taking his sweet old time getting to where I need him to be. His kisses are slow and deliberate, each one sending a jolt of pleasure through me but not giving me enough to reach a climax. His thumb still moves slowly over my clit, but he's only moving enough to make me writhe beneath him.

Finally, after what feels like an eternity, he reaches the inside of my thigh, leaving tiny kisses and causing me to let out a sharp breath and lift my hips off the bed in silent invitation.

Holland's hands move to hold my hips firmly as his tongue swipes over me lightly.

"Holland…" I begin, but when his tongue does another drag, I lose all train of thought. This is what I need.

His tongue is relentless, flicking and swirling, his fingers joining in to tease my clit. Oh my fucking God. I'm going to combust. I'm going to die. This is going to kill me, I think.

My body trembles, my breath coming in short, sharp gasps as the pleasure builds quickly in my core.

"Please," I pant, my voice hoarse. "Please… I need to-"

"You need to what, Lainey Bug? You need to come? Is that what you need?" he asks, his warm breath against my center as his fingers continue to work in and out of me. I nod frantically, hoping to God he'll continue with his magic tongue so I can come.

"Yes, I need to come. Please," I beg again. God, I hate begging. But I am about to fucking lose it and I need him.

Holland looks up at me, his eyes dark with desire, a wicked smile playing on his lips.

"Impatient, aren't we?" he teases, his voice low and husky. "You need to come, Bug? Then come for me."

With a devilish grin, he moves back to his delightful torture, and I come within seconds. Literally, seconds. I'm panting and moaning and writhing, and all I can think about is how I desperately want him inside me right now.

My breath catches in my throat as I feel him line himself up at my entrance.

"Are you ready for me, baby girl?" he asks in a husky tone. I nod, squeezing my eyes shut and waiting for the familiar feeling of him entering me.

"Use your words, Barkley. I know you love to hear yourself talk," he mocks. How is it possible to want to slap someone and fuck them at the same time?

"Fuck me," I demand breathlessly. Without a second thought, he's pushing inside me, his thickness stretching me and filling me completely. "Oh, god."

"That's it, baby. You take me so well," he groans as he pulls out slowly and slams back in. I yelp and moan as his hips begin to rock in a steady rhythm, his hands holding my hips as he gazes down at me.

"You feel so good," he growls, his voice thick with need. "So tight, so wet… fuck, Lainey, you're perfect."

My arms fly up, locking around his shoulders as my body moves in sync with his, my breath coming in short, sharp gasps as the pleasure builds. Holland's pace quickens, his thrusts becoming more urgent, more demanding.

The bed creaks beneath us, and I am actively praying that Haley and Ellie are both still out because they would definitely be able to hear us if they were home. Honestly, I'm so lost in Holland right now that I don't even think I'd care if they did.

"Harder," I practically whisper, my voice a plea, and Holland complies, his hips snapping against me as he pounds into me with a ferocity that leaves me breathless.

The room spins, my senses overwhelmed by the feel of him, the scent of our combined arousal, the sound of our bodies moving together.

Why does this feel so different with him? Why does sex with Holland feel like it's healing everything inside me?

"Fuck, Lainey," Holland groans, his voice tight with restraint. "I'm close… so close."

Fuck, yes. My body tightens around him, my walls clenching as my second orgasm crashes over me, waves of pleasure washing through me, leaving me trembling and gasping for breath. Holland follows soon after, his hips stuttering as he thrusts deep one final time. His release spills into me, his groan of satisfaction echoing in the room.

"Jesus Christ, woman. What are you doing to me?" he asks, and I can't help the small chuckle that leaves my lips. I enjoy that I make him feel good. I like feeling like I have some sort of control.

For a moment, we lay entangled, our naked bodies still joined and our breaths slowly returning to normal. Holland's hand strokes my hair gently, his lips pressing a soft kiss to my forehead.

"Well, Lainey Bug. I don't know about you, but that was… fucking incredible," he murmurs, chuckling to himself.

"Yeah, it was, wasn't it?" I agree, a soft smile on my lips.

"And to think, this happened because I pissed you off. I should piss you off more often," Holland shrugs, his thumb moving a stray piece of hair away from my face.

"Don't worry, you do that a lot," I tell him with a cheeky grin.

"Is that right?"

I nod. "Definitely."

Holland stares at me for a moment, his gaze intense, as if he's looking directly into my soul. I shift uncomfortably next to him, trying to understand why he's looking at me like that.

"Hey, Lainey," he begins. He seems like he's nervous, and I have a strange feeling I know exactly what he's about to say, even though I don't know if I'm completely ready to hear it. "I-"

He's cut off by my door flying open.

"Hey, Lane. Can I borrow your-" Ellie stops dead in her tracks, her jaw dropping as she takes in the sight before her.

Me and her brother, naked, tangled together like vines on my bed. Betrayal and hurt are etched all over her delicate features.

I do my best to scramble up, grabbing my sheet off the bed as I go, but Ellie is out of the room in no time.

"Shit," I hear Holland say as I wrap myself with the sheet, trying not to trip as I follow Ellie out into the living room.

Well, fuck. Now, I'm screwed.

Chapter 38

LAINEY

You know those moments in movies where they freeze frame and the main character says something like 'yep, that's me. You're probably wondering how I ended up here'?

Well, that's me right now. Standing in my living room, covering up my naked body with my bedsheet as my best friend stares at me in complete shock and disbelief.

I don't even know where to begin. I don't know how to explain this to her. This is not how she was supposed to find out.

"Okay, I know I've royally fucked up. Like, incredibly bad, I know. But please, listen to me," I plead, hoping Ellie will let me just explain myself first before she storms out of here.

"How long?" she asks, a tear streaming down her face. My heart shatters as I watch the tear fall to the floor.

"What?" I ask, not completely understanding her question in my panicked haze.

"How long have you been fucking my brother?" she asks, a bit more bite to her tone. I know she's pissed off because she never swears, and she just dropped the F bomb like it was nothing.

Holland steps out of my room, fully clothed, his arms crossed over his chest as he walks up to stand beside me. I want to be pissed at him. I want to place all the blame on him and tell him this is all his fault.

He did this. He made me fall in love with him. But it's not his fault. None of this is anybody's fault but my own. I'm the one that hid this from Ellie. I'm the one that told Holland to keep it a secret.

It's all me, and for what? Because I was too afraid to confront my own feelings? Because I didn't want my best friend to hate me? Well, now look where we are, stupid.

I'm the bitch. I'm the problem. I should have just told her when I started feeling differently toward Holland. I should have gone to her and explained what was happening. We wouldn't be in this mess if I had just said something.

"El, calm down," Holland tries, but Ellie shoots him a death glare so lethal it could kill anyone in its path.

"Stay out of this. I asked her," she seethes, and I've never seen her so… hurt. She doesn't seem angry. She just seems, betrayed. I think that's worse.

Looking back at me, she asks again. "How long?"

Taking a deep breath, I begin to think back at the timeline. It hasn't been that long, but it's been long enough. I've had plenty of time to tell her, and I've been a pussy and chosen not to.

"Since the wedding," I tell her honestly. There's no point in lying about anything now. Everything needs to be out in the open if there is any hope of us getting past this.

Ellie's face falls, her jaw ticking.

"Since the wedding? That was weeks ago!" she exclaims. I wince at the unexpected outburst. "You've been hooking up with my brother since Italy? What the hell, Lainey? You're supposed to be my best friend. Why wouldn't you say anything?"

Gripping the sheet tightly as if it could save me, I shift from one foot to the other. Ellie and I have never fought, never bickered, never had any differences. Unlike Gwen and I, Ellie and I have grown up together. We've been there for each other through everything.

Our friendship has never wavered. It's been the one stable thing in my life since I was a kid.

I'm also not very used to being lectured or screamed at. Since my parents were never around, I never had any actual consequences to my actions. Sure, my nanny would 'ground' me, but she didn't actually enforce it. Mrs. Monroe tried to keep me in check the best she could, but I didn't live with her, so there was only so much she could do.

There's nothing I can say to make this right. Nothing I can do to make this situation better. I've made my bed, and now I have to lie in it. But I'll be damned if I don't try to at least put out the fire.

"I don't know, okay! I don't know. I should have told you, I know. But I didn't know what was going on and I wanted to be sure before I said anything," I try to explain, but she shakes her head, running her hand through her short hair.

"I didn't want you to hate me. I didn't want you to be pissed that I was… hooking up with Holland."

"Well, how'd that work out for you?" she snaps, and I stumble back a bit, bumping into Holland who has been quietly watching our interaction. "I'm your best friend, Lainey. You could have told me. We all knew you two had a thing, it's been so obvious."

Wait, what?

"What are you talking about?" I ask, confused as to what she means by it's been obvious.

Ellie huffs. "You guys have had this weird tension between you for years. We've all seen it. We even made bets last year on how long it would take you guys to finally hook up."

What the actual hell? Is she serious right now?

"Who's 'we'?"

"Gwen, Haley, and me. Mason even put some money in. We all knew it would happen; we were just waiting on you two to figure it out," she explains, and I don't know how to feel about this new development.

My friends were betting on if Holland and I would hook up? They could see something between us? How is that possible when I didn't even see anything there?

"You could have just told me. I'm your best friend, I would've supported you," she tells me, her voice back to the soft, inviting tone it usually is.

I look down at the ground, unable to meet her eyes. I'm not used to this kind of confrontation. This talk about feelings. I'm uncomfortable and I'm trying my best to stay strong. I'm not the one that's hurting right now, Ellie is. I don't get to be hurt. This is my fault.

"I didn't think you'd want me with your brother, El. I didn't know how you'd react. I couldn't risk losing you," I tell her, and her features soften a bit more.

"I'm more pissed now that you didn't tell me, than if you would have just come to me in the first place," she says, and my heart drops because I can't tell if she's going to forgive me for this or not, and I don't know if I'd blame her if she didn't.

"I know, I'm so sorry, El."

"You know I don't care if you're with my brother. You're basically my sister already, but I would have liked to know about it instead of walking in on you two… naked, might I add," she shivers, her face contorting in disgust. "Who else knows?" she asks, and my stomach drops. Shit, I was really hoping she wouldn't ask that question.

I peer up at her, trying not to cry because I know this will break her heart. Not only did I not tell her, but both of our friends found out before she did. She might never forgive me for that.

"Lainey?"

I look over at Holland who is watching me curiously. He doesn't know that Haley found out. I never told him; I didn't see a point.

"Haley and Gwen," I say, ashamed.

"They both knew before I did? What the hell, Lainey?" she asks, and I honestly don't even know what to say.

"Haley just… guessed it! She never really asked, she just assumed. She told me I had to tell you, and I knew I did. I just needed to wait until the right time. And Gwen, I told her about our kiss the day before the wedding because she practically dragged it out of me," I explain, hoping she'll understand.

"Kiss? What kiss?" she asks, and I grimace.

"We… kissed on the plane. Holland was having a panic attack, and I was trying to help-"

"With your lips?" Ellie shrieks, her face twisting in disgust.

"It was the only thing I could think of at the time!"

"I can't believe this," Ellie cries.

"Come on, El. It's not that big a deal," Holland tries, but Ellie doesn't want to hear it.

"*You.* You're supposed to be my brother. My twin, no less. We tell each other everything. Why wouldn't you tell me you were hooking up with my best friend?" she asks, directing her anger at him instead of me for a change.

"It's none of your business who I'm with, El," he tells her, his arms falling to his sides and his hands bunching into fists. I've noticed he does that when he gets mad or frustrated.

"It is my business when the person your screwing is my best friend!" she yells back. Now I feel like I'm caught in the middle of some sibling war, and I want to get as far away as possible.

Holland shakes his head, his brow furrowing as he looks between his sister and me before his gaze lands on Ellie.

"I love her," he tells her, and my heart falls into my stomach. Did he just…?

"You what?" she asks, about as taken aback as I am.

"You what?" I ask, looking at him and almost completely forgetting what this entire conversation is about.

He continues to look at Ellie, who is standing in shock.

"We're not just fucking. She isn't just another girl. I love her, and it's none of your damn business what we do or don't do. Yeah, we should've given you the heads up or whatever, but in the end, it wouldn't matter. Because if you were pissed about it or if you didn't approve, I'd still love her. I'd still want to be with her, and I wouldn't let you tell me I couldn't," Holland defends.

Oh my God. Holland loves me? I mean, I think a part of me already knew that, but he hasn't said it yet.

Ellie looks between us before focusing on her brother.

"Holland, I want you to be happy. I want you both to be happy. If you make each other happy, I wouldn't try to stop that. I just don't like that you hid it from me," she says, another tear falling down her cheek.

"I'm so sorry, El. We should have told you," I say, hoping she can forgive me., forgive us, and we can all move on from this. Holland and I can continue whatever this is between us, and Ellie will know about it so we no longer have to hide.

Ellie nods, wiping her tear-stained cheeks. "Yeah, you should have. But I understand why you didn't," she tells me. I let out a breath, feeling like a weight has been lifted off my shoulders.

"You do?" I ask, hope filling my voice.

"Yeah, I do. Just, next time, if there's something this big happening in your life, tell me, please. I want to know," she says. I nod in agreement.

"I promise, I'll tell you everything," I say, holding out my hand and extending my pinky for a pinky promise. Ellie joins her pinky with mine and we both kiss our thumbs.

"Okay," she smiles.

"So, we're good?" Holland asks, looking optimistic.

"We're good," Ellie agrees, and I can feel the tension in the room disappear as we each begin to calm down. I already feel like I can breathe again knowing that this whole thing is out in the open and my best friend knows.

The front door opens and Haley walks in with her bookbag slung over her shoulder and a small pizza box in her hand. She doesn't see us at first, but when she does, her eyes widen.

"What the hell did I just walk into?" she asks, and I look back at Holland and Lainey hoping one of them will explain. "Why are you wrapped in a sheet?"

I look down at myself, having temporarily forgotten that I am indeed wearing a sheet instead of actual clothes. I can't help the laugh that bubbles out of me. I can't control it, and Ellie's laughter follows. Holland joins in too until all three of us are laughing hysterically at Haley's perplexed expression.

The front door opens once again, and this time, Mason strolls in behind Haley.

"You know, I've been looking all over for you, man. Wait, why are you wearing a sheet?" he asks, looking between Holland, Ellie, and me with confusion written all over his face. "What kind of freaky shit did I just walk in on?" Mason asks, and that causes our laughter to reach a new level of hysterics.

My body feels lighter, my head feels less full, and I feel freer to do what I want and feel how I feel now that everything is out. But there's still something weighing on me.

Holland said he loved me. What the hell am I supposed to do with that?

Chapter 39

HOLLAND

The warmth of the shower has done practically nothing to ease the pain and aching in my muscles. Practice was absolutely brutal today, and I think I was knocked on my ass more than I was standing vertical.

I don't know what's going on with me. My mind is racing, and I feel like there's a huge weight on my chest. I shouldn't feel this was since my sister now knows about Lainey and me.

We don't have to hide anymore. Shouldn't that make me feel less… I don't know… stressed?

Except, there's one thing that's been heavy on my mind this past week since that whole fiasco.

I said I loved her. I told Ellie that I love Lainey, in front of her, and she hasn't said anything since. Nothing. We've been together every day, and Lainey hasn't brought it up at all. Sure, I could bring it up. I am the one that said it, after all.

But how can she know this huge thing and just pretend that it never even happened? Does she just not feel the same way? Does she think I only said it to make Ellie stop her freak out? Why wouldn't she say anything at all?

She has to feel the same way, right? I mean, after everything, there's no way she doesn't. Right?

Stepping out of the shower, I grab my towel and wrap it around my waist. I sit on the edge of my bed, my head in my hands, letting out a deep exhale. What the hell am I doing? Why don't I just ask her how she feels?

For real, dude. Grow a pair; ask the girl if she loves you back.

My phone ringing breaks me out of my thoughts. Grabbing it off the nightstand, I see that it's my mom. I haven't spoken to her in a while, so I decide to answer the call.

"Hello?" I say.

"Hi, honey. How are you?" my mom's sweet voice asks through the speaker.

My mom has always been a sweet, caring woman. She never yells, never fights. When her and my father would get into arguments, she would always be the calmer and more collected one. The one to get to the root of the problem.

"I'm okay. Is everything alright?" I ask, worried that she may be calling for a reason other than to just say hi.

"Yes, darling. Everything is fine. I just wanted to check in on you to see how you were doing. Ellie told me you and Lainey have been spending some time together?" she questions, and I could strangle my sister for telling our mother about my situation with Lainey.

Not that I'm hiding it, but my mother loves to meddle.

"Yes, mother. We have," is all I give her. I'm not going to get into all the gory details with her right now, especially not over the phone.

"Do you love her?" she asks, and the question hits me in the chest like a ton of bricks.

"Mom…" I begin, not wanting to talk about this.

"Holland," she says sternly.

Groaning, I decide it's best to just give her what she wants so the conversation will be over faster.

"Yes," is all I say.

"Oh, honey. I knew it. I always knew you two would end up together. Does she feel the same?"

I shake my head, because I don't know. I don't know if she feels the same because she won't fucking tell me and it's infuriating. I hate not knowing how she feels, ever. She keeps everything so bottled up and she's too afraid to let anyone in. Even me.

"I don't know" I answer honestly. My mom makes a noise on the other end.

"What do you mean you don't know?"

"I mean, she hasn't told me. I don't know how she feels," I explain the best I can.

"You know Lainey. Always so protective of her feelings. She's never been good at expressing herself. Give her time, love. I know she loves you too," mom says. How could she possibly know that?

"Mom," I begin, running a hand through my wet hair. "It's been weeks, and she still hasn't told me how she feels. Maybe she just… doesn't want me the way I want her."

Mom chuckles lightly. "Oh, baby. Trust me, that girl has been in love with you for years. Just as you have been with her. You two have just been too stubborn and hardheaded to admit it."

I scoff. "I have not been in love with her for years."

I haven't. I know I haven't because everything she did annoyed me or pissed me off. I never thought of her as anything other than what she was, my sister's best friend.

"Whatever you say, dear. All I'm saying is give her time. She'll let you know how she feels when she's ready to."

She's right. I can't force Lainey to tell me how she feels. It'll just push her away, and it already feels like she's pulling away as things get more serious.

"Okay, mom."

What has happened to me? A couple of months ago I couldn't even imagine being in love, having a girlfriend, wanting someone to want me just as badly as I want them. Now, all I want is to hear Lainey tell me she loves me too. I'm a little bitch.

I can't tell the guys about this, especially Mason. I'll never hear the end of it. Ryker might understand since he was even more against relationships than I was, but I feel like an idiot.

It's like I'm a completely different person when I'm around her. My guard is down, and I get this weird feeling in my stomach, and my palms get all clammy. I mean, I feel like a little girl with her first crush. This is ridiculous.

But I don't think I care. Maybe my mom is right. Maybe this has been a long time coming, and it isn't as sudden as it feels. Maybe I've been slowly falling in love with her for years.

"I love you, honey. Talk soon, okay?" Mom says, and I nod.

"I love you too, mom. Talk soon."

The line goes dead, and I'm left sitting on the edge of my bed, still dripping from my shower, staring at the wall.

That's the second person to tell me they've seen Lainey and I getting together. How many more have assumed this would happen and never said anything?

Does it even matter? I mean, it did happen, sort of. Lainey is mine now, and she knows I'm hers. I don't think she's planning on seeing anyone else, I've made it pretty clear that I'm not looking for anyone else either.

I just need to talk to her, straighten everything out. I need to know what she's thinking, how she's feeling. I need her to know that I don't plan on going anywhere, and if that's what's keeping her from telling me how she truly feels then she has nothing to worry about.

She has to know that I would never do anything to hurt her. Sure, we've said some hurtful things in the past, but we were always just busting each other's balls. It never actually meant anything.

But I'd never purposely hurt her. I'd never leave her, not like her-

Her parents. Her parents left her. They left and they've only popped in occasionally to check in or have brief interactions with her. Lainey has grown up thinking people just up and leave when they're done with her. But I'm not them.

There're two things I know for certain. I'll never leave her, and I'm definitely fucking screwed if she ends up not feeling the same way because I am one hundred percent in love with her.

Chapter 40

LAINEY

Rain drops pound against the roof of the massive campus library as I sit at a large table with my books spread out in front of me. I have a sociology test tomorrow morning that I had completely forgotten about until this morning.

I've been so preoccupied lately that I haven't been able to focus on my schoolwork. Don't get me wrong, I've never been a straight A student, and I've never really cared about my grades. However, I would like to graduate this semester and start looking for jobs.

I was thinking of taking a bit of a break after school ends, maybe travelling or something while I explored all my options. At least, that was my plan until a certain boy came in and screwed it all up.

Never did I imagine I'd have a boyfriend, especially one named Holland Monroe. I fully anticipated being the fun aunt to Gwen and Ellie's kids. You know, the one that helps them learn how to drive, takes them on fun trips, and teaches them how to live on the wild side occasionally.

Now I'm thinking about a future with this man and how many kids we'll have and where we'll end up living. I think we'd move closer to the city, where Gwen and Ryker live so Holland can be more involved in the clubs.

I'd probably find a job as a school psychologist or something. Maybe at the school Gwen teaches at. Who knows.

My phone vibrates against the table and Gwen's name flashes across the screen. I quickly pick it up and answer it.

"Hello," I whisper, trying my best to stay quiet. There aren't many people around me but it's still a library.

"So, it's official then? You and Holland?" she asks with a teasing lilt to her tone. I roll my eyes. Of course, Ellie called and told her about the new discovery.

"Yup, I guess so" I reply, not exactly sure where this conversation is going. The last thing Gwen knew was that Holland and I kissed before the wedding.

"Finally. It's about damn time. Honestly, I thought you two would never figure your shit out. Thanks for the heads up by the way."

My brows furrow as I rack my brain for what she could possibly be talking about.

"What do you mean?"

"For warning me that Ellie was going to call all pissed off about me knowing before her. She was really upset about it."

Shaking my head, I rest it on my hand as I stare out the large window and watch the rain fall.

"Shit, I'm sorry. I didn't know she was going to call you," I apologize. I guess I should call Haley and see how she's doing considering Ellie must have talked to her too.

Gwen chuckles on the other end. "It's okay. She's over it now. Are you happy?" she asks, sounding genuinely interested.

I think about it for a moment. Am I happy? Does Holland make me happy? Even though I'm scared shitless as to what might happen, I think the answer is yes.

A small smile pulls at my lips. "Yeah, I think I am."

Gwen squeals. "Good. I am so happy you found someone that could break down that wall you built inside yourself. You deserve to be happy, Lane. If Holland makes you happy, then I am so glad you found him."

My smile grows wider as thoughts of Holland and the past weeks play in my head. Maybe I do deserve to be happy. Maybe this is my time, and I need to fully embrace it. Now that our relationship is all out there, we don't need to pretend.

I'm still terrified of the outcome. I mean, fairytales don't exist, right? Noone is happy all of the time, and when things seem too good to be true, they usually are. A part of me doesn't want to let myself feel this happy, this at peace because I know the world can snatch is away at any moment.

This could all come crashing down and blow up in my face. Holland could realize I'm more than he bargained for and decide that he doesn't want to deal with it anymore.

What then?

"Lainey?" Gwen's voice breaks me out of my doom cycle.

"What? Sorry, I-" I'm cut off before I can finish what I was saying by a sopping wet, green eyed God plops down in the seat across from me.

Holland pushes a hand through his wet hair and shakes, water dripping all over my books and papers. He gives me a cheeky grin, and I almost can't be annoyed with the fact that he got my stuff all wet.

"Hey, Gwenny. I'll call you back later, I have to go," I tell Gwen before hanging up the phone and setting it face down on the table. I give Holland a questioning look.

"What the hell? You got my books all wet," I scold. He chuckles a bit, leaning back in his chair and crossing his arms. God, he's so hot.

"I could make other things wet if you'd prefer," he teases, and my clit pulsates at the thought. I clamp my thighs together to keep myself grounded.

Rolling my eyes, I lean on the table. "What are you doing here?"

"I came to see my girl," Holland says nonchalantly. I don't think I'll ever get used to that, being his girl.

"I told you; I'm studying. I have a test tomorrow and Professor Nimmens is a hardass."

Holland moves to lean over the table, landing on my books and inching much closer to me. Our arms touch, and just that small brush of contact makes my hair stand up.

"I'll put something hard in your ass," he says, a bit too loudly.

Slapping his arm, I shake my head and try to contain my laughter. He's like a child. If I laugh, it'll only make him continue.

"You have to go, you're too distracting and I need to concentrate," I tell him sternly, pulling my book toward me and attempting to read the page, but I'm too distracted by the man sitting across from me.

I feel his stare, smell his cologne, sense his presence. It's making it near to impossible to focus.

"I have to talk to you," he tells me, and his tone switches from playful to kind of serious. My stomach drops as I think of every possible thing he could say. Is he breaking it off? Is he over it already, over me?

No, he couldn't be. He just called me his girl; he came to see me. There's no way it could be anything like that, right?

I take a deep breath through my nose before meeting his gaze.

"About what?" I ask, hoping my voice didn't sound as shaky as it felt.

"Us. You," he explains. Oh god. This is it, isn't it? I admitted I was happy and now the universe is about to take it away. I fucking knew it. "It's not bad," Holland says, as if he can sense the tension and worry in my body.

"Okay… well can it wait?" I ask, hoping it can because I don't know if I can handle whatever he's about to say right now. He shakes his head.

"Not really," he says, taking a deep breath and looking around the large space. No one is around us, and I'm thanking God for that right now. "The other day… when Ellie caught us, I said something."

I nod slowly, not understanding where he's going with this.

He lets out a breath before continuing. "I said I loved you… like, as in, I'm *in* love you," he clarifies. Well, that's not exactly where I thought this was going.

"Oh, that," is all my stupid brain can think to say.

Holland chuckles lowly. "Yeah, that. You didn't mention it after that, though."

He's right, I didn't. Part of me didn't know what to say or even how to bring it up, and the other part was too scared to.

Shrugging, I say, "Yeah… I guess I didn't know what to say."

He shifts in his chair, and my nerves feel like they're on fire.

"Well, I mean, do you?" he inquires, and I know what he's asking but I don't know how to answer it because yes, I do think I love him, but I'm terrified to admit it out loud.

"Do I what?" I ask, playing dumb.

"I can't believe I'm asking this. I feel like a fourteen-year-old girl. But… do you feel the same way?"

Time freezes and my heart feels like it stops in my chest. Every memory, every fight, every kiss, every touch replays in my mind in slow motion and I feel like I want to cry. Can I let myself do this? Can I give so much of myself to another person? Can I trust him to not break me?

"I… I don't… I have to go," I stutter in a panic as I scoop up all of my things, toss them in my bag and make a run for it toward the exit.

In my haste, I'd forgotten that it was downpouring, so now I'm soaked and walking home in the rain in the middle of March. Fantastic.

What the hell did I just do? Why couldn't I give him an answer? Why did I just get up and leave? What the hell is wrong with me?

Holland bursts out the doors of the library and storms toward me, looking confused, hurt, and angry. I turn away and head down the sidewalk, walking as fast as I can, even though I know it's no use because he's going to catch up to me. And he does.

He steps in front of me, blocking my way.

"Stop! Lainey, what the fuck?"

The rain pours down around us, and I shiver as a cold breeze passes. Jesus, I should have thought this through.

"What do you want me to say, Holland? That I love you? That I'm in love with you? That I've never felt this way about anyone before, and I don't know what the hell I'm doing? That I'm so fucking scared of letting you in and getting my heart crushed? That I'm terrified you're going to leave just like… nevermind," I yell over the rain before walking around him. Holland's hand wraps around my wrist, stopping me from moving.

"Don't walk away from me, Lainey," he demands, his voice low and rough. I spin on him, my hair wild and wet around my face.

"Then stop following me!"

We stand inches apart, the years of built-up tension and friction vibrating like a live wire between us.

"You think you can just keep pushing me away every time things get too close!" Holland's chest rises and falls, the veins in his forearms prominent as his fists clench. "Why can't you just be honest with yourself? Or me? You never actually say what you're feeling, it's always a fucking guessing game with you!"

My laugh cracks sharp and brittle, startling even me. "What the hell are you talking about? You don't-"

"Don't what? Don't know you?" his voice booms. "Lainey, I've known you my whole damn life. I know the way you chew on your pen when you're about to lie or you're thinking too hard, I know you'll pretend you're fine even when you're bleeding inside, I know you hate letting people in because your parents fucked you up, and I know you've been running from me for years because you're terrified of what this is."

My mouth opens, then closes. I hate how he can see through me, how raw and open I feel standing in front of him with nothing to hide behind.

"This?" I manage, my voice feeling small, despite the frustration I'm feeling inside.

Holland steps closer, so close I have to tip my head back to meet his eyes. His voice drops, rough and ragged.

"Yeah. This. Us. You and me. I get you're scared, so am I. I've never felt this way about anyone either, and I never thought it was actually possible. But here I am. I told you how I felt, and you haven't said a word. I know, I should wait until you're ready, and I will. But you need to give me something. I mean, Jesus, Lainey, I'm in love with you. I think I have been for a while now. I don't know when the hell it happened, or even how. But somehow, some way, I fell in love with you. You can try to push me away, you can try to deny what you're feeling, but I'm not going anywhere. I'm not letting you go," Holland's shoulders move up and down as he tries to catch his breath.

Holy hell.

Chapter 41

LAINEY

My heart slams against my ribs, my throat burning. Fuck, I want to say it back. But the weight of those words, the permanence, the risk…is it worth it?

"Holland…" my voice breaks. I press my hands to my face, shaking my head. "I don't…I've never-"

He swallows hard, his shoulders tight, every inch of him bracing for the blow.

"Say it. Say you don't feel the same. Say it, and I guess I'll walk away. I don't want to. But if that's truly what you want, then I will."

My chest aches, and instead of admitting the one thing I want to say, something else comes out in its place. Something I've never admitted to anyone before.

Holland's eyes search mine, desperate, pleading. My lips part, trembling.

"I'm scared," I whisper.

The anger and frustration seem to slip from his face, replaced with something softer. He reaches out, slow, almost cautious, and his hand brushes mine where it hangs by my side.

"I know," he murmurs. "So am I. But we can be scared together, Lainey."

My hand twitches beneath his, my breath shallow, feeling like every nerve in my body has been set on fire.

"I don't know if I can give you what you want," I mumble. God, I sound pathetic. I've never felt this vulnerable.

"All I want is you, Barkley. Just give me *you*," Holland says, his thumb brushing across my knuckles. His eyes burn into mine, unflinching. "Messy, scared, angry, you. I want all of it."

The words knock the air out of me. For years, I've managed to build all these walls so carefully, convinced that if I let anyone too close, everything I depended on would collapse. But standing here now, the walls feel like paper, crumbling under the weight of his voice.

Tears stroll down my cheeks, mixing with the rain. My chest heaves, a thousand arguments on the tip of my tongue, but none strong enough to push him away. Instead, I step forward, just enough for the space between us to vanish.

I take him in, the emerald green eyes, the wet hair, the small scar above his lip from the time he ran into a pole while playing rugby, the look of pure admiration on his face. Reaching up before I can stop myself, my had caresses his cheek slowly. He leans into my palm, holding my arm in place.

And then I let go. I let go of the fear, of the uncertainty, of the doubt. I let it all go, and my mouth finds his, fierce and clumsy.

Holland groans against my lips, his hands gripping my face like he's afraid I'll disappear. My hands fist the front of his shirt, attempting to drag him closer, needing him nearer, needing to feel the reality of him before doubt swallows me again.

The rain continues to pour down around us as the kiss deepens, not sweet but desperate, bruising, like everything we've left unsaid is being poured into this one kiss. When we finally break, we're both gasping for air, my forehead resting against his.

"I love you, too," I whisper, butterflies taking over my stomach. I can't believe I just said that, but I don't even want to take it back. I mean it, I love him.

Holland chuckles softly, moving my wet hair out of my face. "Now was that so damn hard?"

A small smile plays on my lips, and the heaviness of the situation dulls.

"Yes."

"You're so damn stubborn," Holland says, pulling me in for another kiss.

My throat tightens when I pull back, watching him for a response. "I don't know how to do this."

Holland pulls back just enough to meet my eyes, his palms still framing my face.

"I don't either. But we're going to figure it out, together."

I nod, agreeing with him. "Is this what love feels like?

"What do you mean?" he asks, brows furrowing.

"Like finally finding the one thing you don't want to lose?"

"Yeah, I think so," Holland says before kissing me once again.

A loud crash of thunder breaks the moment, and I jump, startles by the loud, unexpected noise. Holland laughs at my response.

"Wanna get out of here?" he asks, smiling down at me.

"Absolutely," I tell him, and we run toward the parking lot to his car.

Crashing through the front door, we don't make it two feet before we're on each other again. Kissing and touching and dripping water all over the floor after being soaked with rain.

Holland's hands are in my hair, on my body, grabbing at anything he can, and mine match his. It's like we've never felt one another before, and this is the first time we're being allowed to do so.

A throat clears and breaks us out of our desperate embrace.

"Oh, hey, Ellie… hey Hal," I stammer, seeing my friends on the couch and cringing at the fact that they both just watched that. Haley gives a little wave, trying to hold back her laughter. Ellie grimaces.

"Can you guys like, get a room?" she asks, covering her face with a blanket.

I nod. "Yeah, yes. We'll do that."

Holland chuckles from beside me. I pull him to my room and shut the door behind us. Not even a second in the room, he grabs my face and pushes me up against the door.

His lips crash against mine, the kiss desperate and hungry. I melt into him, my hands tangling in his hair as I kiss him back with equal fervor. His hands slide down my back, pulling me closer, our bodies pressing together as if to erase any trace of the distance that had once separated us.

The kiss deepens, and my heart pounds in my chest. I feel like I've run a marathon. When we finally break apart, we're both breathless. Holland's gaze is dark with desire, making me shiver. The mix of being soaked and cold are not helping with the adrenaline coursing through my veins.

The air is thick with anticipation, charged with the promise of what's to come. The world outside seems to fade away, leaving only the two of us alone in my room. Holland moves to pull my sweatshirt over my head, and I begin to undo his belt.

My sweatshirt lands in a wet heap on the floor, followed by my leggings. My fingers tremble a bit as I reach for his shirt and pull it over his head. Holland's clothes join mine on the floor.

His eyes rake over me, and this time, I don't feel so vulnerable. I feel like… like he loves me for me. I've never felt that before. Having someone love me for who I am, flaws and all. I never thought that was a real thing.

My breath hitches as he steps closer, his hands sliding down my arms, over my waist, and down to my hips. He pulls me against him, our bodies flush, his erection pressing against my thigh.

"You have no idea what you do to me, Barkley," he murmurs, his lips brushing against my ear, sending shivers down my spine. His hands move to my breasts, cupping them gently, his thumbs brushing over my nipples, already tight and aching for his touch.

I moan softly, tilting my head back as he kisses his way down my neck, his mouth hot and hungry against my skin.

Reaching for him, my hands roam over his chest, his abs. Holland groans, his head falling back for a moment before he captures my lips once again. Our bodies seem to move in sync as Holland guides me back toward the bed, our lips never parting.

He eases me down onto the mattress, following me down, his weight pressing me into the soft sheets. My legs part for him, inviting him closer as my hands pull him down until our bodies are pressed together, skin against skin.

His mouth trails down my body, kissing and nipping at my collarbone, my breasts. His tongue swirls around my nipples, making me arch into him with a soft cry.

"Holland," I gasp, my hands threading through his hair, holding him close. "Please."

He looks down at me, his eyes dark with desire, a small smirk playing on his lips.

"Please what?" he teases, his voice low and rough.

"You know what," I pant, my hips shifting restlessly against him.

Holland's smirk widens as he moves lower, his mouth trailing down my stomach, his hands spreading my thighs wider. My breath catches as he kisses the sensitive skin of my inner thigh, his breath ghosting over my core, making me shiver with anticipation.

Then, his mouth is on me, his tongue delving into my wetness, his lips sucking and nipping. Oh lord, if he keeps that up, this will be over before it even starts.

"Oh God, Holland," I moan, my hands gripping the sheets as my body arches off the bed. His tongue is relentless, his mouth devouring me as his fingers press into my thighs to hold me steady.

My hips buck against him, my cries filling the room as my orgasm builds. I don't want to come yet, but my body isn't going to give me the choice. My orgasm washes over me in waves of pleasure, and I can't help the loud moan that leaves my lips.

Once I catch my breath and my body stops trembling, he finally lifts his head. His eyes are hooded with desire as he moves back up my body, his lips brushing against mine in a soft, tender kiss.

"You're like, really good at that," I tell him, and that causes him to chuckle.

"I'm glad you enjoy it," he says. My eyes wander down his body and stop on his cock.

"I guess I should return the favor," I whisper, my hands reaching for him, my fingers wrapping around his throbbing cock.

He groans, his head falling back as I stroke him, my touch both gentle and firm. My lips curve into a smirk as I lean down, my mouth closing over the tip of his cock. My tongue swirls around it before I take him deeper, my lips sliding down his length.

Holland's hands tangle in my hair, his hips bucking slightly as I suck him, my tongue teasing and tormenting. I love the way he reacts to my touch. It's nice to know I have this kind of power over him.

"Fuck, Lainey," he groans, his voice thick with need. "You're going to make me lose it."

I hum my response, my mouth never stopping its rhythmic movements. Holland's breath quickens, his body tensing as he seems to fight for control. But I don't let up, and my mouth and hands work in tandem, driving him closer and closer to the edge.

"Stop," he gasps, his hands gripping my shoulders to pull me up. "I want to be inside you."

My eyes meet his, and he looks so needy and desperate for me, it makes my pussy clench.

"Then take me," I demand.

He doesn't need to be told twice. Holland positions himself at my entrance, his eyes locking on mine as he thrusts into me, filling me in one slow, deliberate stroke.

I gasp, my nails digging into his shoulders as he seats himself fully within me. Our eyes stay locked as he begins to move, his hips rocking against me in a steady rhythm.

Holland's hands move over my body, his touch both possessive and tender, his lips brushing against mine with every thrust.

My legs wrap around his waist, my heels digging into his back as I try to meet his movements. I don't care that Ellie and Haley are right outside in the living room. I don't care if they're listening. I only care about the way Holland's dick feels inside me right now.

The tension builds, the pleasure spiraling tighter and tighter, until I'm teetering on the edge once again. Holland's thrusts become more urgent, more desperate, his breath coming in short, sharp gasps.

My cries grow louder, my body arching into him as my second orgasm crashes over me.

"Oh my god," I practically scream out. Holland follows, his release spilling into me as he groans.

"Fuck, shit," he says through gritted teeth.

He pulls out of me slowly, falling onto the bed next to me. My breathing steadies as he turns on his side to look at me.

"You're amazing," he tells me, and a soft chuckle leaves my lips.

"Thanks, I try," I tell him. He shakes his head.

"No, I mean it. You're perfect. You're everything I need, everything I want. You're mine, and I fucking love you."

My heart stutters at his words, and I have to take a moment to digest what he's saying.

"I... I love you."

Holland kisses my forehead, and I wrap my arms around him, my fingers tracing patterns on his chest as we lay entwined. He lifts his head, his eyes searching mine, his expression unreadable.

My heart pounds in my chest, my mind racing as I being to think about where we go from here.

Holland brushes a strand of hair from my face, his touch gentle, his gaze intense. "Lainey," he begins, his voice soft.

I close my eyes for a moment, listening to the steadiness of his heartbeat before replying.

"Yes?"

He places a finger under my chin, forcing me to look up at him.

"We're going to be good. Okay? I'm not leaving, ever," he assures me, and God help me I think I believe him.

I reach up, my fingertips brushing against his cheek, my smile faint but genuine.

"Okay…" I whisper, though I'm not sure if he can promise that.

Holland's hand covers mine, his thumb brushing against my knuckles, his expression a mix of relief and desire.

As we lay in silence, our bodies still entwined, the tension and uncertainty seem to dissipate. I don't know if this will be forever, but I know I want to try. I want it to be Holland. I want this life with him, and as scary as that is, I think it might be worth it.

I've never been the girl to believe in happily ever afters, but maybe, just maybe, I've finally found mine.

Epilogue

LAINEY

"Come on, Lainey! You're going to be late; they're waiting for you!" Ellie's voice rings out as I stare at myself in the large mirror that stands in the corner of the room.

Taking a few more deep, shaky breaths, I smooth down my dress and paste a smile on my face. This is supposed to be a happy day, so why do I feel scared shitless?

"You look beautiful. Now let's go!" Gwen says, pulling me by the arm toward the door.

"Okay, okay. I'm coming!" I say, chuckling at my friends.

"Oh thank god, I thought you were going to flee," Haley says, wiping fake sweat off her brow.

My friends stand in front of me, each wearing their dark, maroon-colored dresses, looking stunning and excited.

"I'm here, I didn't flee. I'm not that much of a bitch," I tell them, taking another deep breath and shaking out the nerves. "I feel like I'm having a heart attack. Is it hot in here?"

Gwen steps in front of me, planting her hands on my shoulders. "Breathe, Lane. You're not having a heart attack. You're just nervous. Take a deep breath," she tells me in an attempt to calm my racing heart.

"You're going to be great, just don't forget to smile," Ellie says, giving me her best calming look.

"And don't trip," Haley chimes in.

We all shoot her a glare.

"Shut up, Haley!" Gwen scolds before turning back to me. "You're going to be fine. Just pay attention to what's in front of you and keep smiling."

"You got this," Ellie says, holding her thumbs up in encouragement.

Music begins from behind the large wooden doors, and my adrenaline spikes. Okay, Lainey. You can do this. It's just some family and friends.

The doors open and before walking through, my friends smile and give me a thumbs up. Gwen gives me one last smile and kisses me on the cheek.

"I'm happy for you, Lane," she says with a sweet smile, tears forming in her eyes.

"Don't cry, because then I'm going to cry and I'm going to have to kill you for making me cry," I tell her.

She chuckles before turning and walking through the doors.

The music changes and I take one final breath before walking through the doors. Friends and family line each side of the aisle, and at the end, my best friends stand with huge smiles on their faces. On the other side, Holland's friends stand beside him, and Holland stands in the middle, waiting for me.

The smile on his face is one I'll remember for the rest of my life. He looks incredibly sexy in his black suit with his dirty blonde hair all tousled.

I finally make it to Holland, and it feels like I'd been walking for an eternity.

"You showed up," he whispers with a smirk. I let out a quiet, shaky laugh.

"Here I am," I say.

"Finally," Holland says, and my heart pounds in my chest. To think, this same man annoyed the living shit out of me for years, and now I'm marrying the guy.

This doesn't feel real. I wasn't supposed to get the guy. He was supposed to be like everyone else and just leave. To be fair, he still could, but I don't think he will.

When it's time for the vows, my stomach churns. I am so not into public speaking. This is honestly one of the parts I was dreading the most. I told Holland we should do private vows, but he insisted on doing them in front of everyone so they could witness how much he loves me.

I couldn't say no to that, and I also couldn't let him be the only one to do it. So here we are, and I feel like throwing up.

"Lainey, I think I loved you before I even knew what love actually was. You were my storm, my rival, my friend, and somewhere in the middle of all our years of arguments and bickering, you became the only person I couldn't imagine living without. I realized a long time ago that I'd always choose you, even when you didn't believe in us, even when you pushed me away. And today, I stand here not because it's easy, but because it's right. I vow to love you with the same certainty I've carried all these years. To fight beside you when you're strong, to hold you when you're tired, and to remind you every day that what we have isn't a fairytale — it's better. It's real. It's ours. It's us. I love you, Lainey Bug."

I can't help the stupid tears that begin to fall down my cheeks as I take in the words he just said. How in the hell did I get so lucky?

Sniffling, I take a deep breath and begin to recite my vows.

"Holland, I spent years pretending I didn't care. Pretending the way you looked at me didn't unravel me, pretending I didn't notice when you were the only one who could make me laugh when I was angry. I thought love was supposed to be easy, and what we had… it scared me because it was real. Messy. Unavoidable. But today, I'm not afraid. I vow to argue with you when I think you're wrong and to fight beside you when the world is. I vow to love you in the small ways and the loud ways; in coffee on tired mornings, in holding your hand when you're restless, in reminding you that you've always been enough. I vow to love you because I don't know how not to. Thank you for not giving up on me and thank you for showing me that real love does exist. I love you."

Holland reaches up, brushing away the tear that slips down my cheek. The crowd blurs into silence. The years of stubbornness and denial have led to this moment. To us. The officiant's voice breaks through the temporary stillness.

"You may kiss."

"Finally," Holland repeats his earlier sentiment. I giggle, and then, his lips are on mine. And for once in our tangled mess of a history, neither of us hesitate.

Even though my parents weren't able to come due to their stint in Paris, everyone who really matters showed up. My nanny, Erika, Mrs. Monroe, our friends, a lot of Hollands family. It's absolutely perfect.

For so long, I believed that this kind of love only existed in the movies, that I was incapable of finding someone that would love me for me. That because my own parents didn't want me, no one could.

Holland had always been there, and for a long time, he was only a background character in my story. I didn't ever imagine that we'd end up here, but God, am I happy we did.

Here's to getting my fairytale, and my happily ever after.

The End

Authors Note

First, I'd like to thank you all for taking the time to join Lainey and Holland on their journey. I never thought so many people would care to read about my silly little characters, but I so grateful that you are here.

I'd like to take a moment to acknowledge the people that have been so supportive and encouraging during this process. Writing is a crazy journey, and I'm so thankful for the people in my life that supported me every step of the way.

Thank you to my beta readers for your time and dedication to reading my story and helping me edit. I couldn't have done this without you.

Thank you to my ARC readers for providing such helpful feedback. I genuinely appreciate your time.

Lastly, to my readers, I wouldn't be here if it wasn't for you. Thank you for your continuous support and encouragement.

I love you all!

Love always,
Rae Quinn

About the Author

Rae Quinn is a romance author, teacher, and screenwriter who lives in Georgia with her pup, Layla. When she's not writing sappy romance novels, she's consuming way too much coffee, reading a book, and travelling.

Join Rae Quinn on social media to keep up to date on new releases, giveaways, and more!

Instagram: @authorraequinn_
Goodreads: Rae Quinn
Facebook: Rae Quinn – Author
Tiktok: _raequinn_

www.ingramcontent.com/pod-product-compliance
Lightning Source LLC
Chambersburg PA
CBHW020234010826
48973CB00006B/1508